# The Last Voyage of The Emir

PSALM 107: 28-29

# THE LAST VOYAGE OF THE EMIR

David Riley

ELM HILL

A Division of
HarperCollins Christian Publishing

www.elmhillbooks.com

## The Last Voyage of The Emir

Published in Nashville, Tennessee, by Elm Hill, an imprint of Thomas Nelson. Elm Hill and Thomas Nelson are registered trademarks of HarperCollins Christian Publishing, Inc.

Elm Hill titles may be purchased in bulk for educational, business, fund-raising, or sales promotional use. For information, please e-mail SpecialMarkets@ ThomasNelson.com.

**Library of Congress Cataloging-in-Publication Data**

Library of Congress Control Number: 2018933344

ISBN 978-1-400329212 (Paperback)
ISBN 978-1-400329229 (eBook)

*For Renee:*
*Without your encouragement and support this book*
*would not have been completed.*

# THE EMIR

The Emir was getting old. Movements had always been slow and ponderous due to great size, but now they were accompanied by creaking and popping noises. Shuddering and wobbling were common, and there were blemishes and stains that would not go away despite vigorous scrubbing. Some days there was a lot of wind, but others hardly any. Many times there was noticeable seepage and wetness in the lower areas where it was not supposed to happen.

This particular Emir was a ship; a large ship from the Egyptian fleet, traveling back and forth across the Mediterranean hauling its cargo of grain. It was about 200 feet long and 50 feet wide, with one tall mast holding a large sail. It could carry as many as 300 people in addition to the cargo.

Most ships were referred to as females but this one was not. The figurehead, strangely enough, was a beautiful young woman, but on closer inspection, you could see that she was holding a baby. Presumably this was the Emir the ship was named after. Details had been blurred as time, weather, and the salt spray of the sea had done their work through the years.

The official name, of course, was in Arabic: Emir al Salaam. Through the years, it had been shortened to The Emir. The crew, not really giving much thought to the name's origin, were happy to just have a job. The captain, however, knew the story, his father having worked on this very ship as it was built in the shipyard. He had heard the story about the ship's namesake several times when he was growing up and could tell his father had been greatly impacted by Him.

This is the tale of the last voyage of The Emir.

# CHAPTER ONE

He rode into Myra just before midday. Three weeks of riding had left him tired, hungry, and in a bad mood. His back was sore and his scarred left arm was aching from overuse since he had wrapped the reins around his stiff and useless fingers.

He had been following the coastline alert for any news. In each dirty little town, he had asked for any news of a ship traveling along the coast. He thought he had found his prey in Sidon. He had news that a ship carrying Roman soldiers and prisoners had docked for a day and some of the prisoners had been allowed to disembark unaccompanied. This was almost unheard of since the soldiers could be severely punished to the point of death if they escaped. The innkeeper was still talking about it after a few days. By the time he had arrived, however, the ship had put to sea again.

He did not have any further news after that, but as he had turned west to follow the shore, the wind was in his face. He had smiled grimly at the thought that a ship would make slow going under these conditions, allowing him to gain on them.

He had been biding his time for more than two years, waiting for an opportunity to exact his revenge. The man had been kept securely locked in the Roman prison in Caesarea, out of his reach the entire time. Initially he had others working with him with similar desire for vengeance. As time passed, their determination had wavered and failed. He alone had persisted, motivated by burning hatred for the man who had destroyed his life. The long jolting ride had only increased his anger.

When he arrived in Myra, he made his way to an inn at the port. He sat down and called for the serving girl to get him food and drink. He was drumming his fingers on the table impatiently when she finally returned and set a plate of meat and bread in front of him.

"It's about time!" he grumbled. He grabbed the cup from her hands and took a quick drink. She was turning to go when he grabbed her arm. "Wait! I need some information. Is there a ship here carrying Roman soldiers and prisoners?"

"I don't know," she said, pulling back from his reach with a frown. "Ships come and go all the time. You need to ask at the port." She turned and quickly walked away.

"Useless woman!" he mumbled.

He ate in silence, looking around at the other tables. There were no soldiers within sight. He finished his plate and gulped down the ale. Wiping his mouth on his sleeve, he got up to leave. He dropped a coin on the table as he surveyed the dwindling funds in his moneybag.

He made his way to the port. There was a ship anchored just off shore, and he could tell by the activity it was preparing for departure. He only saw one other ship anchored in the harbor. His frustration grew as he muttered curses under his breath. He stalked toward the pier intending to question the men working there. He feared he had lost his chance.

As he drew near, he suddenly stopped, his eyes widening. Now that he was closer, he could see there was another ship beyond the first, hidden by its size. It had a familiar appearance. He turned and quickly strode closer to get a better look. His irritation receded as he recognized the ship. It was the one! He had seen it leaving Caesarea carrying his quarry.

"You there!" he called to a nearby sailor. "When did that ship arrive?"

"Which one? There are three ships out there!"

"That one!" he gestured impatiently with his outstretched hand.

"It arrived yesterday."

"What happened to the people on it? The soldiers and the men they were transporting?"

"I don't know. You might need to ask the harbormaster. His office is over there." The main nodded toward a low building nearby as he turned and walked away.

He turned with a frustrated growl and stomped toward the office. He thrust open the door, startling the man inside causing him to jump spilling the cup he had in his hand.

"What do you want?" he said irritably as he brushed away the puddle with his hand.

"Where are the soldiers that arrived on the ship anchored out there?"

It took a moment for the harbormaster to comprehend the question. "Are you talking about the one heading back to Adramyttium? That came in from Caesarea?"

"All I know is there was a ship full of soldiers and prisoners that left Caesarea a few weeks ago. I have been trying to catch up to them ever since. Where are they?"

"Well, they just left this morning! The centurion in charge booked passage on an Alexandrian grain ship called The Emir. They are heading on to Rome. I'm afraid you missed them."

He let out an exasperated groan and slapped the door with a loud bang.

"Hey now! Don't break my door!" the harbormaster scowled. "If you want to try to catch them, maybe you should talk to the captain of the ship getting ready to leave. They are heading along the same route. And since they are smaller, they probably will catch up to them along the way!"

His eyes widened as he considered this. Without a word of thanks, he whirled around to rush to the pier leaving the harbormaster muttering and shaking his head, and he continued to clean up his spilled ale.

# CHAPTER TWO

Gaius leaned against the rail worn smooth by the friction of time. As he watched the frothy surface of the sea, plowed aside by the prow of the ship, he was reminded again that the hope of a restful voyage was not likely to be realized. The noise of a ship at sea engulfed him with the creaking of timber, the slapping of the waves offended by the passing hull, and the snapping and rattling of the pregnant sails laboring to deliver them toward Rome. He could catch snatches of conversations all around him: the crew shouting instructions to one another, men trading good-natured insults, and his fellow soldiers growling at the prisoners in their charge. There were also the smells of the salt tang of the sea and the collective physiology of 200 plus human creatures held in a confined space, thankfully diminishing into his subconscious after several days at sea.

The excitement and anticipation he'd had as they left Caesarea the first day had faded as the monotony and routine of life on board the ship became reality. It had taken him a few days to get used to the movement of the ship but now he hardly noticed it. The weather had been nice but evidently this was not enough to please the captain of the ship. The winds were not what he wanted, so they had to sail to the north along the coast of Asia. This gave them slow progress, and the daily routine overseeing the soldiers under his command became somewhat boring.

Things got more interesting when they arrived at Myra. They had to find another ship heading to Rome, so they had a day in the city while

Julius, his friend and the centurion in charge, secured passage for them. Gaius ordered the men of his cohort to keep a close watch on the prisoners. He was well aware of the severe penalties if one were to escape and did not want that on his record. He knew only too well the life-changing implications of letting a prisoner get away, even a dead one. His father had experienced such an incident and never fully recovered.

They finally left Myra a few days ago. The Alexandrian ship, The Emir, was much larger. He estimated there must be 250–300 people on board counting the crew, prisoners, soldiers, and other passengers. The large mast in the center of the deck held a huge sail, and there was a smaller sail at the front. There were two decks below, the lowest a large hold for the grain the ship was designed to carry. It also held a large cistern for drinking water and an area for the provisions to feed the crew and passengers. The middle deck was divided into three main compartments. One was fitted with several hammocks for the crew and one with a large area for the prisoners, soldiers, and passengers to sleep on pallets on the floor. The third room was used as a common area and had a few tables for the people to congregate together.

With nicer weather, most of the people would spend time on the upper deck. The breeze helped to dissipate the normal smells associated with that many men gathered in one space. After a few days, most were still polite and cheerful, but Gaius knew human nature well enough to know that with a long time in limited space, there would likely be some conflict. He started studying the groups of people around him, wondering who would be the troublemakers he may have to help control in the future.

The crew was ever present, performing their various duties efficiently. They were accustomed to life on board the ship, so he did not anticipate them being a source of trouble. They seemed to speak in their own language and kept to themselves. Some were weathered, with the dark leathery skin brought on by a life in the wind and sun. Rough calluses were noticeable on their hands. They showed the marks of a rough life at sea, with missing fingers, scars, and pronounced limps, but still able to do the work required. A few looked very young, and he could tell at least two or three were likely on their first voyage. He could see their vigilance bordering on fear as they seemed to be ever anticipating a reprimand.

There were several passengers that kept to themselves, some cautiously making overtures of friendship to other passengers. Most were fairly well dressed, and some seemed to have a definite air of superiority as they avoided contact with the crew or the prisoners. Travel to Rome carried a certain status, and some of them wanted it displayed prominently. Gaius knew their type and expected they would be more demanding as the trip wore on.

The largest group were the soldiers. One cohort was being transported back to Rome after their deployment in Asia. There was also the cohort commanded by the Centurion, Julius, with Gaius as the second-in-command. The two groups, now combined under the command of Julius, spent much of their free time sharing stories of where they had been stationed, often inflating tales of their acts of bravery when on duty and other more prurient conquests off duty. They quickly developed a level of camaraderie during the first few days.

The soldiers were trained for a life of discipline and following orders. For Gaius' men, this particular assignment was in many ways desirable. They had no reason to fear death due to battle while on the voyage. Any hard labor on the ship was done by the crew who knew the equipment and the work required to maintain the ship. The prisoners really had nowhere to go, so the guards could afford to be less vigilant during the trip. Gaius had to keep reminding them that escape was not the only problem they had to guard against. Mutiny was a possibility as well. He tried to keep a regimented schedule of rotating their shifts and requiring some upkeep of their weapons and uniforms, mostly to keep them on their toes. Complacency and tedium could be dangerous around prisoners, and he was determined to keep trouble at bay.

The final group was the prisoners. These prisoners were a lot different than those he had been around before. Roman prisoners could be violent and difficult but this group was more docile. Twenty-two in number, several of them had been imprisoned in Caesarea, some for two years. It seemed this group was more political rather than violent. Gaius was of the opinion that they really posed no significant threat and he did not understand why they had been imprisoned for so long. He and Julius both felt a certain respect for them. In fact, when they docked in Sidon, Julius went so far as to let one of the prisoners leave the ship with his traveling companions, one of whom was a physician, so they could provide care for him before resuming the long journey to Rome. Gaius was taken aback by the freedom allowed by Julius, but knew he had been with them in Caesarea before the journey started, and he trusted Julius' judgment implicitly. He still breathed a sigh of relief when they boarded again.

During the first leg of the journey, this small group of prisoners and their traveling companions took to sitting on the deck each day, talking. The main prisoner, a man named Paul, was educated and had a gift for teaching. Those gathered seemed to be in rapt attention as he taught them, and over time other prisoners, and even a few of the guards, joined these times of teaching and discussion.

Gaius became curious and stood nearby on a few occasions to see what was being said. He wanted to be sure there was no scheming or plan for mutiny being discussed. Paul seemed mostly to keep repeating themes of holiness and living life in a way pleasing to his god. His favorite words seemed to be "grace" and "peace." When he heard Paul mention the name Jesus, however, he wanted no more part of the discussion. That name had caused nothing but disruption in his family, and he was not interested in hearing more about it. He kept his distance after that, watching from afar to be sure the soldiers were acting appropriately.

All in all, the voyage had been uneventful. He was glad of that but at the same time hoped for something to break the humdrum monotony. Within reason of course. No need to wish for trouble!

His reverie was interrupted by someone calling his name.

"Gaius! There you are."

He looked up to see his friend and commander, the centurion of their cohort.

"Hi, Julius! What is happening? Please tell me there is something to do! This boredom is beginning to take its toll!"

"I'm afraid I don't have much to tell you. I was just talking to the captain of this wooden rat trap. I was hoping we would be making quick progress. I, too, am getting tired of this standing around and waiting. I hope the soldiers are keeping up with their assigned duties?" Julius said.

"I think they are growing weary as well. I had to reprimand Cassius and Porcius from the Asian cohort for their sloppy appearance. They seem to like going off on their own, whispering and laughing at their private jokes. I'll need to keep an eye on them," Gaius reported. "What did the captain have to say?"

Julius scowled. "I think we may be stuck on board for longer than we had hoped. The winds have been contrary and slowed our progress. The captain was hoping to have been much further along by now, but we have been forced to follow the coastline instead of a more direct route. We should have reached Cnidus in just one or two days with the right winds. He hopes we can be there in the next few days and then we may have a better chance of favorable winds."

"Aargh! Maybe I should just swim!"

"You know you are afraid of the water!" Julius said with a laugh. "It was all I could do to get you to follow my orders to come on this journey!"

"True. I still hate being trapped on this wooden raft so far from solid ground! But, I know better than to disobey a direct order. Besides, I am ready to be done with Palestine. It is dry and dusty, and I have always wanted to go to Rome." His smile faded. "Plus getting away from family memories may be a good thing."

Julius studied his face for a moment. "Gaius, your troubles with your father will fade. Don't be too quick to turn away from your family."

"That is not for you to judge," he said, more sharply than he intended. "You could not understand what happened between us. I would prefer you stay out of my business." He turned to survey the deck. "I better make my rounds to check on the men and the prisoners," he said as he turned to go.

He winced slightly. "I'm sorry Gaius. Someday maybe we can talk more about this. I'll see you soon." He watched as Gaius waved halfheartedly and walked away.

# CHAPTER THREE

The sun was hot on his back but one good thing about the ship was there was always a breeze. The wind was vital to its progress across the sea, and on warm days like this, it served to cool down the crew. It was stifling down in the hold. Being on deck meant he was working, but he had learned to sneak a rest now and then, sitting with his back against the railing of the ship in the shade. There were rare times he had been caught and his ribs still ached where he had been kicked as an "incentive" to do his work.

Temeros had been on board now for a few days. Initially, he felt queasy as he adjusted to the continual rocking of the ship. He quickly adapted, and by the third day, he had felt much more at ease. He had started to win over the crew with his willingness to work, but mostly he kept to himself.

When he was alone, his mind naturally went back almost three years to the events that changed his life. The scars on his body may be visible, but there were also invisible scars on his soul, with anger and a desire for vengeance that would well up in him at various times. The attack that disrupted his family was a horrible memory. His father was dead, so anger toward him was futile but still simmered in him, occasionally flaming hotter and brighter until he could regain composure. More than once he had lashed out at people around him, with the result being more time on the road, traveling from town to town looking for a place to heal and forget the past. It was hard to form any semblance of friendship as he pushed others away and continued moving.

His father was the direct cause of his exile from home and friends, but two other names were associated with his pain. His father had been consumed with anger, screaming about Paul, and his teaching about the prophet, Jesus, ruining his life as he in turn ruined those around him. Temeros had not forgotten these names linked to his scars.

In his quiet moments, lying on his pallet trying to sleep, he would subconsciously trace the irregular shape of his ear and the firm scar tissue around it. No hair would grow there, so he learned to keep his head covered with a head scarf. Sometimes, if no one was nearby, he took out the silver pendant and looked at his reflection in its polished surface. The physical pain had long since faded. In fact the scars on his head were numb now. The ache in his heart had not resolved, however. The simmering pang of loss was always with him.

————

The scabs and oozing of the sores had taken several weeks to heal, with so much pain at the first. He was on his own and had run away after that awful night. His memory was a blur now but he ran north. He had some realization that Smyrna was that direction and was a center for medical training. He might find someone who could help him. After hours on the road, he was weak, unsteady on his feet, and he must have looked awful with the side of his head so scarred. He found a dry place by the road and laid down, pain searing into his consciousness until he passed out.

He was not sure how long he was unconscious, but he awoke in a room with low light provided by a lantern. He still had pain but it was muted. He reached toward his head and felt a damp cloth covering the painful area.

"Don't touch it!" a man's voice had said. "I just put the salve on it and it will take some time to calm down the swelling. Just rest. I will get you something to drink and to soothe the pain."

He turned his head toward the speaker and saw a tall dark-haired man, with a look of concern on his face. The man rose and went to a nearby table, poured some water into a cup, and picked up a small parcel, returning to the bedside. He reached an arm under Temeros' shoulders and helped him sit up.

"Here, drink some water. Your mouth is very dry," the man said, holding the cup to his lips.

He remembered the water was like a magic potion. He had never had such a satisfying drink before that point in his life. The act of swallowing, however, increased his pain and he winced, groaning with pain.

"Let me give you some medicine to help the pain," the man said

"Who are you?" he croaked, barely recognizing his own voice.

"My name is Luke. I'm a doctor. What is your name?"

"I am Temeros. Where am I?"

"I found you by the road as I was returning to Smyrna for my studies. We are at an inn near where you had fallen. You have been badly hurt. It looks like a burn. Can you tell me what happened?"

The memories flooded back, and for a moment he could not speak. "There was a fire at my home. I... I ran away."

Luke's brow furrowed slightly. "Where is your family?" he asked.

Temeros turned away, shaking his head slightly, and then wincing with pain. "They perished in the fire," he said, beginning to weep.

Luke put his arm around his shoulders. "I'm so sorry. Let me give you something to help your pain. This is a paste of willow bark, and if you chew on it, the juice will begin to help in a few minutes." He placed a pinch of dried, crushed bark into his cheek.

Luke paused, looking at him. "I want you to know that there is a God who loves you and will help you through this."

At these words, Temeros' face clouded. "I don't want to hear about any god. My family was very religious in the temple in Ephesus. Artemis took over my father's life. All religion only causes more suffering."

Luke was silent for a moment. "I will not force this discussion on you when you are hurting so badly, but I hope we will have a chance to discuss this further when you are healed. For now, you need rest."

Temeros calmed a bit, lying back against the pillow. The paste in his cheek left a bitter taste but he was beginning to feel less pain. After a few minutes, his breathing deepened and his mind wandered. The low light and warmth in the room allowed him to drift off to sleep.

The next few days were a blur. His pain was sometimes severe and delirium accompanied his fluctuating fever. The man, Luke, was ever present with a cool cloth for his face, water to drink, and bread when he was able to take it. Gradually the pain was less and he was able to stand and walk around. Luke taught him to wrap the burned area, as the blisters slowly stopped oozing. After about four days, it was still tender and swollen but the pain was tolerable. They did not return to the subject of religion.

Luke was trying to help him find a place to stay or to contact relatives who could help him. Temeros was not interested in returning to any family. There were too many deep hurts and bad memories. His mother was gone, and his father too. He was overwhelmed with a mix of grief and anger, sometimes crying, sometimes silently fuming inside. He did not want to talk to this stranger about what happened, not yet. It was too fresh. He needed time to process it and to decide what his next move would be.

He was only seventeen. He had been helping his father, the silversmith, and learning to craft various items. He had not developed any other skills he could do at his age, especially with no resources. He needed to get away from here, to find a place where he could hire himself out to earn money for food and shelter. He did not want to depend on this stranger for help, although he did not want to tell him that.

On the fifth morning, he awoke to an empty room. Luke must have gone out for some supplies. Temeros dressed and got a drink. He took one more dose of the willow bark to help his pain, although it was not bad now. He let himself out of the small room and looked around. He did not see anyone in the hallway but could hear voices in the next room, and he recognized Luke's voice. He turned the other way and quietly opened the door at the end of the hall and left.

If he went north to Smyrna, he was afraid he would be found by Luke. He wanted no further obligation to him. He had no desire to return to Ephesus. There was nothing for him there but painful memories and grief. He decided to aim for the coast. Maybe he would find escape from his painful life there.

From that day on, he had been on his own. He had traveled in the region stopping at various towns. In some places he was able to find work cleaning at an inn or helping on a farm in exchange for food and shelter. He never stayed long in any one place. His pain faded as the scar matured. His left ear was misshapen but his hearing was still fairly good. The numbness became a minor inconvenience as time passed.

He slowly made his way south to Myra, on the coast. It was a hub of activity, and he was able to find work fairly easily. Over time, he became more fascinated with the port and would spend time watching the ships enter and leave the harbor. In his quiet moments, he felt so alone and displaced that he began to imagine what it would be like to just get on a ship and leave.

The months had turned into years and now, after two years, he started watching for an opportunity. He hired on at the port to load and unload the ships, giving himself over to his work. On his off days, there were drinks, and women to entertain him, but the feeling of emptiness and longing for another life and a new start never left.

Finally, he saw the huge grain ship. The mast in the center of this ship stood tall, and the front of the ship had a large figurehead that had been weathered over time. Although it had been repainted, the once bright colors had faded under the sun and salt spray of the sea. It appeared to be a carving of a beautiful woman holding a baby. This seemed strange since the men said the ship was called The Emir, or The Prince, but he only considered that for a moment and then quickly forgot about it. It was the largest ship he had seen in the port since he had been there. He was intrigued by it and decided it was time to leave Myra.

He approached the master of the ship and worked up the courage to ask him for a job. He was in luck, as three of the crew had been injured in a fall from the mast. Since an injured crewman is useless on a ship, they were quickly sent ashore and told to find their own way home. Temeros was given a spot to put his meager possessions down in the crew quarters and was put to work.

He was so busy learning what was expected of him that he was only dimly aware of other passengers arriving and making arrangements for passage. He did see several soldiers on board and thought that was odd, but he was kept busy in the hold stacking the sacks of grain and filling the water cistern and loading other supplies as they prepared for a voyage to Rome.

Rome! He had not even bothered to ask where the ship was going, being more interested in just getting away and leaving his painful past behind him. But he never imagined he would have the chance to go to Rome! His heart leaped at the thought of all the possibilities ahead, changing his fate.

Now, after a few days at sea, the routine of the ship was beginning to set in. As he went about his work, he started to look more closely at the others on board. All told, there must have been over 200 people on the ship, so he had to be careful not to stumble over the passengers sitting around on the deck.

He noticed a group of people that tended to congregate in the prow of the ship. About fifteen or twenty sat in a group with several Roman soldiers close by. He finally asked another crew member about them and was told they were prisoners being transported to Rome. This fascinated him!

He walked closer to the group, wondering what a Roman prisoner looked like. Surely they must have done something horrible to be sent so far under guard! Maybe they were heading to the Coliseum to fight to the death! But he realized with some disappointment that they were pretty docile. In fact there seemed to be one prisoner speaking while the others were listening as though in school. He could not see very clearly since others were standing around.

As he got closer, he could see that the prisoner was gesturing to one of the Roman soldiers standing guard nearby. The guard did not appear very happy to be the center of attention of the prisoners, but the man did not seem to be inciting the prisoners to rebel. Rather, Temeros could hear him talking about the way the soldier was dressed.

"You see, he has a helmet to guard his head and a shield and sword as well as a breastplate. The prophet Isaiah once talked about his people seeking justice and salvation and then God responding by sending an intercessor. He described that intercessor as having 'righteousness as a breastplate, and a helmet of salvation on His head; He put on the garments of vengeance for clothing, and was clad with zeal as a cloak.'[1] In the same way, we who follow Christ are in a battle. Not against Rome! We battle against rulers of darkness of this age, spiritual hosts of wickedness. We, also, need to be wearing armor in the battle. We need the breastplate of God's righteousness and the helmet of His salvation but also His truth as a belt and faith in Him as a shield. With these, we are protected by God from the spiritual attacks we will face as we follow our Lord Jesus."[2]

At the mention of that name, Jesus, Temeros lost interest. He did not want to be reminded of the troubles in his life related to that name. He began to back away from the crowd. As he did, he glanced at the others standing around and stopped in his tracks in shock! One of the men was slim, tall, and dark haired and so familiar to him. He subconsciously reached for the scars on his ear as he stood gaping in surprise. Without a doubt, it was Luke, the doctor that had nursed him to health so many months before.

[1] Isaiah 59:17

[2] Based on Ephesians 6:12–17

# CHAPTER FOUR

H is shock lasted for a few seconds before his mind began to work more clearly. He realized he had been staring at Luke and quickly averted his gaze. As he did, he noticed Luke look over at him and he braced himself for an uncomfortable confrontation, but it never came. Luke did not show any recognition. Temeros realized it had been a couple of years since their painful meeting, and since then he had grown and become more muscular, now having a short beard and weathered skin. Of course, the head scarf covered the scars that could have identified him to the doctor. Luke glanced at him curiously and then looked away.

Temeros wandered toward the other side of the ship as his thoughts whirled. Should he go talk to him? Would Luke be angry that he had disappeared without any word or sign of gratitude? Would he demand some sort of payment for the care he provided? (Doctors could be so arrogant and greedy at times!)

His thoughts were interrupted by his boss, the foreman in charge of the ship's crew.

"Sabbi!" he yelled. "What are you doing? Stop daydreaming. Come here and help rig the sails!"

His boss was from Egypt, where the ship was based. He was known as Rayiz (Arabic for boss) and could be very strict but was also fair. He had taken to calling him Sabbi, which he learned meant "boy" in Arabic.

Temeros' heart skipped and he hurried over to the mast where Rayiz was pointing. He feared he was in trouble but the chief had already moved on to yell at another crew member, so he figured he would be saved any punishment for now.

One of the crew, Erastus, was looking up at the sail. He had been sailing on this ship for a few voyages and was well respected by the other crew members. He looked over at Temeros.

"Sabbi!" he called out. "I need your help. The rigging for the sail needs to be tightened. There's not enough wind, so the cloth is just hanging and it starts to loosen the support lines. I need you to climb up with me so we can adjust the ropes and tighten them."

Temeros swallowed hard. He was not fond of heights but knew he could not back down from this or he would definitely be punished. Even worse, he would be thought a coward by the rest of the crew. He nodded and said "Ok, just tell me how I can help."

"Just follow me and put your hands and feet where I do. Once we reach the crossbar up there, we will each take a side. I'll talk you through it." Erastus noticed his clenched jaw and the film of perspiration breaking out on his forehead and his expression softened. "Don't worry. It is always scary the first time but it is much easier than it sounds. Just keep your eyes focused on where you are climbing, and don't look down. If you start to get dizzy, let me know."

He nodded, the fear relaxing its grip on him ever so slightly. He took a deep breath and said "Ready when you are."

Erastus smiled reassuringly and turned toward the mast.

Temeros watched, paying close attention to the handholds he used. After Erastus climbed about ten feet off the deck, he stopped and looked down.

"Ok, come on up," he said.

He watched as Temeros reached for the handholds and started his climb. After a moment, he turned and continued toward the crossbar called the yard. The large square sail was hanging from this supported by thick rope lines at regular intervals.

Temeros was much slower and deliberate in his climb but focused on where he was reaching, just as instructed. He was relieved that the stopping point was steadily getting closer. There was a gentle breeze as he rose above the deck that made it almost pleasant. After a few minutes, he reached the crossbar where Erastus had been patiently waiting.

"See, that wasn't so bad, was it?" he said as he reached out a hand to help Temeros up onto the bar.

He found his footing and held tightly to the nearest rope as he looked around. He made the mistake of looking down and immediately gasped as he held tighter. They were about sixty feet in the air and the ship that had seemed so large when down on the deck suddenly seemed small. Also, the wind was more noticeable, and the motion of the ship that he no longer noticed down on the deck was magnified at this height. He became acutely aware of the swaying of the mast, side to side, several feet at a time. His eyes widened and his breath became shallow.

"Hey, look at me!" Erastus said. "Keep your eyes up here, Sabbi! It will be ok. Look at me!" he repeated.

Temeros tore his eyes away from the deck so far below and looked at Erastus. He blinked a few times and tried to calm his breathing. After a moment, he was able to feel more in control, and he slightly relaxed his white-knuckled grip on the rope.

"There, that's it," Erastus said encouragingly. "Just take it slowly, one thing at a time. First, we need to attach the safety rope, and then we will sit here for a minute to get settled. Take the rope you are holding onto and loop it around your chest under your arms. That can save your life up here!"

Temeros nodded sheepishly and did as instructed, keeping a strong hold on the rope the whole time. "I'm sorry," he said. "I think I'll be ok in a minute, now that I know I am attached to this lifeline!"

Erastus gave a reassuring smile. "You're doing fine. Everyone that climbs up here feels this way their first time. Don't let them fool you. Even Rayiz almost wet himself when he first started! But if you tell him I told you that, I will deny it!"

That drew a quick laugh from Temeros and immediately he felt better. "Thanks," he said. "I think I'm okay now. So, what's next?"

Erastus grinned. "Good!" He looked to his left at the rope that was a few feet out on the crossbar, just beyond Temeros. "Let's start with the easiest one first. See that rope just a foot or so from your left foot? You are going to slowly bend down while holding onto the safety line and reach out for it. Keep focused on the rope, not on what is below it!"

For the next several minutes, they focused on the task at hand. After a short time, he was able to push his fear to the edges of his consciousness. They moved from rope to rope, pulling each one tight and securing the riggings. The crossbar was wider than it had first seemed and he did not lose his footing. After making sure he was comfortable with the job, Erastus turned to his work, leaving him to do the last one on his own.

When he finished, he returned to the center mast and watched as Erastus did the same thing on his side. Temeros watched with envy as Erastus moved nimbly from one rope to the next, appearing to barely hold onto the safety line. When he finished with the furthest one, he surprised Temeros by grabbing the safety line and leaping outward, swinging in an arc back to the center.

"That was fun!" he said. "Days like this are great because there is no wind to blow you off balance. It is so hot down on the deck; I try to take a little extra time up here to enjoy the view and to cool off!"

Encouraged by watching his easy manner up in the riggings, Temeros cautiously looked around. From this height, he could see the coast in the distance to the north. There were no whitecaps since the wind was so light, but the wake stretched out behind them as they made slow progress in their voyage. The bright sun was ahead of them now as it continued its slow, steady descent toward the horizon. The sail blocked the view to the west, but it also provided some shade and they could see the brightness of the sun's glow behind the thick fabric. There were a few seabirds nearby, following the ship. They would occasionally perch on the top of the mast and the sail above them. He could see the appeal of being up here away from the noise of the crowded deck.

"Well, we better not stay too long or I will get accused of slacking off!" Erastus said. "Besides, we have been on this tack for a while so I imagine they will be turning soon. That can be a little tricky for your first time!"

They untied the safety lines and begin the slow, cautious descent. Or rather, Temeros began the slow, cautious descent as Erastus made fairly quick progress, moving easily downward and stopping frequently to wait on him so he was nearby for support.

When they reached the last eight feet or so, Erastus jumped nimbly to the deck and turned to guide Temeros for the last section.

"This part can get a little tricky, Sabbi!" he called up. "The rungs have a different spacing and are smaller. Watch your footing!"

Temeros, now about fifteen feet from the deck, reached out his left arm to wave in acknowledgment. As he turned to look down, his balance shifted and his foot slipped. He waved his free hand wildly trying to grip one of the handholds. Just as his fingers began to get a grip on it, his other foot slipped and he found himself holding on for dear life, supporting his body weight only with his right arm still gripping the handhold. He panicked as he felt himself swing away from the mast, scraping his left side on one of the handholds as he did. He felt his right shoulder twisting under his weight and his hand slipped. He fell the last several feet to the deck, landing with a grunt. His right hand was stretched out trying to break his fall, and he felt his shoulder pop painfully as he cried out in pain. The breath left his lungs and he found himself gasping like a fish out of water. His head started spinning and his vision darkened as he gave way to unconsciousness.

# CHAPTER FIVE

L uke checked the cloth bandage binding the sailor's wound and felt it was secure. The bleeding seemed to have slowed to a trickle with Luke's attention and had not seeped through the bandage. The edges of the wound were straight enough and the cut shallow enough that it should heal although the man would be left with a nice scar on his lower leg as a result. However, Luke had discovered over the years that the rough men who populated the sailing crews of the ships in this area usually took pride in their scars as evidence of surviving life's battles and coming out on top.

Luke once again checked to see that his foot was pink and warm and that the man could move his toes. He had him stand and although the man was sore, he felt he could be up and continue working.

Luke stood and stretched his back, stiff from bending over the man's leg. He gave instructions to keep the bandage in place for the next two days and then come to let him redress the wound, but it did not appear the man would have any complications. Infection was an ever-present risk, and Luke had learned that keeping the wound clean would help prevent such an occurrence but was a difficult thing to do on board a ship. He prayed silently for healing, as he always did after seeing someone who needed his attention, and watched the man limp back to his post.

His training as a doctor was widely known among the crew, and even the soldiers were now aware of his availability to treat the various ailments that may occur on a trip such as this. He had been on many ships, some as Paul's traveling companion and personal physician and some as the ship's doctor on various voyages in the area. His reputation for his skills in treating the sick and injured and for his compassion toward his patients was becoming well known at some of the busier seaports. Some captains had begun to ask for him by name, requesting that he serve on their ships as they traversed the seas between ports.

His time at sea had given him an education in sea travel, and he was well aware that the winds were contrary on this voyage making it slow going. The short distance from Myra to Fair Havens on the island of Crete could be accomplished in one or two days if the winds were favorable, but they had spent almost a week so far tacking to the north and south to combat the wind that was blowing from the Northwest. Every day on board could carry risks unique to sea travel, so prolonging the voyage due to contrary winds could lead to more trouble for him to address. His days were becoming very busy, but he was able to make time to enjoy the sunshine and light breeze on deck each day.

Luke made his way back over to the group at the forward part of the deck. About twenty people were gathered there, mostly prisoners. A few of the passengers had joined them to pass the time. The soldiers standing by, presumably on guard duty, could be seen listening as well to the short, bald man seated on the box with his back against the gunwale. The crowd was listening in rapt attention as he taught them. Luke smiled as he thought back to all of the adventures he had shared with this man, Paul, over the past few years.

———

Luke had grown up in Antioch. As a young man, he developed an interest in science and medicine. He was apprenticed to a local physician and learned the art of evaluating patients and formulating various balms and poultices to aid in treatment. He was taught bloodletting and could diagnosis ailments by evaluating the humors just as well as his teacher after a few years. He had heard of the centers for medicine in Smyrna and the sources of eye salve in Laodicea. He dreamed of someday traveling there to learn more about those treatment options as well.

Over the years he became well known throughout Antioch. His gentle but confident nature and his skill in treating his sick patients caused his good reputation to spread to the surrounding areas as well. He became fairly busy and settled into a comfortable existence.

His passion and focus on medicine changed when some strangers from Jerusalem arrived. They began to teach in the Jewish synagogue about the incredible things that had happened in Judea and Galilee, teaching about a man named Jesus. This was no ordinary man, they said, but rather the savior of the world, the Messiah long awaited by the Jews.

Luke was a Gentile and had no interest in converting to Judaism, so the synagogue generally held no interest for him. He was not present to hear firsthand the amazing accounts of the miracles. There were tales of people being healed of incurable diseases, and some even said people had come back from the dead! He laughed at this when he first was told of this story by one of his patients. As a doctor, he was well aware that was impossible. How gullible were these people to believe such lies? But, the group continued to grow, much to his surprise.

The more devout Jews were very resistant to this new doctrine. They were trained in the Scriptures and traditions of their fathers, and they knew what God would do. The Messiah was going to be a conqueror and throw off the Roman oppression, not live in poverty and be killed by the Romans. This Jesus that was being taught actually opposed the Jewish leaders in Jerusalem! It was preposterous to believe He was doing anything on God's orders. And to hear that people were actually worshipping Him?! This just could not be tolerated! They began actively resisting these men to regain control of their synagogue.

The growing group of believers responded by leaving the synagogue, gathering at other meeting places and forums. As their numbers increased, many Gentiles joined them. Surprisingly, the Jewish converts welcomed them. This was incredible in itself. Jews and Gentiles did not mix. This further offended the Jewish priests, but there seemed to be an inevitable decline in the number of people attending the synagogue.

Soon, word spread to the Church in Jerusalem about the church in Antioch. Barnabas, a devout member of the church there, was dispatched to encourage the congregation and teach them further of God's grace and Jesus' sacrifice for them, as well as to tell them of the Holy Spirit.

After a few weeks, Barnabas departed, indicating he was going to bring back another teacher to assist him in the work of the church. He left for a few months and returned from Tarsus with another man named Saul. The two of them ignited the fervor of the congregation catching the attention of the entire city.

Luke began to hear reports of people claiming to be healed of diseases. He laughed this off as mere religious hyperbole until one of his own patients with an incurable skin disease returned completely cured. Some diseases could be hidden, but not this. It had been clearly on display, a weeping ulcer on his cheek for several weeks, beginning to spread to his ear. Luke had given several courses of treatment with various poultices but finally had told the man he could not do anything else for him. To see him standing there now, completely cleared just one week later and with no trace of scar, was unbelievable.

Luke decided to go himself to hear firsthand what was being said, intending to defend scientific facts and refute some of the wild stories he had heard. He well remembered his first visit. The people were not ignorant or simpleminded as he expected. The teacher, Barnabas, was a devout, gentle soul, a model of morality and compassion. The other man, Saul, was more forceful in his teaching and displayed a logical mind, obviously well-educated and trained in debate. Luke found himself at times irritated by the man's confidence but then surprised by his humility in sharing his own background and failures. Despite his intentions, he found himself drawn to these men and desiring to hear more.

He continued to come back, ostensibly to investigate and gather more evidence. Over the next several weeks, it became obvious that Saul was the primary preacher. He seemed to have great skill in pointing out truths seen in nature and in life around them, relating them to the truth of God's existence and always coming back to grace and peace related to this man Jesus. Surprisingly, he believed that Jesus had risen from the dead, and he offered many convincing proofs of this.

Most compelling was his own story of conversion. He was not just an average, every day sinner. He was a notorious and widely feared persecutor of the early believers, working under the authority of the Jewish high priest. His goal was to seek out these followers and bring them back to Jerusalem in chains to be punished. He was traveling to Damascus for this purpose when he was suddenly blinded by a bright light from the sky and knocked to the ground. Those traveling with him saw the light and saw him fall, and they were afraid. Saul was talking to someone they could not see or hear. Saul professed to have actually heard the voice of Jesus Christ!

He was sent to a specific place in Damascus to await further instructions. He was completely blind for three days until a believer named Ananias was sent by the Lord to teach him. Immediately after Ananias prayed for him, his sight was restored. He was forever changed by that encounter and knew he could no longer follow the path of persecuting believers when he himself now believed.

Luke was skeptical, but the evidence offered by Saul, as well as the proof in the changed lives of the people in the congregation (many of whom were known to Luke from his past treatment of the injuries and illnesses that resulted from their sins), were undeniable. Luke was not one usually ruled by emotion. He prided himself on logically considering facts and making informed decisions. In this situation, although Saul offered compelling arguments and the others in the church supported and agreed with what he taught, eventually there was a point where facts fell short and he had to decide to make a leap of faith. For several days, Luke wrestled with this, feeling the weight of his own sin and realizing his need for a savior but still wanting some sort of proof. He felt that giving in to stories of miracles and resurrections would tarnish his reputation as a man of science, but he could not go on living the way he had after being confronted by God in this way.

He resisted until he could no longer stand it. Sleep eluded him and he felt a sense of turmoil inside. He could not keep going on this way. He sought out Saul one night, waking him from sleep and asking that he pray with him. Saul was eager to do this and after a simple prayer and laying hands on Luke's head, something unexplainable happened. There was an immediate and overwhelming sense of peace and healing and Luke was overcome by emotion. His turmoil ceased, and his mind was clear with a sense of joyful purpose. He could barely put into words what had happened, but Saul recognized immediately that he had encountered the Lord. As the Holy Spirit began to work in his soul, he began to understand more and more why Saul continued to speak of grace and peace.

From that point on, although he continued to work as a doctor, his priorities shifted. He wanted others to know that this life was not the end, that eternity awaited, and that only through Jesus' sacrifice could they someday have eternal life. As Luke interacted with his patients, he was more acutely aware of how many of them were following after pleasure, living for the moment. This was a source for so much of their pain and physical ailments, but so few of them were willing to acknowledge this. Even if they agreed that pleasure-seeking was the source of their troubles, they continued on the same path. It was hard to understand at times.

Saul and Barnabas stayed in Antioch and taught the Christians many things. Saul was well trained in the Jewish Scriptures and showed how the prophecies pointed to Jesus. They instructed them about living a Christian life and about the teachings of the Lord himself. They lived in anticipation of Jesus' imminent return, and new converts were continually joining them.

As Saul's ministry became increasingly oriented toward the Gentile believers, he made the decision to stop calling himself by his Jewish name, Saul, but rather by its Roman equivalent, Paul. To the Gentiles, his Roman citizenship led to opportunities that a Jewish man would not have had, and this simple but profound change in his name was a way to further the kingdom among the Gentiles.

Luke and Saul (now Paul) had become close friends over the ensuing months. They had many long discussions, each admiring and respecting the wisdom and logical nature of the other. Through their discussions, Luke learned more of the early days of the Church in Jerusalem. He peppered him with questions about Jesus, wanting more details about his life than just what he taught.

"I really want to know more about Jesus, His life, and the things He did. Where was he born? Where did he live? What about his family? All of it! If I am to follow this Way, I need to learn. Any suggestions?"

"Well, all of the information we have has been passed on to us by oral tradition. Aside from his teachings that we have been sharing, we know of some of His miracles of healing and of course of His resurrection. The details on his life are not as widely known. We don't have a written record at this time."

"I think it is very important to have this in writing. I'm sure there are many others who want to know this information other than me. Oral traditions are great, but we all know that over time there can be changes in how the details are communicated. This is too vital to trust to imperfect memories!"

Paul considered this. "You are right. It would be helpful to commit this to parchment so all can be given the same information." He thought about this for a moment. "I know many of the Twelve are still in Jerusalem. They walked with Him and listened to His teaching in person. They would be the logical ones to give this information. His brother, James, is even leading the church there now."

Luke became excited by this. "His brother?! You are kidding! Can you imagine the stories he may be able to share? I would love to travel there and interview these men face-to-face! It would be amazing to meet people who were actually in His presence. They would have so much to tell us!"

"Wait, that's not really what I meant," Paul said. "I just meant if they would send us their written memories of Jesus we could learn more from them."

Luke had already latched onto the idea of researching and writing this biography of Jesus and was already planning his strategy. He started making arrangements with another physician to be available for those who needed care and arranging travel. He asked Paul for letters of introduction to the Jerusalem church. He could scarcely contain his excitement at the idea of meeting them and learning more about the Lord.

Over the next few years, Luke made several trips to Jerusalem. The initial discussions with the Apostles were amazing. Luke was in awe of being in their presence, knowing that they were friends of Jesus. They were able to provide so many details of his life and ministry. When Luke's questions stumped them, they usually knew of others who could provide answers. Eventually, he even had the glorious opportunity to interview Mary, Jesus' mother. What an amazing discussion they had! He made copious notes and then began organizing them as he considered how to write this life story of the Good News of Jesus.

As he was doing this, Paul and Barnabas began to travel around the region. They preached in the cities throughout Asia and Macedonia and Greece, establishing churches and teaching them about Jesus. Luke was able to joint them on some of these missionary travels. As they traveled by ship, he became more familiar with the seaports and the various medical needs common among the sailing crews. He began to work with the captains and gained a reputation as a good doctor to have on board for their voyages.

Now, with Paul's imprisonment for the past two years, the future of the church was hard to see. It seemed that Paul would surely be released. He was not guilty of the crime of which they had accused him, but Roman politics seemed to conspire against him. He was interviewed by the governor and the Jewish high priest, and then his sentence was extended until the new governor decided to question him. Finally, Paul took the bold step of appealing to Caesar, and as a Roman citizen, this could not be denied him. That led to their current situation on board this Egyptian grain ship, making slow, slow progress toward Rome.

———————

As Luke approached the group of prisoners and passengers, one of them seated at the edge of the crowd looked up and smiled.

"Hello, Dr. Luke!" he said quietly, so as not to disturb the others. "Have you been out torturing the sick and injured again?"

Luke laughed. "Aristarchus, you know I reserve that treatment only for ungrateful prisoners like you! At least I am making myself useful!"

Aristarchus grinned in return. "Hey, my job is very important. Someone has to keep this box from blowing away," he said pointing to his seat. "Besides, Paul might need me to explain some of the finer points of our faith if someone asks him a tough question he can't answer!"

At this, both men had a good chuckle. They well knew that everything they had come to know about Jesus and the Christian Way had been taught to them by Paul. His knowledge and depth of insight into God's kingdom and topics of discipleship were unfathomable. They knew there was nothing they could teach him on these subjects.

Aristarchus was one of Paul's traveling companions on his most recent missionary journey. He was almost always in a good mood, and as his faith had grown, he had learned to trust God in all situations. Even when the rioting crowd seized him in Ephesus, he was reminded of Paul's view of the various hardships and dangers they faced as light and momentary. He was quick with a smile and he and Luke had become good friends. Now, he was numbered among the prisoners, having been caught up in the persecution of the church. He was arrested and held in the same prison as Paul in Caesarea. It was providential that he was now traveling with Paul to Rome on their current voyage.

"What is the topic today?" Luke asked him.

"So many things! One topic raises questions that lead to other topics. Some of the group believe, but there are some who are here just to pass the time or to try to challenge what he is teaching. Of course they are no match for Paul!"

They turned their attention to what was being said. Paul was recounting his conversion story on the road to Damascus. Even though Luke and Aristarchus had heard this many times, it still amazed them to think that Jesus had actually spoken to Paul, setting him apart for this ministry to Gentiles that had reached them and forever changed their hearts.

# CHAPTER SIX

As he stood at the edge of the crowd surrounding Paul, Luke glanced around at the various people scattered about the ship. Earlier, when the group had first gathered, he thought he had seen one of the younger crew members looking directly at him. He was wearing a head scarf and had a startled expression on his face, but he turned quickly to his work and did not look back. He was puzzled by this but thought it must be his imagination. Now he was not so sure. Something in the man's bearing seemed vaguely familiar. As he looked around now, though, he could not see him anywhere. He shrugged and turned back to Paul.

Suddenly, someone cried out and pointed to the mast. Luke turned to see a group rushing toward the base of the mast and the sight of someone lying on the deck unmoving.

He quickly made his way there and pushed through the crowd.

"What happened?" he asked the men standing nearby.

One of the crew said, "We had been up on the mast attending to the sails. We were climbing down, and when he was close, he tried to turn and answer me when he slipped! I'm afraid it is my fault! Will he be ok?"

"I'll do my best to help him. Let me take a look," Luke responded.

As he knelt down by his side, the man began to moan and move his head. Those standing around let out a sigh of relief at these signs of life.

"Wait!" Luke said to the man. "Don't move yet. Let me make sure you are ok." Turning to the man he had just talked to, Luke asked, "What is his name?"

"We call him Sabbi. I don't know his real name. He is new and I have just begun to get to know him," the man replied, still with a worried look on his face.

Luke gently felt the man's head and neck. There was no bleeding and he did not feel any shifting of the bones of the skull. His neck seemed to be ok. He quickly assessed his extremities. It was immediately obvious to Luke that his right shoulder was not properly aligned. As his fingers probed around the joint, the man, Sabbi, cried out and tried to withdraw.

"Sorry," Luke said. "I think you may have dislocated your shoulder. I need to check it and see if we can get it back in proper position before everything begins to tighten up."

He gently lifted the man's arm and rotated it to see how well his range of motion was. The exam confirmed his suspicions.

"Sabbi," he said to the man lying on the deck. "Can you hear me?"

The man tried to nod his head but immediately grimaced in pain.

"It's ok, don't try to move. Your shoulder was dislocated when you fell. I need to get it back into the socket before everything gets more stiff and tight. It may hurt a bit, but just try to relax and I will do all the work." He patted his other shoulder reassuringly.

As Sabbi lay on the deck, Luke gently straightened his arm and began to lift it slowly above his head as he placed his other hand on the front of the shoulder. He felt the upper arm bone under the skin and was relieved when he felt it clunk back into proper position. Sabbi gave a whimper and then relaxed as the shoulder pain quickly felt better. Luke put his arm back down by his side.

"We need to put your arm in a sling for a few days to allow it to heal fully. Let me use your head scarf," he said as he reached to remove it from the man's head.

Sabbi tried to stop him, raising his other arm and turning his head, but again he felt the ship begin to spin around him and had to lie back on the deck again. "No, please don't," he said.

By that time, however, Luke already had removed the head scarf and was placing it around the man's neck to support the right arm. As he did so, he saw the reason the man tried to stop him from removing the scarf. The left ear was partially deformed and the side of the head was scarred, appearing to have been burned.

Immediately, Luke recognized his patient. "I know you!" he said. "I helped to treat you the night you were burned! That was at least a year ago, wasn't it?"

The man called Sabbi tried to respond, but as he turned toward Luke, he immediately groaned and laid back. He felt sick and took some deep breaths to calm his stomach.

"Take it slowly!" Luke instructed. "You must have hit your head pretty hard. Don't worry about talking. There will be time enough for that later. Let's get you to a more comfortable place."

He asked the men standing nearby to help carry Sabbi to his sleeping quarters.

"Slowly! Be gentle!" he instructed them. "Try to keep from jostling him too much."

They made it to the area designated for Luke, as the ship's doctor, and placed him on the pallet. Then Luke sent them out, telling them his patient needed rest.

About that time, Aristarchus came to the door to check on him. "Where did you go?" he said. "I turned around to talk to you and you had disappeared. The crew said someone had fallen, so I assumed you were there somewhere to help!"

Luke stepped outside and spoke quietly. He told him of the fall and the injury.

"Now, he needs to rest. He hit his head pretty hard so it may be a few days before he can do much." He paused. "Aristarchus, it is pretty amazing but I know this boy! I recognized the scars on the head from the night we met!"

Aristarchus started to tease him about his poor treatment leaving permanent scars, but let it pass. He could tell this was troubling to Luke. "Tell me about what happened," he prompted.

Luke related the tale of finding him by the road and treating his burns. As he talked, he began to recall more details. It was near Ephesus, and the man's father was involved in the temple worship somehow in Ephesus. His family had perished in a fire and he recalled the sadness and anger he displayed.

"I tried to gently point the way toward God but he was very opposed to any discussion of religion. I had planned to resume that discussion after he recovered, but one morning after I had gone to get some supplies, I came back to the inn and he was gone. No one could tell me where he went."

Aristarchus considered this. "You said he spoke of Ephesus and the temple and then of fires. This was a couple of years ago? That was about the time of the riots, where I was seized by the crowd. Do you think this could have something to do with that mess?" he said, intrigued.

"That might be!" Luke said. "It would sure fit the circumstances. I wish I could remember his name. It will come to me."

They considered this silently for a moment.

"Maybe we should tell Paul. He can pray for him and lay hands on him," Aristarchus suggested.

"That is a good idea," Luke said. "He surely needs to know Jesus and the healing he can bring to his life. I'm just afraid he is not quite ready to hear that. I'll need to see if he indicates any openness to such a discussion now. First, I need to let his body heal. I'll get him something for his pain when he wakes up."

"Well, he seems to be in good hands," Aristarchus said.

"I'm shocked!" Luke said, acting surprised. "I think that may be the closest thing to a compliment I have ever heard from you!"

Aristarchus chuckled. "Don't flatter yourself!" he said, a broad grin spreading across his face. "I was talking about me. I'll be watching closely to be sure you don't make his injuries worse!"

Luke laughed. "I knew it was too good to be true!" he said. "Let's go back to the deck and let him rest. I'll check on him again later."

Temeros heard them walk away. He laid on the makeshift bed, his shoulder aching, his head throbbing, and tears in his eyes as he thought about the conversation he had overheard. His emotions were conflicted. These men seemed to have a genuine concern for him. He longed for the kind of friendship they seemed to have with each other. At the same time, they spoke of Paul. That name brought a flood of memories accompanied by anger, hatred, fear, and loneliness as he felt anew the grief over losing his family.

——————

Memories of the night that left his life so scarred came rushing back uninvited. He clearly recalled his father, Demetrius, railing against this man, Paul, who had disrupted the city of Ephesus along with the rest of the region. He had become enraged by the fact that his business was decimated as people turned to this Jesus that Paul taught about. They no longer were buying the silver shrines to Artemis that had been his main source of income. He had been in the city center all day, stirring up the other silversmiths and artisans into a frenzy. The crowd became an unruly mob, rioting in the theater. Temeros had been at the edge of the crowd watching the excitement as some of the men who had traveled and worked with Paul were seized. The crowd was demanding justice, calling for Paul to be punished, but he was nowhere to be found.

After several hours his father returned home, still seething with anger. He was fuming about Paul and about Jesus and how they had ruined his life. As he was going on about Jesus and the problems from this "cult" of his followers, Temeros' mother had said something to defend Paul and Jesus which caused his father to become even more irate, now that anger targeted at her.

When it was revealed that his own wife had become a follower of this Jesus, it had pushed him over the edge. Even the memory now, a few years later, caused Temeros to feel anew the fear mixed with anger as his father shouted at his mother. There had been other fights, but this was the worst and it became physical. He grabbed her and shook her violently and even went so far as to slap her across the face. Temeros tried to intervene but then he became a target of his father's wrath as well, being knocked to the ground.

There was no way to reason with him and they tried to get away, running together to the small storage room and closing the door. The barricades were not strong but were enough to keep him from reaching them.

But then, in his blinding fury, he must have thrown a lighted lamp at the door. The oil in the lamp splashed across the door and the walls, igniting. The fire quickly spread.

His father was screaming maniacally, saying "Where is this Jesus now? Let's see if He will save you from this! You will never be my wife again! Go to this precious Paul that you seem so devoted to!"

They could hear him on the other side of the door throwing more items against the wall, and then his voice faded as the roar of the fire increased.

The smell of fire and billowing smoke began to spread under the door. In his terror, Temeros began frantically searching the room for anything that may help save them. It was a small room barely larger than a closet. There were no windows to crawl through. He could barely see but as he felt along the wall opposite the door, he bumped into the shelf where the food was stored. He knew that was not going to help, but as he searched through the items on the shelf, he felt cloth, evidently aprons that his mother wore when cooking.

He grabbed two of them and tried to squeeze some of the fruit onto it, anything to wet it. It wasn't much but it was all they had. He gave one to his mother, and they both wrapped the aprons around their head and shoulders.

He knew the door was their only way out. The fear of facing his father was still very strong but the fire was a more immediate threat. They had no choice. He quickly cleared the barricade from the door and yanked on the handle to open it, but it would not budge. He tried again, but then the horrible truth became clear. They were trapped. His father must have latched the door from the other side!

At this news, his mother began to cry, apologizing to him.

"Now is not the time, mother!!" he said in response. "We have to get that door open or we won't survive!"

She mumbled something then, and moved back to the far wall. Temeros' attention was focused on the door. It was made of thick pieces of wood and he was not sure how to get it open. He rattled the handle, beginning to feel some warmth on this side of the door. He pushed forcefully on the middle of the door and thought he could feel it give slightly.

He steeled his courage as he kicked the door. The heat from the fire was increasing, now radiating through the door, but the wood had not weakened enough to break. He kicked a second time and felt it crack and a small piece of it fell away. The heat of the fire was more intense now, not impeded by the door. He knew time was running out. He rammed the door with his shoulder, and it collapsed under him, sending him sprawling on the floor on top of it. The cloth fell from around his head. He immediately was surrounded by fire, feeling the intense heat on the side of his head and smelling burnt flesh and hair. He cried out in pain but was able to jump up quickly and move back from the flames.

He turned to his mother and yelled. "We must go now or we won't make it!"

She was kneeling against the wall, eyes closed, praying fervently that Jesus would save them. Temeros knew there was no time and that they must save themselves. He grabbed her by the arm and she nodded to him with a determined look.

"I'm ready" she said, her voice steady. She appeared calm, almost at peace.

Temeros wondered at this but did not have time to dwell on it. Together they took a breath and ran as fast as possible through the wall of flame blocking the door.

The intensity of the fire was terrible but only lasted a moment. Then they were on the other side. He looked around quickly for his father, readying himself for a fight, but he was not there. He must have gone to the workshop where he kept his tools as well as some weapons.

The far wall had not yet started burning, but the flames were licking the ceiling and beginning to spread above their heads. Smoke filled the room. Temeros half dragged her to the far wall where the door to the outside was located. As he let go of her arm to open the door, she collapsed on the floor, coughing. He pulled the door open, allowing a rush of fresh air into the room and giving him hope of escape, but when he turned to help his mother, the fresh air mingled with the flames causing an enormous ball of fire and rush of hot wind that knocked him from his feet throwing him outside onto the ground. As he jumped up, he saw fire filling the doorway where he had just been.

He could see his mother's form, surrounded by the flames, but now she was standing, with arms raised and eyes looking up. He was not sure but it sounded like she was singing. He was sure it was the fire playing tricks on his vision, but he had imagined he saw a second person standing with her. This form was taller than his father and seemed to have a more regal bearing. Temeros had the fleeting impression this form was somehow protecting his mother. He knew that could not be. There was no one else in the house. All of this lasted just a moment before the house collapsed, destroying the room.

He was stunned, tears streaming down his face as he called out to her, but there was no hope. She was gone. He sobbed for a moment and then had a pang of fear. What about his father? Even with his rage and violence, Temeros knew he could not just leave him. He had no other family.

He made his way around the burning house to the workshop in the rear. It, too, was beginning to burn. The fire was climbing the wall adjacent to the house, and flames were licking at the thatching that comprised the roof.

Temeros yanked open the door and called out. "Father! Are you in here?"

There was no answer. He quickly surveyed the room, walking around the large workbench. He saw the silver pendant he had been making for his mother and snatched it up as he searched. The light from the burning roof was getting brighter and he knew there was not much time. He did not see his father anywhere.

He turned to go back out, and just then a section of the roof crashed down to the floor. The brightness of the falling flames illuminated the dark corner furthest from him. He saw a glimpse of his father slumped against a barrel, a bottle of ale next to him. Before he could get to him, however, the wall began to crumble and a large section fell directly on his father as the blaze filled the room. There was a muffled scream that quickly stopped as the fire incinerated that corner of the workshop.

He turned and fled into the night pursued by the intense heat.

—————

Now, even a few years later, the pain of his father's rage and his mother's death was fresh. He missed his mother, and at times even his father. His mind wandered back to memories of his home and his childhood. After a few minutes, his mind began to grow dim and he drifted off to a fitful sleep.

# CHAPTER SEVEN

When he woke up the next morning, he felt much better. Then he tried to move and immediately his shoulder screamed in pain and his head started throbbing. He sagged back onto the sleeping mat and took a few deep breaths for a moment before trying again, much more slowly. It took him a moment to get his bearings and he remembered that he was in Luke's sleeping quarters. Light filtered in through a small window, and he could see that the room was empty. He could hear distant voices and the creaking of the ship.

After the pain subsided, he attempted to get up. That was a struggle as he could not use his right arm and the strain of movement caused him to feel pain in parts of his body he did not realize were injured. He groaned in pain and ceased his efforts, deciding rather to rest a bit longer. He was sitting with his back leaning against the bulkhead when the door opened.

"Good morning!" Luke said as he entered the room. "I'm glad to see you're awake. Last evening you were pretty groggy. I checked on you a few times in the night and you seemed pretty restless. Do you remember what happened?"

Temeros considered this. "I think so. I remember being up on the mast and climbing down. I don't remember how I got there, but I remember lying on the deck with people around me. You did something to my shoulder and then I was carried here. How bad was I hurt?"

Luke crossed over to where he lay and knelt beside him. "Your shoulder was out of place, but I think I was able to get it back in the socket.

You had a nasty bump on your head, but I don't think you did any lasting damage. Let me take a look at your shoulder," he said as he began to gently loosen the sling.

As the sling came off, Temeros realized it was his head scarf and he self-consciously reached up to touch his ear and the scars on his scalp.

"Sorry, I had to borrow your head covering to support your arm. I noticed the scars and I think we've met before. Aren't you the young man I found hurt along the road near Smyrna a few years ago?"

"Yeah," Temeros said, his eyes dropping. "You're Dr. Luke. I remember you."

"Remind me of your name," Luke said as he palpated the structures of his shoulder.

"Temeros," he said as he winced.

"That's it!" Luke said. "I have been trying to remember. It is good to see you again!"

He supported the elbow and said, "Bear with me. I need to check on how well your shoulder moves. This is going to be a little sore, but try to relax as much as you can."

He gently moved his upper arm out from his body as he kept his other hand on the top of the shoulder. Temeros gasped and whispered an epithet.

"Ok, good!" Luke said, a pleased expression on his face. "I apologize for the pain, but I think your shoulder is in good position and it will start to heal in the next few days. Now let me check your head. Can you move your eyes for me?" he said as he moved his finger from side to side, watching closely.

Temeros complied but as he did so felt slightly queasy and the room seemed to swirl around him briefly. He closed his eyes after a moment.

"Looks like you will be resting for a couple of days," he said, "but I don't think there is any major problem."

Luke reached up and felt the back of his head around the bump that had arisen after the fall.

"I think that seems to have gone down a lot over night!" he said encouragingly. "I think everything will be good after a few days."

"What about my work here on the ship?" Temeros asked. "I am afraid they will send me ashore and replace me at our next port."

"Don't worry about that right now," Luke said. "I know the captain and I think I can convince him that this is temporary. I'm pretty certain he would rather keep a crew member that has already become familiar with the ship than start over with one he does not know. Besides, as late as it is, sailing season is about spent. I imagine we will be spending a couple of months in port until the winter dangers are over."

Temeros relaxed at that. "Thank you, Luke." He paused a moment and then added, "I am sorry about sneaking away the first time we met. I am grateful for what you did to help, but…"

Luke interrupted him. "Hey, don't worry about that. It was a long time ago. I'm just glad to see you have recovered. You seem to have found your way these last couple of years. You can fill me in on what you have been doing sometime. For now, let's see if we can get you up. You can come out to the deck and rest. I think there is a group up there talking."

It took some effort but Luke was able to support him and help him to his feet. Temeros put his good arm across Luke's shoulder and tried to steady himself as they walked slowly. The short walk to the deck was an ordeal, but by that time, Aristarchus had joined them. Between the two of them helping him, he made it.

Out on deck, the sun was shining brightly and the gentle breeze was blowing. The bright sunshine hurt his eyes and reawakened the dizzy feeling for a moment but he quickly adjusted. They helped him cross over to the group that was sitting together at the bow of the ship and got him settled on a blanket with a place to lean back and rest.

"Sorry to interrupt, teacher," Luke said to the man at the center of the group.

"No problem, Luke," he responded. He stood and walked over to where they were, kneeling down beside Temeros. "Hi," he said, reaching out his hand to touch his shoulder. "I'm Paul."

At this, Temeros stiffened and his jaw clenched. His brow furrowed ever so slightly. Luke noticed all of this and made a note to inquire about this later.

"This is Temeros," Luke answered for him. "He is on the ship's crew but fell yesterday afternoon. He will need to rest for a couple of days to let his shoulder and his head heal. I thought he may want to join the group and have some company." He watched Temeros' expression closely as he said this. He did not respond.

"I am very glad you can be here with us. I will pray that your injuries will heal quickly. I know how it can feel to have injuries like this. It seems even if you only hurt one part of your body, you ache everywhere!" Paul said.

Aristarchus interrupted. "Teacher, what have you been talking about while we were away?"

"I was just commenting on how this ship can be out in the ocean, away from any landmarks, and yet the captain and crew are able to read the position of the sun and stars and still direct us to our destination. In the same way, we may be in unfamiliar circumstances in our lives, with none of the things that are familiar to us, like family or home or friends. In that situation, we need to have something we can look to for direction, a constant reference point. For us, God provides that in His words in the Scriptures but also through the teachings of the Living Word, Jesus. In addition, the Holy Spirit is living in us to give us inward guidance when we are lost. Just as the ship needs wind to propel it through the sea, the Spirit provides the spiritual power to move forward as God directs."

As he spoke, Temeros watched closely, expecting to see signs of hatred, arrogance, and destruction. This was the picture his father had painted of Paul in Ephesus, leading to loss of his business and his horrible anger that led to the tragic death of Temeros' mother. So far, he saw none of this, but surely Paul was putting on an act for those around him. He burned with anger, desiring vengeance for the loss of his family and of his comfortable, familiar life. But as Paul continued speaking, his anger began to waver.

He tried to appear uninterested in what was being taught, but the words Paul spoke resonated with him. Here he was, alone in an unfamiliar place, no friends or family. Many times he had wondered how he got here and where he was trying to go. He did not know who to turn to for advice.

"I never cease to be amazed at how you can take normal everyday

things around us and see something that points to God and his kingdom!" Aristarchus said. "Luke and I were talking about that the other
day. I think you could take anything we mention and find some spiritual
truth to teach us!"

Paul smiled at that. "I don't think that is entirely true! However, God
is all around us and sometimes we just need to open our eyes to see what
He is doing. Even King David wrote in the Psalms 'The heavens declare
the glory of God; the skies proclaim the work of His hands. Day after day
they pour forth speech; night after night they display knowledge. There is
no speech or language where their voice is not heard.'[3] I think if we medi-
tate on Him, the Holy Spirit brings to our mind these truths."

"So what else has He brought to your mind?"

"Well, I was just thinking a moment ago about our friend's injuries,"
he said, pointing toward Temeros. I think of the church as the body of
Christ, our Lord, here on earth. We are His hands and feet of flesh until
he returns. When the body is injured, it is not able to function as it should
and we cannot perform the duties we are called to be doing. When there
is an injury like this, even though only one part is injured, it affects the
whole, and all of the body suffers and aches with it."

The group around him was listening attentively, nodding in agreement.

"As we think of the body, we also know that there are many parts to
the body, all of which serve a different purpose. Some are more promi-
nent and active, while others have smaller roles to play. But each one has
to play the part it is designed for. If I am a toe in the body of Christ but all
I do is try to do the duties of the eye, the body will not walk very well. If
the eye wants to be the mouth and speak for God, refusing to do its designated part, the body will be blind stumbling around without direction."[4]

This analogy brought chuckles from those listening.

"We in the body are instructed to support each other, lifting each
other up, with each one serving where God has placed us. We should not
seek the visible, important places of service for our own glory. If God

---

[3] Psalm 19:1–3 (NIV)

[4] See 1 Corinthians 12:12–26.

wants us to serve in that capacity, it comes with greater responsibility. Many times I have felt the weight of that charge, wishing God had made me just a toenail in His Body rather than what I am. But I cannot deny that He has directed me to proclaim His grace and mercy even to the Gentiles. The Holy Spirit has allowed me to spread this truth across Asia and Greece and Macedonia and, now, to Rome as well!"

As Temeros listened, this did not sound like the words of a trouble-maker. There was no arrogance or pride or self-promotion in his words. Maybe his father had been wrong. But surely something had caused his father to do what he did. It must have been something Paul had done.

This conversation continued for the rest of the morning, and as the afternoon wore on, various people would leave the group and others join. There was no specific agenda but just an ongoing conversation sprinkled with easy-going laughter.

Temeros dozed in the afternoon sun, enjoying the fall breeze. Luke helped him stand and stretch a few times and he walked around the deck. He and Luke went to the supervisor to talk about his restrictions and Rayiz was not happy about it. He agreed to give Temeros a few days to recover but then would expect him to begin doing some work. They agreed to this with the understanding that he had to be cleared for work by Luke.

They were making progress toward Fair Havens, expecting to arrive the next day. This late in the season, there was debate about whether they would be going any further or if they may need to winter there. If so, his injuries would have plenty of time to heal before they could sail in the spring. Temeros began to look forward to being off the ship for an extended period of time.

After meeting with Rayiz, Luke helped him to a less crowded area and sat down by him.

"I noticed that you appeared to have heard of Paul," he said. "I get the feeling you were not happy about what you have heard. Would you like to talk about it?"

Temeros' countenance darkened at this. He clenched his jaw and considered this question. "I would just say that Paul has been the subject of much pain in my life."

Luke was silent for a moment. "I have known Paul for several years and I know he can be exasperating and very firm in his language, but his entire focus is on sharing the Gospel of Jesus Christ. He is motivated by love, but some have a hard time seeing that. Are you comfortable sharing any more information with me about what happened?" he asked.

Temeros glared at Luke and gestured to his burn scars as the words poured out. "This is all due to him. My family disintegrated, my mother was killed, and my father lost his mind in anger and perished in the same fire. I am all alone, with no home, no family, and no friends!" he said angrily. "Paul caused all of this!"

Luke took a breath and chose his words carefully. "I know you are from Ephesus. Paul shared with me that the city was overtaken by riots in protest to his ministry. Even my friend Aristarchus was seized by the crowds during that time and feared for his life. Do you mean that affected your family as well?"

"My father was the leader of the silversmiths, faithful to the temple of Artemis. And yet my mother heard Paul and began to follow this Jesus that he spends so much time talking about. When my father heard of this, he was angry. Not only was his business ruined by Paul and his influence on the people in the town, but my mother betrayed him by joining the very ones who were the cause of his troubles." As he spoke, his anger gave way to tears. "My father was the one that called the town together to protest. When he came home, he found out about my mother's belief in what Paul taught and he lost his mind with rage. He lit the house on fire and then went to his workshop, drunk. I saw the burning roof of his workshop collapse on him, killing him. I was burned trying to save my mother, but she... she..." his voice faltered as he let out a sob.

Luke put his arm around him as he wept. "I'm so sorry," he said quietly. He said no more for a moment as Temeros cried, his hands to his face, head bent in grief.

After a short time, the weeping subsided and Temeros sat with his head bowed forward.

"My friend, I am sorry you have suffered so much. All I can tell you is that our Lord has defeated death and there is great comfort in knowing that your mother believed before this terrible act occurred. I can assure you that she is in paradise with God as we speak. Jesus has overcome the power of death in our lives. When we who believe in Him lose a loved one, we miss them terribly, but we do not grieve as people who have no hope. We know that we will see them again if we trust Him to guide us and believe that he has paid the price for our wrongdoing."

Temeros sniffed, listening. "Do you really believe that? Aren't you a doctor? Isn't death irreversible?"

Luke nodded. "Yes from a human standpoint, we cannot avoid death. But I have spent the last few years researching the life of Jesus and learning from Paul. Paul himself had an encounter with Jesus in person, hearing His voice, and this was long after His death. There are many witnesses who saw Him alive after His crucifixion. I have talked to them and I believe their report. I can't explain it but I believe it. I just know beyond doubt that Jesus is divine and is my Lord and Savior."

"If He is so holy and good, why does He cause so much pain?!" Temeros asked, still with some anger in his voice.

"I can assure you," Luke responded, "that Jesus did not cause this to happen. When we began to turn away from our selfish pursuits and worldly ways and focus our lives on Jesus, our enemy, Satan, fights back. The ones we have left behind as we pursue Him sometimes get angry or try to change our beliefs. Doing what is right and good can sometimes cause division. Our Lord Himself said that in our lives with Him, we will face tribulations, but He promised He has overcome the world! Can you imagine that? Even Paul has taught that we cannot be separated from God's love, no matter what happens to us in this life. And he would know! He has been stoned and attacked and left for dead, as well as being stuck in a Roman prison for the past two years. The Jewish people hate him, as do the followers of false gods, even the followers of Artemis in the temple in Ephesus."

Temeros sat silently as he processed all of this. He knew this made sense and that the tragedy in his home was not something Paul caused, but he still felt angry and wanted vengeance on someone. But everything he had heard pierced his heart and he recognized truth in Luke's words.

"I miss her," he said quietly. "I tried to save her. Why was I saved and she was not? I don't understand and it makes me angry."

Luke answered, "In the times when I don't understand why God allows something painful to happen in my life, all I can do it trust in what I know. God is good, God is just, and God is all-knowing. His ways are not my ways but His ways are perfect. I choose to believe that He will work all things together for some sort of good in His timing. I know that He has saved me through the sacrifice and resurrection of my Lord and one day I will see my loved ones that have died. I find great comfort in this."

"I wish I could have that same comfort. I need time to think about all of this," Temeros responded quietly, his anger gone and replaced with longing for the peace and certainty he saw in Luke.

"I will be praying that God will direct you. I am always available to talk more when you are ready," Luke said with a gentle smile. "I will give you a break and go check on my other patients but I will be back later."

He got up and walked away, leaving Temeros lost in his thoughts. The anger and desire for vengeance had faded as they talked. His head was spinning as he considered their conversation. As he sat there in the shadow of a stack of crates, two Roman soldiers stopped near him on the other side, deep in conversation.

"I don't trust him," said one. "I tell you, Porcius, he is up to something. That crowd that he has gathered around him all the time could cause big problems if they banded together."

Porcius answered with a sneer, "What do you expect to do about it, Cassius? You know he is the favorite of our Centurion. In fact, I think Julius secretly believes all of that stuff about Jesus that he keeps spouting. Surely he can't be naïve enough to believe someone came back from the dead?! That is ridiculous!"

"Definitely! I don't know why he is so enamored with a prisoner! Just because he is a Roman citizen! Why would a lowly prisoner deserve that honor? I have not been granted that privilege myself, and I am a soldier of the Empire! It is disgraceful."

"I agree!" Porcius said, nodding. "I don't think he should be commanding Roman soldiers if he is giving that much influence to a common criminal! We need to keep an eye on him. Gaius is not much better. He is always yelling at us for one thing or another. As for that prisoner, we should teach him a lesson in humility!"

Cassius glanced sharply at him. "What do you have in mind?"

"Well, you know that we are almost to port in Fair Havens. I have it on good authority that since it is so late in the year, there is a good possibility we may have to winter there. Surely in the next few weeks or months, a lone prisoner could quietly disappear or have an 'accident.'"

"Hmm," he said, rubbing his hands together. "I think you may be on to something. That way we could remove that risk of rebellion as well as his power over Julius. Of course we could not have it traced back to us."

"We have some time to think about it. Let's keep this to ourselves but we will talk more," Porcius said as they walked away.

Temeros was stunned by what he had overheard. As he sat there mulling over the conversation he had heard, his mind was in a jumble. What should he do with this information? Just a short time ago, he would have been glad to join in the schemes he had overheard. His opinions about Paul had been darkly colored by his father's rantings.

Now, however, his anger and desire for revenge had given way to longing for the hope the believers seemed to have. His mother had died with this hope in Jesus and he now realized it was because of the ministry of Paul. Thinking of her brought deep sadness and the desire to see her again. Luke was certain he could see her again if he, too, believed. He wanted to hear more about Jesus and the eternal life He offered.

# CHAPTER EIGHT

The next morning, Julius met with the ship's captain. They were approaching port in Fair Havens and would likely be anchoring there that afternoon. Arriving at any port required a plan for managing the prisoners under his care. There must be tight control over each one. Roman law was strict and there were severe penalties even to death for the soldiers who allowed any prisoner to escape. The confusion and tumult of the arrival process and of the crew and supplies being transferred on and off the ship were prime opportunities for prisoners to slip away.

Julius was the ranking officer onboard, but he understood the importance of delegating authority to his officers. They knew the men best. At the same time, he wanted to protect Paul and he knew some of the soldiers did not share that sentiment. He pulled Gaius aside. As his optio, his second-in-command, the responsibility of organizing this activity fell to him.

"Gaius, I want to be sure Paul is not mistreated by the men. I know some of them have been grumbling. Can you oversee that for me?"

"Of course, Sir," he said, keeping his manner more formal as he glanced at the soldiers walking by. "I've been keeping a close eye on them, especially Cassius and Porcius. They seem to spend a lot of time in secret conversation and are quick to stop talking whenever I come around. I have heard that they feel Paul is being treated with favoritism and I get the impression they want to change that. I'll be sure they are assigned elsewhere."

"Thank you," Julius responded. "I respect Paul very much, even though he is a prisoner. As a citizen of Rome, he deserves our protection while he is in our custody."

"I have heard some of the crew say we are not likely to continue the journey from here, due to the lateness of the season. Did the captain tell you if he plans to winter at Fair Havens?" Gaius asked.

"At our discussion this morning, I asked him that. He definitely feels it is too late in the season to push on to Rome. However, Fair Havens is a busy port. He wants to see if they are overcrowded before he decides. The other option would be Phoenix a few hours further west. He will speak to the master of the port and then make a decision. If we decide to go there, then we will relax the guard."

Gaius smiled. "I will be glad to be ashore for a few months. Life onboard a ship gets old after a period of time. It will be nice to walk around on solid ground and not bump into the same people every few minutes."

Julius nodded in agreement. "Shore leave is always a welcome relief. I think I have forgotten what it is like to be off duty and be able to relax in an inn and sleep in a real bed. Let's gather the men and make the announcement."

Gaius gave the order for all of the soldiers to gather for their assignments. It took several minutes for them to arrive and line up in their ranks. The group of prisoners were seated on deck in plain sight so all of the soldiers were gathered. The men were called to attention, and a head count was taken to be sure all were present and accounted for.

Julius addressed the gathered men with a loud voice.

"Soldiers of Rome, we will soon be arriving in the port of Fair Havens. The prisoners in our charge must be accounted for during this process. I don't need to remind you of the severe penalty if any should escape! Discipline has been relaxed during our voyage but that will change now. Gaius will be assigning guards to each prisoner until the next step in our journey is decided. As you are aware, it is late in the season. The captain has informed me we will not be able to go to Rome at this time. We will be considering the best option for wintering in port. After talking with the port master at Fair Havens, we will determine whether to disembark there or to go on to Phoenix, a few hours west. Until the decision is made, we will expect you to be on alert and fulfill your duties to the Emperor. As always, complaints and insubordination will be met with the severest discipline."

He stepped back and gestured to Gaius to take over. Gaius began giving commands. He ordered them to gather all of the prisoners in the main compartment below decks upon his command, approximately two hours prior to arriving. At that time, each would be shackled between two soldiers until further notice. The soldiers groaned at this but knew the drill. They had been through this before. Each secretly hoped he would not be chosen to guard the prisoners during the transfer to shore. It made for a difficult and awkward time for both the prisoners and the guards.

He dismissed the men after ordering them to check the posted guard assignments in one hour's time. The junior officers were then given the task of making assignments. Gaius spoke privately to the junior officer in charge of Cassius and Porcius. He made it clear to him that they were being closely watched and in danger of reprimand if they stepped out of line. Gaius ordered him to keep them separated from Paul for the time being and then went on to his other duties.

Within a few hours, there was a noticeable air of excitement spreading around the ship. The ship's crew fell to their assigned duties quickly and efficiently. The foreman was calling out orders as various crews were assigned to the main sail, others to the foresail, and some to the anchors at the bow and stern, and the oarsmen took their position to maneuver to their mooring site. The boat, which had been towed behind the ship, was reeled in and readied for the captain and Julius to go ashore when the time came.

The passengers lined the rails on the starboard side of the ship watching the approaching shore and the activity in the port. There were three other ships anchored in the port as well, but none as large as theirs. The soldiers that were not assigned below decks with the prisoners were on deck watching as well.

Temeros found a place on the rail near the stern. His head was no longer throbbing but his shoulder still ached. He was not able to assist with the arrival of the ship but was fascinated as he observed his coworkers performing their tasks. Luke walked over to where he stood and greeted him.

"It's good to see you today, Temeros. Glad to see you seem to be feeling better," he said.

"Hi, Luke," he answered. "Yes, my head feels much better, but my shoulder still aches. I think the pain is a little better today."

"Good!" Luke gestured toward the crowded deck. "It is always exciting to see the activity of pulling into port. I've been on many ships and never cease to enjoy watching this."

Temeros nodded and was silent for a moment as he thought once more about the conversation he heard the day before. "Luke, I need to tell you something," he said.

Luke turned toward him expectantly. "What is it?"

"Yesterday after you left me on deck, I overheard two soldiers talking. They were talking about Paul and it sounded as though they were planning to hurt him."

"What!?" Luke said in surprise. "Why would they want to do that?"

"I think they envy his citizenship. They feel he has influence over your centurion, and they did not like that. They said they fear he may try to overthrow the ship since he has so many followers on board."

"That is ridiculous! He is a prisoner! How could he do that?"

"I don't know. It sounded silly to me, too."

"What are they planning to do?"

"They were not specific. They just said when the ship is wintering in port, it would be easy for a prisoner to have an accident."

Luke considered this with a grim expression on his face. "I'm glad you told me. I will speak to Paul and also alert the centurion."

"Please don't tell them it was me who informed you!" Temeros said.

"Of course not! I will talk to you again soon," he said as he turned to go.

Meanwhile, Cassius and Porcius were at the bow of the ship, leaning on the rail to the port side, away from shore. Their heads were together as they conversed quietly.

"I've been thinking," Cassius said. "Fair Havens is a busy port, with people everywhere. It may be harder to do what we are thinking here."

Porcius nodded. "I was thinking about that too. I have a friend who has been to Phoenix and it is more isolated. Plus, they have more inns and more women willing to sell their wares over a long winter!" he said sneering.

Cassius leered at that. "I think we need to try to somehow convince the captain it would be better to go on to Phoenix instead of staying here. Not only will it make our winter more enjoyable, but the town would lend itself more to our purposes, with fewer witnesses who would question what we were up to!"

"I have a few friends on the ship's crew, and I think they could be easily swayed to get more of their crewmates to push for going on!"

"Let's see if we can do that before the captain makes up his mind!" Cassius said. They pushed back from the railing and walked away to find the crew.

—————

The idea of going on from Fair Havens to winter in Phoenix with all of its "amenities" caught on rapidly with the crew. Soon the word spread to Rayiz, the foreman. As he made his rounds among the various work crews, he heard several of them mention this. He finished his checklist and went to report to the Captain.

"Sir," he said. "There is talk among the crew that Phoenix is a much better place to winter in than Fair Havens. Several of them seem to know it well."

The captain considered this for a moment. "Have you ever been there Rayiz?" he asked.

"No, I have not. I have talked to others on past voyages who have, though. They tell me it has a variety of inns and places for lodging." He did not mention other sources of entertainment.

"Well, Fair Havens is very nice but also crowded. There are already three other ships here. I will take the Centurion, Julius, with me to talk to the port master before deciding, but it may be best to go on."

Rayiz nodded, smiling inwardly and already imagining a few months of relaxation and indulgence in port. "Yes sir. I will wait to inform the men until I hear from you." He went back to check on the men again.

———————

In the midst of the activity on deck, Julius and Gaius were discussing the plans as they walked. They stopped for a moment near Paul. As they conversed, Paul stood and made his way over to them.

"Excuse me, Julius!" He called out to them. "Do you have a moment?"

Julius paused and turned to him. "Hello, Paul. I am pretty busy. Can it wait?"

"I just need a minute of your time. I feel it is important that I talk to you before you go ashore with the captain."

He sighed and motioned for Gaius to wait a moment. "Ok. What can I do for you?"

"I know we have taken much more time in our journey than was intended. Now that it is late in the season, after the Jewish fast, it is becoming more dangerous to continue to Rome. I heard you speaking to your troops earlier about plans for wintering."

"Yes, go on."

"In my prayers today, God spoke to me and I feel I need to give you a message." At this, Gaius rolled his eyes. Julius kept his expression neutral.

"I'm not sure why God would want to give me a message but please continue," Julius said.

"I know that if we continue further, we will be faced with disaster and the loss of the ship and cargo, as well as risking our lives. I believe strongly we should winter here in Fair Havens."

Julius and Gaius looked at each other with puzzled expressions.

"Thank you for your input but we have not yet decided. When the captain and I go ashore, we will have more information on which to base our decision."

Paul nodded. "I understand, and I appreciate you listening. Please understand this is not just my opinion but I feel truly this is God's leading. Even if the captain wants to go further, you are the highest ranking officer and he will have to obey you. I believe as you have been with me, you have heard God's teaching. I pray that you will come to know Christ and His saving power. I don't want you to be in danger of losing your life by continuing on before you have given your life to Him."

"Ok, Paul, we will consider this. I appreciate your sharing this with me," Julius said, noncommittally.

As Paul walked away, Julius raised his eyebrows and shook his head as he smiled at Gaius. "Well! I guess I have my orders!" he said jokingly.

Gaius chuckled slightly. "Good luck with that! How are you going to tell the Captain that the prisoner thinks we should stay here?!"

"Maybe I'll let you take on that task! It will be good training for you!" Julius said with a grin.

"I think I better go check with the officers on how the guard assignments are coming along!" Gaius said with a laugh. He excused himself and walked away still smiling.

Julius turned to look out at the port, bustling with activity. His smile faded as he considered Paul's words. Paul spoke with authority and was very convincing. Maybe he should not be so quick to dismiss what Paul had said. He mulled this over in his mind. Paul appeared to have personal experience with unexplainable miracles and a profound connection to his God.

He had felt moved many times as he overheard Paul's teaching. Julius was intrigued by Jesus and the amazing things He was reported to have done. He had seen the lives of the prisoners change as they had confessed their belief that Jesus had returned from the dead. He had even heard stories that had spread through the Roman army about the crucifixion and then the body disappearing.

When Julius was ordered to Caesarea a few years prior, it was to replace another centurion named Cornelius. Rumors had spread that Cornelius had become a follower of Jesus[5]. Before meeting him, Julius was angry that such a high-ranking soldier would turn his back on the emperor to follow another god. When they met to transfer command, however, Julius was surprised by the man. He was humble and confident and carried himself with dignity and authority without seeming arrogant. It was evident that there had been a profound effect on his life, and he was preparing to travel to teach others about Jesus. Julius had considered this a waste of training and did not understand why Cornelius would throw away his life on such an endeavor.

Now, after hearing Paul's teaching, he saw Cornelius' decision in a different light. Could there really be some truth to the claims that Jesus had actually come back to life? It seemed so unbelievable! Surprisingly, Gaius was his closest source of information on this.

Gaius was a third-generation Roman soldier. His grandfather served under Herod the Great, but something had happened that had caused him great depression and anguish, leading him to drown himself in alcohol. Growing up in such a contentious home, Gaius' father had left as soon as he was old enough to join the army.

His father had served for many years and eventually was assigned back in Jerusalem, just as his father before him had been. His promising career was derailed, however, by the events of that momentous day.

Initially, Julius had dismissed the rumors about Jesus as tall tales. However, they did not fade with time, but instead the stories about Jesus had spread as His followers had dispersed through the Empire. Then, when Gaius had related his father's firsthand account, Julius began to reexamine his initial impression. Now, he had heard Paul teach with authority about the same topics. His mind whirled when he considered the possibility it could actually be true. He would need to talk further to Gaius and to Paul when he had time, but not now. He had to prepare to go ashore with the captain.

---

[5] See Acts chapter 10.

# CHAPTER NINE

As the deckhands held it steady, Julius and Captain Sahaq climbed down the rope ladder to the small boat bobbing alongside. The captain had ordered one of his crew to row them ashore for their conference with the harbormaster.

"Captain, have you had any more thoughts about where to wait out the winter?" Julius asked as they made their way past another ship anchored nearby.

"It seems many of the crew prefer going on to Phoenix," the captain answered. "Seeing these other ships in port, I am inclined to look for a less crowded place to stay. And they tell me there are many good options for lodging and for food there. We'll know more after we talk to the harbormaster."

Julius considered this, recalling Paul's admonition about the dangers of going on. "You know, I have heard from some under my command who feel it is safer to stay here rather than risk going any further," he said, choosing his words carefully.

Captain Sahaq looked at him with raised eyebrows. "Is that so? And what is their basis for this opinion? Do they have as much experience with sailing in these waters as my crew?" he responded, his tone defensive.

Julius lowered his gaze. "No, no, that is not the case. They just expressed a concern and I wanted to pass it along."

"Well, I think they would be wise to leave such decisions to the sailors," the captain said dismissively. "Phoenix is only a few hours further, and if my crew vouch for it, I am inclined to give it some consideration."

"Of course, captain," Julius said. "I'm just passing along one opinion. We can reserve judgment until we get more information."

"I imagine since it is already almost midday that we will be here at least overnight. That will give us an opportunity to see what accommodations they have to offer here."

As they made their way to the dock, Julius took in all of the activity around them. There were two other ships in addition to the one they just passed, all three smaller than their own. The decks were lined with crew and passengers watching the hubbub. There were several small boats ferrying passengers and supplies back and forth from ship to shore. The single dock in the port was crowded with men carrying bags and boxes of supplies. The air was filled with shouts and conversations and creaking of ships as well as lapping of water against the oars. Cries of birds surrounded them as the seabirds swooped down to the water and strutted on the shore. It was more entertainment than he had had since leaving Myra.

They came to the dock and waited as another dinghy pushed off to return to their ship. Then they tossed their line to the dock worker who deftly tied it to the bollard and leaned down to offer a hand as they climbed ashore. The captain instructed his crew member to return to the ship and to tell Rayiz to send men ashore for fresh water and food for the crew and passengers.

As they strode down the dock to shore, Julius was surprised by the odd, unsteady feeling of walking on solid ground. He almost stumbled a few times and had to catch himself against the captain, apologizing.

The captain chuckled. "It takes a little time to readjust to land after being on the ship! You'll get used to it soon. Just widen your stance a bit until you get your land legs back."

Julius nodded, a bit embarrassed. He felt a little silly walking that way, but it did keep him on his feet and he was able to walk more or less in a straight line. Within a few minutes, it was less noticeable.

Captain Sahaq headed for a building to the east of the dock. The sign on the door indicated it was the office for the harbormaster. There were three men waiting at the door. As they approached, the door opened and a man exited as the first man in line entered.

They greeted the remaining men and learned that they were from the ship anchored closest to theirs. They had just arrived in port earlier that morning and the crew was eager for shore leave. They had come from Sicily, and it had been slow going with the unpredictable winds. They had come through a squall two days before that had caused a lot of concern at first but it had quickly subsided. They had to bail water for a day after that but the ship had come through it unscathed. The crew, on the other hand, were young and many were on their first voyage. Several of them were seasick and they were still recovering.

Captain Sahaq shared with them the details of their own voyage. They were impressed by the size of the grain ship and began discussing technical aspects of the ship and its operations. Julius felt like he was listening to a foreign language and he could tell this conversation could go on for a while. He decided to walk down the street to see what was nearby.

There were several open stalls selling fish and fruit to the seamen gathered around. A little further inland, there were a few inns that offered rooms to rent as well as food. It was a nice-appearing port. He was aware of a few passers-by staring at his uniform and realized there were no other Roman soldiers in view. He made a mental note to ask about the nearest garrison.

He returned to the harbor office and found that the captain was waiting alone, the other two men having entered the office.

Captain Sahaq greeted him as he approached. "It seems the ship those men are with will be staying here for the winter. The other captain that came out as you were walking is also planning to winter here. He was expecting a companion ship to arrive this afternoon, joining them. It appears this will be a fairly crowded port!"

Julius cringed at this. "I guess we will have to see what other options we have," he said.

A few moments later, the door opened and they were summoned in to see the harbormaster. He was a rotund, bearded man with a gruff voice. He seemed to have a permanent scowl, but as he talked it was apparent he was actually quite jovial, with a dry wit that set them at ease.

The captain made introductions and gave him the information about their ship, its crew, and the soldiers and prisoners it was transporting. When he mentioned the number of people onboard, the harbormaster interrupted.

"Whoo!" he exclaimed, subconsciously tugging on his beard. "You have 275 people? That will be a challenge. We already have three other ships before you that are wintering here and a fourth that has been registered by the captain that was here just an hour ago! We will have to do some checking on what is available for supplies and food, but there may not be lodging available for your passengers who don't want to winter onboard the ship! I'm sure we can make do, but I'll need to make arrangements for further supplies," he said as he scribbled some notes on a parchment.

The captain frowned at this. "I feared that may be the case. Some of my crew had been through these parts before and mentioned Phoenix. What can you tell me about that harbor?"

The captain put down his quill and looked up grinning. "Phoenix, you say! They do have certain, ahem, "amenities" that the crews find appealing. That is true!" he chuckled. "They have a nice harbor. Not nearly as nice as mine, mind you! But it can accommodate a ship like yours just fine. Last I heard, they only have one small ship planning to winter there."

Julius spoke up. "What do you mean by amenities? Are there facilities that could accommodate a squad of my men on shore leave for a short time if we rotate them?"

"Yes, they have three inns near the port and I'm sure your men will find the women there quite eager to accommodate them," he said with a wink.

Julius' expression hardened at this as he imagined the discipline problems this could cause with his men. He glanced at Captain Sahaq but could tell from his expression that the captain had already made up his mind to move on.

"It sounds like we would be best to go on to Phoenix," the captain said. "We will anchor here for the night and replenish our water supply before moving on tomorrow."

The harbormaster nodded. "I hate to lose your business but I understand, and I fear we may struggle to meet your needs here. We'll be happy to have you here for the night. You'll find the inns have good ale and Eunice just down the street is a great cook. I have been there many times as you can see!" he said, rubbing his ample stomach.

The captain and Julius laughed at this. "A hot meal sounds wonderful," Julius agreed, and Captain Sahaq nodded in agreement as Julius pushed back his chair preparing to stand.

"One more thing," the captain said, and Julius settled back in his seat again. "Any more information about the weather? One of the captains that was here before mentioned a squall that sickened some of his men and caused them to take on water."

The harbormaster frowned. "Aye, I've heard from a few that it was a pretty strong blow, tearing some sails and putting some water in their holds. Of course you've sailed these waters enough to know how bad the storms can be. This was nothing but a sprinkle compared to some. We've had a good stretch of fair weather and only light rain two days ago. I don't expect any problems. I can usually feel it in my knees when there's something about to happen and I feel well enough to go dancin'! I think we'll be fine for a good stretch."

"Good to hear," the captain said, relieved. "We will spend the night and plan to depart in the morning."

With that, the men stood and thanked the harbormaster for his time and left the small office.

# Chapter Ten

J ulius and the captain walked back toward the dock, and then the captain excused himself to return to the ship to inform his crew of the
plans.

Julius walked on down the dusty street to inquire at the inn about a
room for the night. He was eager to spend a night off the ship, back on
more stable ground without the constant rocking motion.

He found the place the harbormaster had mentioned and went in to
get something to eat. It was fairly crowded with a few tables full of obvious
sailors from one of the ships in port, noisily discussing their travels and
adventures. There were a couple of tables where some townspeople were
eating quietly. In the corner was a table where a lone, disheveled-looking
man was hunched over his meal.

Julius found a table against the wall and sat down. He could see the
kitchen area and saw a middle-aged woman working over the oven, wiping her brow. He guessed that must be Eunice. A teenage girl hurried over
to his table and asked what he wanted to drink. After taking his order, she
rushed away to the kitchen.

Julius stretched his neck back and forth and sat back in his chair. It
felt good to be alone after the weeks on the ship with soldiers, prisoners,
sailors, and passengers. The hubbub in the inn around him was in some
ways soothing background noise compared to the noise on the ship. He
let his mind wander, thinking about Rome. He had not been there for

years. He was excited to see the center of the World's power once again. However, his excitement was tempered by his memory of the decadence he remembered seeing there, including the carnage of the Coliseum. He was embarrassed now about his enthusiasm for watching the gladiators slaughter each other. Even more troublesome to his soul were the memories of how the crowd cheered as the Christians were executed by sword and wild beasts. He was keenly ashamed of joining in the cheers. Now, having spent time with Paul, his prisoner, he had a new appreciation for the courage and faith with which the poor victims faced their certain death, some of them even singing or kneeling in prayer. There were none of the screams or pleadings or weak attempts at self-defense offered by other prisoners that faced similar fates.

His reverie was interrupted by the girl bringing a mug of ale for him. She quickly ran down the choices for food, and he gave her his request as she quickly moved on to another table.

As he settled back in his chair, he glanced around again. He saw two men rising from a table further back, appearing to have come to some agreement as they shook hands. Now that his eyes had adjusted, he could see more details. He was surprised to see one of the men was a Roman soldier. As they walked across the room, they passed by Julius and the soldier paused, surprise on his face. Julius raised his arm in salute as the soldier returned the gesture.

"Greetings!" he said. "I am Darius, Centurion of the Athenian regiment."

Julius smiled as he rose, holding out his hand in greeting. "I'm Julius, from the Augustan regiment. I wondered if there were other soldiers around. Are you traveling on one of the ships in the harbor?"

Darius shook his hand, smiling in return. "Yes. I received transfer orders to go to Palestine. It seems the governor there is troubled by some religious conflict between the Jews and some new sect. I just received my promotion and am being transferred there to meet my new regiment. I paid for passage on a ship heading that direction, but with the season being so late, they decided to winter here. I finally found someone willing to transport me to the mainland so I can continue my journey overland. I just made the arrangements. He wants to leave in the next hour so I am heading back to the port. What about you?"

"What a coincidence! I just left Caesarea in northern Palestine. My cohort is transporting a group of prisoners to Rome," Julius answered.

"Ah, Rome!" Darius exclaimed. "I would love to go back there again. There is so much to do there! So much excitement! Are your prisoners bound for the Coliseum?"

Julius shook his head. "No. In fact I think they may have something to do with your future post. The main prisoner I am transporting has become rather well known around Asia Minor. He has traveled extensively, preaching a new religion. He does not seem to be a troublemaker from what I have seen, but I have heard stories that he was thrown out of several towns. In fact, he was the main focus of the riots in Ephesus a few years ago that you probably heard about. He escaped before being attacked, but one of the other prisoners in my charge was imprisoned in Ephesus as well."

"Oh, I wish I had time to sit and talk with you about this!" Darius said. "I would love to hear more. I am curious, though. Why is a religious prisoner being transported to Rome? It seems unnecessary."

"He exerted his rights as a Roman citizen to stand trial before Caesar," Julius answered. "He had been threatened by a group of Jews that had lain in wait, hoping to kill him, so my cohort is tasked with seeing that he arrives safely. I must say I am eager to get there. I am not cut out for sea travel. It is very nice to be on land, even for a night."

"Only a night?" Darius asked. "Are you not going to winter here?"

"No, we are on the Alexandrian grain ship, and there are more than 250 people. The harbormaster told us he is fully booked with ships wintering here. The captain wants to go on to Phoenix."

"Phoenix has quite a reputation around here," Darius said with a smile. "You may have your hands full keeping your soldiers in line over the winter!"

Julius nodded with a slight frown on his face. "I have already heard about the pitfalls to be found there. My optio is helping me immensely to discipline the men and prepare for potential problems."

Darius looked to the door where his companion was waiting impatiently, beckoning to him. "I'm afraid I have to go or I will be left behind. I hope to get to the mainland in a few hours so I can continue my journey tomorrow. I wish you well!"

Julius smiled. "And you also! Keep an open mind over the conflict you are going to help with. I have found that these 'Christians' are not the troublemakers that some make them out to be."

Darius looked somewhat surprised by this but nodded in agreement. "I will! I am glad to hear you say that. There is surely more to this than is being told. Good bye and good travels!" He turned and walked to the door.

Just then, Julius' food arrived, so he did not look around to see the rough-looking man in the corner watching him with keen focus, leaning forward as he overheard their conversation. He had an odd greedy expression on his face. He rose from his table and made his way to the door by a circuitous route, making sure to avoid any eye contact with Julius.

Julius ate in silence, enjoying a well-cooked meal for the first time in several days. He had to remind himself to slow down and savor it, rather than shoveling it in as he had been in the habit of doing lately.

After he finished, he paid for his meal and inquired about rooms for the night. They directed him to an inn two doors down and he made his way out and walked leisurely in that direction.

The accommodations were nice enough but nothing fancy. He spoke to the lady in the main room and was quoted a price he thought was far too high for the amenities offered. However, she was firm on the price, indicating that many other people would be happy to pay this sum for one of the few remaining rooms in town. He grumbled under his breath as he gave her the coins for payment.

The one good thing was that she could offer him a hot bath for just a small amount more. He eagerly paid the extra for that luxury, reserving a time later in the evening, and made his way up the wooden staircase to the room she indicated. The meager furnishings were lavish compared to what he had been living in since leaving his garrison in Caesarea. It was only midafternoon so he had time to take a brief rest before going to the ship to leave further instructions. He took off his cloak and breastplate and lay down to take a short nap.

He had trained himself through the years to limit his naps and wake when he needed to. His training did not fail him this time and he woke after an hour surprisingly well rested. He wiped the drool off his face and stretched. He put his uniform back on and headed back toward the port, leaving word with the innkeeper that he would be back later in the evening for his bath.

The port was just as busy late in the afternoon as it had been when they arrived. Julius walked out onto the pier where the individual tenders were ferrying people back and forth to their ships. After waiting a brief time as one tied up to the dock and a sailor jumped nimbly ashore, he asked the man in the boat for passage back to the ship. He climbed awkwardly into the boat settling onto the wooden bench and holding on tightly as the rocking of the boat diminished.

The pilot of the boat was efficient in rowing toward the grain ship. "This must be the most popular ship in the harbor!" he said, making small talk. "I think you are the fifth person in the past two hours that has asked about getting to the ship."

"Oh? Who else besides the captain?" Julius asked.

"There was a sailor from the ship that I brought to shore and also another person, probably a passenger."

"No soldiers, I hope!" Julius said. "They are supposed to be waiting for my approval before leaving the ship."

"No, no soldiers came with me. I could see a few of them on the deck looking like they hoped to come ashore, though! There was another man on shore that was asking about the ship, but he was kind of an odd-looking guy in dirty clothes. He definitely didn't look like he belonged on that ship!"

Julius nodded absently, his mind occupied reviewing what he needed to do.

"It was kind of strange that he was so interested in who was on board. He asked if I knew if there were prisoners being transported. I told him…"

"Wait, what did you just say?" Julius asked, turning to face him. "Did you say he asked about the prisoners? Did he say why he wanted to know?"

"No," he responded. "I told him I did not know who was on the ship other than a bunch of soldiers."

"Did he say anything else?"

"Not really. It was odd that he asked if I would be around after sunset. I told him I would not be working that late."

Julius thought about this, feeling uneasy. It would make no sense to have someone on this island interested in helping to free his prisoners but he did not want to take any chances. He would have to talk to Gaius to alert him.

"Thanks for the information. If you see him again, I'd like to know where he is so I can interview him. I'll be heading back to shore in an hour or two. I have a room at the inn just down from Eunice's."

The pilot expressed agreement. They were just arriving at the ship and he was preoccupied with tying up next to the ladder, so the conversation ended and Julius made his way up the rope ladder to the deck.

# Chapter Eleven

Demetrius had arrived earlier that morning and was disheartened to learn that The Emir, the grain ship he had been pursuing, was not in the harbor. He had occasionally seen ships in the distance on the voyage from Myra but never close enough to identify the one he was seeking. He was afraid he had lost them. It seemed his chances of actually finding his objective were fading.

He sat in the back corner of the inn, scowling at his plate. The food was barely tolerable, and the girl that brought it was worthless. She was rushing around like she had no idea what to do. He had to yell at her a few times to bring him his food and his drink. She had plopped it down on the table in front of him and disappeared again, like she was in a hurry to get away from him. The only good thing was that she had a nice figure. He had leered appreciatively as she walked past.

He glanced around the dimly lit room at the people. All of them looked ignorant, like they belonged in such a rotten place. How had he ended up in this dung heap? He used to be important. He had wealth and power. People respected him. Now, here he sat, one hand useless, eating this gruel and wearing rags. He had dipped into his money stores to make it this far, and now it looked like he would be stuck here for a few months.

When he saw the Roman soldier come in and find a table, he wondered if perhaps it was not hopeless after all. He watched warily from the shadows, weighing his options. He could tell by his uniform that he was a centurion. They were not useful to him. They were too honorable and committed to be bought. Back before his life was ruined, he had several soldiers that were quick to do his bidding. Even on that terrible day, they had arrested the men who had ruined his business. Their ringleader, however, had run away, leaving town before he could be apprehended. That was the man he hated that needed to suffer for what had happened.

Another soldier had arisen from a table in the back, and as he walked toward the exit, he stopped to speak to the centurion. He strained to listen as they greeted each other, and he overheard them talking about prisoners on one of the ships. His breath caught and his pulse quickened as he listened intently. Could it be? Maybe his stop here had not been so worthless after all. The man he had been pursuing since Caesarea might actually be here, anchored in the harbor. He could be close to ending his quest and making him pay for what he did.

After the second soldier departed, he watched the centurion closely. His food had just arrived and it appeared he would be there for a while longer. Demetrius left a few coins on the table and made his way to the exit being sure to stay out of sight. Once outside, he hastened to the dock and searched for someone who could give him more information. He saw a small boat tied to the dock, a passenger having just disembarked.

"Hey, you!" he called to the boat's pilot.

The man looked up, a slight frown on his face as he saw the man's shabby attire.

"Yes? Do you need something?"

"Yes! I need you to tell me what you know about the big grain ship in the harbor! Who is on it and where are they headed?"

"I don't know a lot of details but I know there is at least one regiment of soldiers as well as some other passengers. I overheard some of the passengers saying they are headed to Rome, but it sounds like they are looking for a place to winter."

"Did they say if they were transporting prisoners?" he demanded.

He shook his head. "I did not hear anything about that, just the soldiers. Why do you ask?"

"None of your business!" he growled. "Can you take me to the ship later this evening, after sundown?"

The pilot's expression hardened slightly. "No, I don't think I will be able to help you. I will be stopping soon. I'm afraid you'll have to check somewhere else."

Demetrius sighed in disgust and muttered under his breath as he turned abruptly and walked away. He walked back up the road, but he could see the centurion ahead of him, so he quickly turned down a side street out of sight. He watched surreptitiously as the soldier entered the inn across the street. After waiting a few minutes, it appeared he would not be coming back out for a while.

He walked on to the edge of town, deep in thought. He found a small grove of trees and sat down in the shade, leaning against the tree trunk to rest and plan his next move. He rubbed his left hand as he once again inspected the ugly scars. The aching still flared up frequently but he had grown accustomed to it. Drinking wine helped when he was able to get it. Two of his fingers were useless, half gone, and the remaining nubs scarred and fused. The remaining fingers were still there but stiff and covered in the irregular ridges left behind from the fire. At least he still had his thumb and it worked well enough to grasp things but not enough to allow him to do any detailed crafting like he used to do.

As he once again considered his losses, his anger began to rise. His work was gone and his wife and son dead. He would not allow himself to think about the events of that night. The twinge of guilt that rose with their memories had mutated with time into anger that burned inside. He blamed the Jewish teacher, Paul, for ruining his life. After three years, the anger had matured to a deep desire for vengeance, driving him to pursue an opportunity to kill this man, Paul.

Initially, he thought he had found some others who could help him achieve his goal. There were about forty Jews who had vowed to kill Paul and had taken an oath to not eat or drink until this had been accomplished. Unfortunately, they were weak in their resolve, and when Paul was imprisoned in Jerusalem out of their reach, they were about to give up. He was the one who had come up with a plan and urged them on, feeding their desire for vengeance out of his own deep stores of hatred for Paul. At his urging, they had gone to their Jewish leaders, who hated Paul as much as they did. They asked the Jewish council to request that Paul be brought before them for more questioning, but this band of zealots would be lying in wait for him along the route, ready to end his life.

The Jewish conspirators were idiots, however. They had been talking about this plan in an inn and were overheard. Somehow, word got back to the soldiers and the commander arranged to transport Paul under cover of darkness with two hundred horsemen guarding him.[6] So much trouble over a worthless prisoner, but it kept him out of reach. He was moved to Caesarea and was imprisoned there for two years. The Jewish conspirators lost their resolve and gave up quickly. Only he kept the flame of hatred stoked, waiting and waiting for some sort of opportunity.

Finally, Paul had appealed to Caesar, so they would need to transport him to Rome. By then, however, Demetrius had let some of his information sources lapse, and by the time he was aware of what was happening, the soldiers were able to get the prisoners onto a ship. He quickly packed a few belongings and gathered his stores of silver, but the ship departed before he could find a way to sneak aboard.

That had led to his journey overland to Myra and then to his slow frustrating voyage to Fair Havens. The ship was uncomfortable and crowded, and he had been treated with no respect whatsoever. The contrary winds had made the journey maddeningly slow, despite his complaints to the crew. They had arrived in Phoenix just yesterday, and the captain and crew had made it clear he was no longer welcome to travel with them. Besides they were going to stay put and winter in this ugly place, afraid of a few storms and winds.

He had felt acutely the failure of his quest and had resigned himself to trying to find a way on to Rome before spring. Then, his gods (though he despised them) had smiled on him, sending that centurion to the same

---

[6] See Acts 23: 12–24.

inn where he had been eating. This had to be Paul's ship. There was no way there would be another grain ship headed to Rome carrying prisoners, especially one causing religious uprisings. He must find a way to get on that ship.

He laid his head back against the rough bark of the tree. The sunlight was filtered through the leaves and the afternoon breeze was warm. His mind began to wander as his eyes grew heavy and his breathing deepened. As his mind relaxed, memories of that horrible night flooded in.

––––––

He rarely allowed himself to remember. It was too painful even after a few years had passed. But now, as his fury against Paul was fresh, he relived his rage over his wife's betrayal in following Paul's teachings about Jesus. Images popped in and out of his mind unbidden in a chaotic replaying of those events.

He recoiled as he recalled the rapidly spreading flames. Seeking a way to douse the flames, he had run to the workshop to find the water barrel he used for his work. By the time he reached it, however, smoke filled the room. His intoxicated brain was reeling, and he collapsed to the floor next to the barrel and briefly passed out. He did not know how long he had been out, but surely not long. When he regained consciousness that evening, the roof above him was fully engulfed in flames, and he could see that it was starting to disintegrate and sag dangerously low. He remembered in his panic his eyes darted around the room for anything that could help.

He had grabbed the top of the water barrel against which he was leaning and pulled with the last of his strength as he felt the intense heat burning his left arm. Then the glorious sensation of the cool water flooded over him dousing his flaming cloak. At the same time, the weakened wall behind him gave way. He had rolled back out of danger as the rest of the ceiling collapsed to the floor where he had been only moments ago.

He crawled to safety and struggled to his feet. He started to return to the house but it was gone. All that remained was flaming rubble. He could see the smoking remains of a body where the front door used to be and as he drew closer saw the silver bracelet on the wrist identifying his wife. A large pile of burning debris was next to her, and he gasped at the thought that his son was buried under the rubble.

As he stood transfixed by the sight, he became aware of a burning sensation in his hand and arm. Bewildered, he looked at his left arm. In disbelief, he saw the damage to his left hand. His flesh was blistered, hanging loose in parts, and his fingers appeared destroyed. His mind could not make sense of this. It was like he was seeing another man's hand. But then, the pain roared to life and there was no doubt it was his own.

The rest of that night had been a blur. He knew he needed help for his burns. With no aid to be found here, he had staggered as quickly as he was able toward the temple a few blocks away.

He had become very close to one of the temple priestesses, causing significant strife in his marriage when his wife became aware. He followed the familiar route to her quarters and pounded on her door. Her happiness at seeing his face had transformed to panic at seeing his wounds. She had helped him to her bed and called a doctor. After various poultices and treatments, his pain was still intense and they made arrangements to transport him to Smyrna. After several days at the medical facilities there, he had been transported on to Pergamum for the rest of his treatment, finally recovering to his current condition.

————

He startled out of his reverie to a hissing sound. It took him a moment to remember where he was. The hiss sounded again and he looked to his right to see a green and black snake just a few feet away. It was about two-feet long, and it was coiled up on a flat rock warming in the sun.

He froze as he focused his attention on it. He was not really afraid of snakes, not anymore. When he had traveled to Pergamum to the center for medical training, he received much of his treatment in the Asclepion.

This temple to Asclepius had a room full of snakes, an homage to the god of healing who took the form of a serpent. Part of his treatment involved spending time surrounded by the snakes. His initial aversion to them was eventually replaced by a cautious respect, and over time he began to learn the characteristics of the snakes that were dangerous.

As he studied this specimen before him, he could tell it was a poisonous viper. He cautiously moved his left hand toward his canvas bag lying on the ground nearby. His clumsy, scarred fingers were able to grasp the bag and slowly bring it to his side. The snake continued basking in the sun, its head swaying back and forth trying to sense him as its forked tongue tasted the air for his scent. He reached slowly with his right hand, pausing when the snake turned toward the movement. He carefully removed his few belongings from the bag as he shielded the movement with his body. Once it was empty, he slowly brought it up to his lap and turned it inside out.

He reached for a small pebble and placed it carefully in his left hand. Then he put his right hand into the inverted canvas bag, always watching the snake for any sign of danger.

He took a deep breath, readying himself for action, grasping the fabric of the bag as his palm began to perspire. He clumsily tossed the pebble over the snake, and as it landed with a clatter on the hard ground, the snake turned its head. At that moment, he darted his right hand out, covering the snake with the bag and gripping its writhing body through the canvas.

The snake's body whipped around and the hissing increased. He was able to get a strong grip on it somewhere near its head to keep it from turning and biting him. With his left hand, he was able to pull the edge of the bag up around the snake, and then he quickly tied a knot in the canvas so the snake could not escape.

He sat back again to catch his breath, keeping a wary eye on his prize as the snake's movements subsided. He knew the snake would stay quiet in the dark confines of the bag. He was quickly formulating a plan.

The problem he faced was trying to get close enough to Paul to kill him. If he was guarded by soldiers all day, that would be nearly impossible. If he could get aboard with this snake, however, he may be able to smuggle the snake into the prisoners' quarters while they were on deck and let it do what it was made to do. If that did not work, at least it may create a distraction for the guards and he would still be nearby waiting for an opportunity to do the job himself.

He stood up and dusted himself off as he picked up his meager belongings, making a pouch with his cloak and wrapping it around his waist. Then he picked up the bag, feeling the snake moving again with the activity, and began walking toward the port. He needed to find a way onto the ship that night.

# CHAPTER TWELVE

Julius found Gaius on board. He was given report on the soldiers and prisoners. All prisoners were confined to the hold under continual guard. No trouble noted so far. He had also inspected the soldiers in the regiment, keeping them sharp, enforcing discipline where needed.

"Well done," said Julius. "I knew you would have it all under control. It looks like we are going on to Phoenix tomorrow and planning to winter there. The harbormaster was to send word ahead so they will be prepared for a ship of this size. I have already made arrangements for a room ashore tonight. I'll need you to be in charge here tonight, but for the next several hours, you are free to go ashore as well. Stretch your legs, and get some real food, even a bath if you want."

Gaius' face brightened at this. "Julius, you are truly a great centurion! I would love to get off this ship even for a few hours! Thank you!"

"You have earned it. You make my job much easier. Go make arrangements for one of your best lieutenants to take command while you are gone. After that, you are free for the next several hours."

Gaius saluted and turned to go. Julius walked on to his quarters to gather some things for the night.

A half hour later, they climbed down the rope ladder to the skiff bobbing alongside. The crew member manning the skiff rowed back to the dock. After clambering up onto the dock, Julius reminded him to pick him up at sunrise. Gaius promised to find his own way back to the ship with one of the many small boats acting as a ferry to the ships in the harbor.

Julius told Gaius of his plans to return to the inn and enjoy his hot bath. Gaius went his own way to find a hot meal. After enjoying his meal in solitude for the first time in many days, he leisurely made his way to the inn Julius had told him about. He was looking forward to trying out the bath.

He made arrangements with the innkeeper and waited for his appointed time. Julius emerged after a few minutes appearing more relaxed than Gaius remembered him looking for a long time.

"Well, it's not quite like the bath house in Caesarea, but it sure was nice!" he said, a blissful expression on his face. "I am relaxed and ready for a good night's sleep now."

Gaius smiled. "You deserve it, Julius. Thanks for allowing me to get off the ship for a few hours."

"Enjoy it," Julius responded. "Sorry you have to go back to the ship tonight instead of sleeping in a real bed for the night, but I appreciate having someone I can trust being in charge." He suppressed a yawn. "I am going to my room to relax and enjoy the quiet. I'll see you tomorrow."

"Good night, Julius," Gaius said as he turned to go.

Gaius waited a few more minutes as the innkeeper refilled the bath with fresh hot water. Soon, he was soaking in hot water, forgetting the stresses of the journey and the struggles involved in keeping the men in line. His mind wandered as he relaxed.

His thoughts meandered but eventually focused on Paul. Gaius had heard several of his informal discourses on Jesus. He had been intrigued by the way Paul referred to him with such reverence, to the point of calling him the Son of God. Even the talk of Jesus coming back to life after being crucified almost seemed plausible the way Paul discussed it.

Gaius knew how awful crucifixion by Roman soldiers was. He had acquaintances that had been assigned to execution detail, and he had seen them transformed from normal soldiers to some of the most callused and hardened men, even joking at the suffering they inflicted on the condemned. There was no doubt the prisoner would have been dead after they finished with him.

Of course, once the prisoners were dead, they were no longer a problem. Jesus was different, however. The Roman governor of Jerusalem had actually placed his body under guard! He must have been amazingly powerful to warrant that level of concern.

Gaius had heard stories about Him when he was growing up. Surprisingly, the most memorable stories had come from his own family, coloring his upbringing as long as he could remember.

———————

Gaius' grandfather was always gruff and strict but somehow Gaius had grown fond of him. He had died when Gaius was just a young boy, about ten years old. He knew his father did not share much love for the man. Their anger seemed to stem from his father feeling judged by his grandfather, as if his military career had not measured up to his grandfather's expectations. Whenever they were together during Gaius' childhood, sparks would fly. Both men seemed to carry a great deal of anger. When the arguments got heated, Gaius would leave the home and wait outside until it got quiet. At times, his father would storm out, muttering and cursing under his breath stomping off to find a place to drink until the anger faded. When that happened, Gaius knew things would finally begin to settle. Several times, after such episodes, his grandfather would come out, a somber look on his face, and find him. He would kneel down beside him, apologizing for what had happened. On a few occasions, he told him stories about his years as a soldier. Gaius always enjoyed these moments, and over time he learned a few things about his grandfather.

When he was a young soldier in Jerusalem, he was fortunate enough to be assigned to the garrison closest to Herod's palace. Gaius always loved the stories about Herod and the luxurious things in the palace. Now, however, soaking in the tub, his memories were of another story. It was one that his grandfather had only told him once, and Gaius could tell he had immediately regretted saying anything about it.

On that occasion, Gaius remembered the night was clear and the stars especially bright. He had been lying in the grass near the house, staring up at the stars as he waited for the argument to subside. Finally, his father had stormed off, as usual. A few minutes later, his grandfather had come out to check on him. He found him lying there and sat down beside him. Initially he just sat quietly, looking at the sparkling stars spread across the sky.

"You know Gaius, this reminds me of a story," he had said. Immediately Gaius had sat up and scooted closer, excited to hear the story. "Years ago, when I was just a young soldier at Herod's palace, there were some men who had traveled a long way because they had been studying the stars and following one that had been particularly bright, brighter than any of these."

He had gone on to tell him about these men, appearing to be royalty of some type, very wise and learned. They started asking people throughout the city about the birth of a king, wanting to know where he had been born. That was the reason they had been following this bright star, because they had become convinced it was leading them to this powerful king. The people knew nothing of this and told him to ask at the palace, which seemed like a reasonable place for a king to be. When they went to the palace repeating their questions about this king who was supposed to rule over the Jews, of course Herod felt very threatened (and everyone knew that when Herod felt threatened, it was a dangerous time for everyone around him!).

At this point in the story, his grandfather had paused, trying to decide how much more to say. Gaius had peppered him with questions about this king. Where was he? Did they find him? Was he a famous king? Did grandfather meet him? And on and on.

To end the barrage of questions, his grandfather had gone a little further with the story. He told Gaius that Herod had asked some of the palace guard to secretly watch these men very closely. If they could find this king, he wanted to dispose of him before he became more powerful. Gaius had gasped at this but still waited with anticipation to see how this story ended. "What happened? Did they find him?"

Herod found out the Jewish king was prophesied to be born in Bethlehem. He had called the stargazers to him and informed them of this. He told them to go find this king and bring the child to him so he could pay his "respects" as well. But they did not return to the palace. They had departed from there to return to their home in the East.

His grandfather was looking down at his hands, a faraway expression on his face, a mixture of sadness, shame, and anger. He stopped talking and would go no further with the story. Gaius had begged for more but he would not budge. He had abruptly stood up, clearing his throat and wiping his eyes. Gaius had stood as well but could tell there was something about this too painful for his grandfather to share. He had briskly said good night and turned to go. As he walked away, Gaius followed quietly and overheard him talking to himself, muttering "The babies! Why did he make us kill so many babies?! I don't want to remember anymore!" and he hurried away to drown his sorrows.

Later, after Gaius grew older, he heard stories about Jesus. Some referred to him as the King of the Jews. It was a few years before he could put the clues together to realize Jesus was about the right age to have been born when his grandfather was serving Herod. He wondered what was so special about this Jesus that such learned men had traveled so far just to see him when he was only a baby. Now, Paul was teaching about this same man.

Gaius' fondness for his grandfather was more than balanced by his disdain for his father. When he was just a baby, his father had been a soldier in Jerusalem. From all he could determine, he had been respected and a good soldier. But Gaius never knew him like that. Something happened that caused his personality to change. After that, he had become gruff, suspicious, and defensive.

As Gaius grew older, he became aware of people whispering as his father walked by. He had heard taunts from his friends about his dad being a bad soldier. Even his grandfather made frequent pointed comments that caused his father to bristle and become angry. There were rumors he had let a prisoner escape but instead of being executed for this, which was the typical punishment for such a crime under Roman law, he had instead been paid a huge amount of money to cover it up. When he was old enough to understand the implications of this, he had asked his father about it. His father had become angry, yelling at him, red faced, cursing. Then he had threatened to beat Gaius for bringing this up. Fortunately, his mother had intervened.

The relationship between his parents had never fully recovered. His father had spent more and more time at the inn, drinking. When he came home drunk, Gaius knew enough to keep quiet and out of his line of sight or he would be rewarded with a beating.

There were times, however, when being drunk had caused his father to be sad and full of self-pity, defending himself to anyone who would listen. When he had come home in that condition, Gaius began to piece together the events that had led to his father's personality change.

From the information he was able to glean, Gaius learned that his father had been called in to his centurion's presence urgently one day and given a very strange assignment. A man had been crucified because he had offended the Jews and claimed to be their King. (Surely this "King of the Jews" must have been the same one in his grandfather's story!) The Jewish leaders had demanded that his tomb be guarded. They wanted to be sure no one stole the body.

On the surface, this had seemed like a simple job. The man was thoroughly dead, having been scourged severely and then crucified, having a spear thrust into his side. Then, although he was poor with no resources of his own, one of his followers who was apparently rich had donated a tomb for his burial. Gaius' father had never heard of such a thing but who was he to judge. He was only there to guard a dead man's grave for a few nights. The Jewish leaders had claimed that this man had predicted he would come back to life on the third day. They feared the man's devout followers may try to steal the corpse and spread rumors that he had done it. The soldiers laughed about this, thinking it was a ridiculous idea. But orders were orders.

The tomb had been covered with a large heavy stone, and there were three men designated to watch over it. When they were assigned to this duty the day after the execution, they checked the tomb to be sure it had not been tampered with, even moving the stone to be sure the body was not gone. They had seen the bloody shroud covering the corpse. Then they sealed it thoroughly with the stone and settled in, preparing for a slow and boring couple of days. They made sure to have at least one of them awake at all times (they were not ignorant soldiers, and they knew sometimes the commanders made surprise inspections).

Then, everything changed. Gaius had heard his father relate this story a few times, every time with a tone of awe and fear even years later. Early the next morning, the earth shook violently. The soldiers were scared, but then what really terrified them was that the stone which blocked the tomb rolled aside and a searing bright light poured out! All of the soldiers fell to the ground, their hearts pounding, their mouths dry, and their hands trembling. Their breath was fast and shallow and they became light headed as their vision began to darken. They all succumbed to unconsciousness, but just before his vision faded, Gaius' father swore he saw a figure surrounded by the light emerge from the open tomb. As he reached this point in the story, the terror on his face was still evident even after several years. He never wavered in this belief even after years had passed, but the few times he related this story, it was only to his family. He always told them to never tell anyone, afraid he would be thought insane.

When the soldiers regained consciousness, the tomb was empty and no one was around. They huddled together wondering what to do. They knew they would be executed for losing a prisoner. How could a dead prisoner disappear like this? (Gaius' father did not tell the others what he had seen.) They decided to go to the Jewish leaders first, since they were the ones who had been suspicious the man's followers would steal the body. They would know the prime suspects to interrogate. Maybe the soldiers could find the corpse quickly and no one else would need to know.

When they talked to the chief priests, however, their response was much different than expected. They had hastily called together the other leaders and then called in the soldiers again. They instructed them to only say that the man's followers came in the night while they slept and stole the body. At first this seemed like a stupid plan. Admitting to sleeping on guard duty was bad, but a missing prisoner, even dead, was likely to result in their own death. However, the Jews paid them a huge amount of silver, more than any of them ever hoped to earn, and also guaranteed to vouch for them if the governor or their superior officers questioned it. It was a deal too good to pass up.

After that, his father was reassigned away from Judea. This conveniently kept him from sharing this story in Jerusalem. The money allowed them to purchase a large plot of land, and he resigned from the Roman army a year later. He could never put his heart into it. He was isolated and his colleagues were constantly whispering and pointing at him. When Gaius grew up and left to join the army, it was against his father's wishes. He would not be deterred from this, however, so his father's parting advice was to avoid prison guard duty at all costs. He had not been in contact with him since.

As he mulled this over, Gaius recalled another key piece of information, which did not mean much to him when he was a child. The man's name was Jesus. Back then, he did not really know the significance of this, but now, after the other information he had learned and after Paul's teaching, it was astounding to him that his own family had inadvertently taught him from his early childhood that Jesus was a special person, so special that even foreign rulers had sought Him out, considering Him a king. His birth had caused fear even in Herod's palace. And the story of His coming back to life, seeming to be so unbelievable, had been corroborated by his own father.

———

Gaius sat in the tub, pondering all of this. Soon, he became aware that the water had cooled and his fingers were wrinkled from soaking for so long. He climbed out of the water and dried off, dressing in his uniform once again.

He settled up with the innkeeper that had arranged his bath and walked out to the street. It was dark, and the streets were mostly quiet. People were in the inn or settled into their rooms. The shops were closed. There were still a few people making their way to the dock. Some sailors who had indulged in too much ale were weaving their way down the street singing out of tune.

Gaius was still lost in his own thoughts, mulling over the things he had been pondering during his bath. There seemed to be evidence from more than one source that Jesus had risen from the tomb after being crucified. What should he do with this realization? If this was true, then the other things Paul had been teaching may also be true. Could Jesus really be the Son of God?

All of his life, on the rare occasions his mother and father had spoken of Jesus, it had been to blame Him for their difficulties and strife—the lack of advancement for his father's military career, the need to move away from friends and family, the ridicule, the alcohol, and so on. As a child, when your parents have such strong opinions, it is natural to share these same feelings. When he grew older, he never really had a reason to rethink this opinion until now.

He knew he would need to learn more to be able to sort this out. Maybe he should try talking to Paul directly. The more he considered this idea, the better it seemed. He would try to find a private time to talk to Paul, preferably when the other soldiers (even Julius) were not around to overhear.

He arrived at the dock and began to look for someone who could transport him back to the ship. There was a small skiff that had just departed, full of passengers, to take them back to their various ships. There did not seem to be anyone else at the dock at this time. He was about to find a place to sit and wait for the skiff to return when he heard something. He walked toward the end of the pier where the sound seemed to be coming from and realized there was a boat tied up in the shadows. He could see a shadowy figure bending over in the small craft placing a bag in the bottom of the boat.

"Excuse me!" he called to the man.

The man jumped, startled by the presence of a soldier nearby. "What!" he answered.

"I need you to take me out to the large grain ship. I need to be there soon and there are no other boats available. What do you charge?"

"I'm off duty," the man said dismissively, turning away.

"Hey, I'll pay you more than your usual rate if you'll make an exception. I really need to get to that ship."

At the mention of money, the man paused and turned back. He pondered this for a moment and then nodded. "All right. I'll make an exception. But we need to go now so I can get back to what I need to do!"

Gaius rolled his eyes at the man's response but felt it was his only option. He climbed into the small boat and helped to untie it and push off.

The man seemed to be somewhat clumsy with the oars and struggled to get them moving in a straight line. Gaius began to regret asking him for a ride. Finally, they got moving in the correct direction. They traveled in silence, each lost in their own thoughts.

# CHAPTER THIRTEEN

After ten minutes of bobbing on the water in distracted silence, the grain ship loomed ahead. A few lanterns could be seen on deck and the movement of shadows as the crew went about their duties. Voices could be heard speaking in low tones, but overall the ship was quiet. Gaius handed the pilot a few silver coins and thanked him for transporting him. He grunted in response as he carefully counted the coins, a suspicious look on his face. Gaius shook his head in disgust at the man's attitude, and he was about to reprimand him when a voice called out, interrupting them.

"You in the boat! Identify yourselves!" It was one of the soldiers on watch duty.

"It's Gaius, your commander," he responded, turning away from the ungrateful pilot.

"Welcome back, commander! Stand by for the ladder."

He lowered the rope ladder, dimly visible in the faint light from shore. There was also a rope net nearby, draped over the side to the waterline. This was the crew member's preferred means of climbing between the deck and the water, but Gaius preferred the relative stability of the ladder. The boat's pilot clumsily maneuvered closer, bumping against the ship as Gaius grabbed for the ladder. After a lot of bobbing up and down, swinging against the side of the ship and almost falling into the water, Gaius was able to get both hands and both feet on the ladder, holding on tightly.

He caught his breath and began awkwardly climbing as the small boat drifted away from the hull, the pilot not uttering a word.

Gaius lunged over the bulwark, the watchman lending a hand. After collecting himself, he looked around taking a quick survey of his men.

"Anything to report while I was gone?" he asked the man.

"No sir. All was quiet. The prisoners have remained in the hold as ordered."

Gaius acknowledged this and dismissed him. As the man returned to his duties, Gaius made his way to the soldiers' quarters. He found his lieutenant and received his report and officially resumed his duties as the officer in charge. After a quick tour of inspection to check on the prisoners, as well as his men, he headed to the sleeping quarters.

He stretched out on his pallet, remembering how relaxed he felt during the bath. His mind started to wander over all he had been considering, but fatigue won out and he drifted off to sleep. Sometime during the night, he had a dream of a stone rolling aside from a tomb, an unbearably bright light shining out, and a booming voice calling his name. Of course, he only remembered bits of this dream when he woke up the next morning

––––––

Meanwhile, Demetrius was still rowing the small boat around the stern of the grain ship, trying to figure out his next move. The rope ladder was not an option since the watchman had raised it after Gaius had boarded. The net would be his best choice but might be difficult with his weak hand. He stopped in the shadow of the rear deck angling outward above his head. He found the line to the anchors and tied his small boat up, deciding to wait until a later hour. He settled back against the seat of the small boat and once again checked to be sure the snake was secured in the bag. He removed his cloak and folded it up behind his shoulders to act as a pillow and closed his eyes for a few minutes.

When he awoke, he was disoriented at first. His neck and shoulder ached from leaning uncomfortably against the bench seat of the small boat. He sat up and looked around, feeling movement in the bag next to him. He quickly took in his surroundings. It was darker, the faint light from the shore now mostly extinguished. There was a layer of clouds obscuring any stars. Above him, the dark shape of the ship loomed quietly. He no longer heard voices from the deck and it seemed the men had turned in for the night.

He untied from the anchor line, careful to make as little noise as possible. He dipped his oar in the water slowly to make his way to the net he had seen earlier. He cringed with every splash or creak but no one seemed to notice. When he arrived at the net, he studied it in the dark, considering his next move.

Suddenly he froze as he heard footsteps on deck above his head. He grasped the net to keep himself in the shadow of the ship as best he could. He held his breath as the footsteps walked past. Evidently the watchman was making his rounds. After a moment it was quiet again on the deck, and Demetrius knew this would be his best opportunity to get aboard before he came back.

He picked up the bag holding the snake and tucked it into his belt, being sure to secure it tightly. He carefully placed the oar in the boat and reached out for the net. There was a slight thumping as he lifted himself out of the boat but no sign of discovery from the deck.

He used his foot to gently push the boat away toward the shore and began his slow climb upward. He used his scarred left hand to stabilize him as he reached up with the right hand and carefully raised his feet to the next part of the net. It was slow going and after a couple of minutes, he was perspiring and breathing hard. He knew he could not stop, since he was not sure how long before the guard came back.

He finally reached the edge of the bulwark and surreptitiously raised his head to survey the deck. There was a soft murmur of voices coming from the stern to his right, and he could see a lantern there and the outline of two soldiers speaking. He knew the lantern would hamper their night vision and they were far enough away to allow him time to cautiously climb up and over the top of the bulwark. The sounds he made tumbling onto the deck were soft and swallowed up by the normal creaking of the large ship.

He lay in the shadow long enough to be sure the soldiers were still at the other end of the deck. As they continued to talk and laugh, they began walking toward the other side of the ship. He waited until he was sure they were preoccupied, and as they passed behind the mast, he carefully scurried toward the hatch to his left. He paused at the opening, listening for any sound but only heard snoring.

This was a grain ship and there must be a grain storage room in the depths of the ship. That should be a good place to hide, but he would have to go down through the sleeping quarters to get there. He knew he could not delay since the watchmen would be making their way around the deck soon. He took a deep breath, cinched the snake bag tighter to his belt, and began to slowly descend the wooden ladder to the deck below. As he climbed, the shadows grew deeper and when he arrived at the bottom of the ladder, he could only make out faint darker shapes scattered around the perimeter of the room in the murkiness. He could feel a sense of a larger room and heard gentle snoring and deep breathing coming from all around.

He fumbled around at the base of the ladder, trying to guess where the next ladder to the lower deck may be. He had a momentary panic as someone nearby mumbled in his sleep. About that time, the hatch above him grew brighter and he knew the guards must be approaching. Thankfully, the light spilled down enough for him to see the hatch to the lower level and he carefully stepped over to it.

Just as he reached the ladder to the lower hold, the man closest to him rolled over and sat up abruptly, eyes open and looking directly at him. He had a cloth wrapped around his head like a turban and one arm supported in a sling. Demetrius froze, his heart pounding, and he reached for his dagger ready to use it quickly.

"Mom! Why is the room on fire! Get out of there!" he cried out, anguish in his voice. Then he mumbled incoherently and lay down again. The man rolled over and immediately resumed his heavy breathing.

Demetrius exhaled slowly, realizing the man was talking in his sleep. He had strange, unsettled feeling of familiarity as he watched him. After waiting a minute to be sure he was asleep again, and to allow his pulse to return to normal, he shook his head and moved on to the ladder to the lower level. He slowly climbed down into the inky blackness, feeling his way as he descended to the silence of the hold.

At the bottom of the ladder, he paused. He was met by the musty smell of grain and a scurrying sound of some unseen creatures that made their home in the darkness with him. After a couple of minutes, his eyes started to make out some of the shapes around him. He felt his way over the bulkhead away from the ladder and slid to the ground. He pulled his cloak around him and settled in to wait until the light of day to get a better sense of what was around him.

Once he was quietly seated, the scurrying around him increased. There must be rats that had been feasting on the cargo of grain. After his initial revulsion, he began to accept his situation, knowing that it would only be a day until they arrived at Phoenix and he could somehow make his escape. He felt movement by his right thigh and could tell there was a rat beginning to climb onto his leg. His right hand shot out quickly feeling its furry body squirming in his grasp. He held it tightly and fumbled to open the sack with his clumsy hand. He crammed the rat into it, knowing the snake would feast on that and be good for a few days. He tied the sack quickly and tried to ignore the battle going on inside as the snake writhed and hissed and the rat squealed and twisted. Within minutes all was quiet and there was a wet spot on the bag lying next to him.

# CHAPTER FOURTEEN

The next morning, the ship was bustling with activity. The captain had left orders for the crew to restock the water supply and some provisions. Although it was to be a brief voyage to Phoenix, Captain Sahaq always wanted to be prepared for the worst. Nothing was certain. The small boat was shuttling back and forth loaded with several casks of fresh water, and the crew members were hauling them up and handing them down to the lower hold to fill the cistern located there.

Demetrius had slept fitfully, waking several times to the numerous noises natural to a ship full of people. Very little light found its way down to this level of the ship, and he finally fell into an exhausted sleep in the early morning hours only to be startled awake to the sound of someone climbing heavily down the ladder. The sailor was holding a lantern in one hand and focused on gripping the ladder with the other. He quickly scooted into the darkest corner of the room as quietly as he could. The man was making so much noise he did not notice the additional scurrying.

When the man reached the bottom of the ladder, Demetrius was sure he would be discovered, and he gripped his dagger tightly. Fortunately, he turned away and went through an open doorway into the next compartment. As soon as he was out of eyesight, Demetrius hastily moved some of the grain sacks in front of him and covered himself with his cloak, leaving a small opening through which he could peek. He finished this task

just as another sailor was climbing down the ladder. He stationed himself
at the bottom of the ladder and called up to the next level.

"Ok, I'm ready."

Demetrius heard the sound of something scraping along the deck
above and then the grunting of someone struggling under the weight of
a heavy burden. Then, the man at the bottom of the ladder reached up
and guided the cumbersome object to the deck below. He paused to catch
his breath and then begin to half scoot and half roll a small barrel toward
the next room. The first man reappeared in the doorway to help and they
both disappeared for a minute or two. He could hear the sound of water
sloshing as they poured the fresh water into the cistern next door. Then
they reappeared and passed the empty container back to the floor above.

This process was repeated several times over the next half hour.
The men were so focused on their routine they did not notice the cloak
behind the grain sacks in the corner. Nor did they see the small cloth bag
nearby with the bloody-appearing stain on it. If they had paid attention,
they would have noticed that it moved at times with the writhing of the
snake inside.

Finally, the men above called down. "This is the last one!"

The job was repeated one last time and this time, the men reappeared
from the adjacent compartment holding the lantern. Demetrius thought
he was home free and was beginning to relax when the men looked in his
direction.

"Hey, what is that?" he heard. His heart skipped a beat and he quickly
drew in his breath.

⊠ looks like a bag," the other man said. At this, Demetrius held his
breath, trying very hard not to move.

They took a step in his direction but stopped a few feet away where the
bag was lying.

"I think it moved!" one of the men said, startled.

They stood watching it for a moment, holding the lantern closer.
Finally, one of the men cautiously reached down to pick it up, holding it

at arm's length. He shook it gently and was rewarded with more vigorous movement from the bag and a hissing sound could be heard.

"I think it's a snake!" the man exclaimed.

The other man reached out for the bag. "Let me see," he said. He took the bag. "Hold the lantern for me!"

He untied the string that cinched the bag opening and carefully opened it. Both men peered down into the bag as he held it under the lantern.

"I can't see anything," the braver of the two said. "Hold the lantern closer."

The man moved closer and bent down to see in the light of the lantern, just as the snake jumped toward the light with a loud hiss.

"Ahhh!" he cried out as he jumped back, striking out at the bag with his free hand and knocking it to the floor. He panicked and swung around quickly, causing the lantern to go out.

"Hey, watch out!" the other man said, jumping back as well. "I think it is loose!" Both men jumped quickly toward the ladder.

"I'm staying out of this room!" one said, laughing as they climbed up to the next deck. "You should have seen the expression on your face!" Their voices and laughter faded as they climbed and the room was once more dark and quiet.

Demetrius could hear the faint rustling sound of the snake slithering into the pile of grain in the opposite corner. He sat up and listened closely to be sure the men were not returning. He was relieved, realizing the story of a snake loose in the hold would likely keep him from being disturbed by any of the crew for a long while. He was not particularly worried about the snake, knowing that if he kept to himself, the snake would not have a reason to bother him. The rats, on the other hand, would definitely have something to worry about.

———————

While this was happening in the hold, the preparations for departure continued on the main deck. Luke had left early that morning on one of the first boats ashore. He needed to get some supplies to replenish what he had used so far, and he was glad to get off the ship for a short time.

He spent the morning walking through the village at the port. He had a good meal with fresh bread and fruit and cheese for breakfast. He found a market at the end of the road that carried the herbs he needed. He purchased more willow bark, knowing that for controlling pain it could be very useful on a ship. They also had a small supply of mandrake plant. This was more potent, and he had read in his studies that a wine made from this could be strong enough to make a man unconscious in the event that surgery was needed. Ginger root was a good treatment for nausea and there was great demand for that on any voyage.

He tried to always keep a supply of these on hand. Paul had been susceptible to severe headaches at times, ever since he was temporarily blinded by the light from heaven when he met the Lord. These would come on suddenly, causing him to have a sensation of flashing lights in his vision and vomiting. They would last for several hours at a time. Usually, he had to find a dark quiet place to lay down and rest, which was hard to do when he was traveling.

Luke had been present during one of these episodes and found that a preparation of ginger root was effective at calming the nausea and also that the tea made from willow bark was fairly effective at controlling the pain and shortening the duration of his headaches. Unfortunately nothing was fully effective at stopping them and Paul had suffered with this pain many times. Thankfully, these headaches were infrequent, but they happened enough that Paul had begun to refer to them as his "thorn in the flesh." It seemed they would be something he had to endure for the rest of his life.

After replenishing his pharmacy, Luke ambled slowly back to the port, savoring his time on land. The day was overcast but the clouds did not seem ominous. There was a good breeze. All in all, it seemed like a good day to set sail for the short voyage to Phoenix. It would only be a few more hours on the ship before a good long time ashore for the winter. This fact made the prospect of boarding the ship tolerable.

Luke and the ship's captain rode back to The Emir together and were the last to arrive. The remainder of the passengers, officers, and crew that had gone ashore had made their way back shortly before them. On the way back to the ship, Luke asked the captain about the weather.

"The wind is in our favor today. I talked to the other ships' officers in port, and the squall they faced a couple of days ago should be long gone by now. There should be fair seas and I expect we will be in port by supper time," he answered. His confidence was reassuring.

Luke went to his quarters to put away his new supplies. On deck, the crew were all working with purpose, making ready to depart. All were eager to make this short, easy trip to Phoenix so they could relax on shore for a few months. He passed by Temeros and greeted him.

"Hey, my friend. How's the shoulder feeling?"

Temeros subconsciously rubbed at the shoulder, wincing slightly. "I think it is better today. I'm hoping to be able to get back to some useful work soon." He yawned and stretched cautiously.

"Did the pain keep you awake?" Luke asked, noticing the tired expression on his face.

"Not really. I think it was a bad dream." He responded.

"Well, we should be in port this evening and able to have a couple of months on dry land during the winter to rest and recover," Luke said, turning toward his quarters. "See me later and I'll check the shoulder again."

"Ok, I'll come by soon."

Temeros turned to watch the activity on the deck. He had an unsettled feeling when he woke that morning. He knew he had dreamed about the fire again that night and had tossed and turned a little. But he felt there was something more. For some strange reason, he was thinking about his father, and it was not a happy thought. As hard as it was to lose him in the fire, he still had a lot of anger toward him. Theirs had been a tumultuous relationship.

He sighed as he shook his head, clearing his thoughts. He still had his arm in a sling, but the pain was much better. His headache was better as well.

He moved over to the side of the deck where he would not be in the way, as he watched the sailors preparing. There was a small group of older sailors nearby and he could overhear them talking about the weather.

"I tell you, my knees are aching today more than they have for weeks! I think we are in for some rain!"

"I heard there had been some squalls west of here in the past few days, but the captain is sure they have cleared up," another responded.

"I don't care what he says. Something is in the works and we better be ready!" the first said again.

Another sailor joined in. "I think you're right! The sky was pretty red this morning, and we all know what that means!"

"I'm just glad we only have a short journey to Phoenix and then we can stay anchored there for the winter."

Temeros listened to this exchange distractedly, not really paying attention. He was already thinking of spending time on solid ground for the winter.

# Chapter Fifteen

By midmorning, their preparations were complete. The captain barked out orders to weigh anchor and trim the sails as he stood at the helm ready to steer out of the harbor. The sails snapped and billowed, catching the wind, and the ship began to move slowly toward the sea, the small boat tethered to the stern following them.

The breeze was a welcome change, and the mood on the deck seemed bright with anticipation. The clouds had become heavy above them, but the crew, for the most part, did not seem to notice. They were all focused on their assigned tasks.

The ship cleared the mouth of the harbor and turned west. Fair Havens was open to the south of the island and the Harbor was not very protected. As they proceeded along the coast of Crete, they could see a promontory of land extending into the sea, far ahead in the distance. Phoenix lay many miles to the north and west with natural protection from the shoreline creating a partial barrier to the weather in the windward zone near the coast. As they saw the contour of the island, the captain and crew were more confident they had made the right choice in moving there for the winter.

After about an hour, the ship was approaching the spit of land where the island turned sharply north. The captain planned to angle northwest after passing by that point rather than hugging the shoreline as he had been doing so far. He glanced at the sky and frowned. The clouds had darkened with some storm clouds to the north, but the wind still seemed to favor their course. He gave the men orders to trim the sails setting the desired course.

———————

After the excitement of preparing for the journey had worn off, Temeros had decided to find Luke. He found him in his quarters organizing his supplies, cataloging what he had on a sheet of parchment.

"Hi, Luke!" he called as he stuck his head in the doorway. "Is there anything I can do to help you? What are you working on?"

Luke glanced up briefly. "Oh, hi, Temeros. I'm just trying to take an inventory of my supplies as we get ready to anchor for the winter. It is always good to be organized! Maybe you can help me sort them and put them in their proper place."

"Sure. I need something to do. Do you always keep a list like this?"

"I have learned the hard way that it helps to know what I have and where it is. There have been a few times through the years that I did not have what I thought I had and patients suffered because of it! Anything I can do to keep track of what I have used may be important the next time someone is in need."

Temeros began sorting the bandages, roots, herbs, and so on. Luke was a patient teacher, pointing out what treatments were best to keep together. The work moved along quickly and soon the list was complete.

Luke carefully placed the parchment in a leather folder and filed it on a shelf next to the table. Temeros noticed a larger bundle of similar parchments on the shelf as well.

"You must have been doing this for many years to have that many lists of supplies!"

Luke was momentarily confused but then saw the papers Temeros had indicated. He smiled. "No, that is not my medical papers. That is something much more important!"

"More important than treating the sick?"

"Yes, I believe so," Luke responded, a more serious expression on his face. "For the past couple of years, I have been gathering as much information as I can about Jesus. I have been traveling, talking to the disciples that lived with Him day in and day out. They actually saw Him do miraculous works, healing the sick and raising the dead. They heard His teaching from His very lips. And they were there the night He was betrayed and executed by the Romans."

Temeros listened in rapt attention as Luke continued. "There have been many accounts of His life passed along to the churches, but no one seems to have a complete narrative of His teachings and actions. I wanted to go back to those who could give a firsthand accounting, the eyewitnesses, to ensure that we know for certain what He taught and did. I have gathered the information and now I need to organize it so it can be circulated. I hoped to have time to work on it on the ship, but I imagine I will be able to make some progress over the winter in port."

"I would love to know more. Would it be possible for me to read it when it is done?"

"Of course," Luke answered.

The ship gave a sudden lurch and the deck slanted down slightly as it fell into the next wave. Temeros had a startled expression on his face.

"We must be getting further out from shore. The weather must have changed as we have been in here working." Luke patted his arm reassuringly. "Don't worry! I'm sure it will smooth out soon. We should only have a few hours until we arrive in Phoenix. Let's go out on deck and take a look. We can talk about this later."

———

Julius and Gaius were on deck watching all of the activity, glad to finally have some wind in the sails and actually feel the progress as the ship plowed through the water. They noticed the dark clouds but trusted the experienced sailors enough to feel safe in their hands. The prisoners remained below, closely guarded so they would not be in the way of the crew.

The ship passed the point of land at Cape Matala and began to move further away from shore as it angled toward the north. The waves seemed choppier as they reached the deeper water, and the ship began to bob up and down a bit more. Gaius gripped the railing tighter.

"Oh, great!" he said, breathing deeply. "I was enjoying the calmer seas we've been having up until now."

Julius chuckled. "Calm seas may be more comfortable but we don't make much progress in them. At least we have a good strong breeze to get us there quicker! You just need to endure this for about three more hours and we will be home free."

Gaius nodded and faced into the wind. He began to feel better after a few minutes, anticipating a nice long stretch on land.

————

Thirty minutes later, the clouds were noticeably darker, and they were all startled to see lightning flashing in the distance to the north over land. The wind still seemed to be favorable, but the captain and crew wore a more concerned expression and their actions were more focused on the task at hand as they frequently looked to the north and east.

The mountains along the coast had blocked their view of the gathering clouds, but now as they sailed further west, there was a sudden burst of wind from the north and west that had gathered strength as it blew through a narrow valley opening to the coast. This came with enough force to cause the ship to turn further west than north, and the deck slanted down to the port side.

Over the next hour, the sea became rougher and the clouds darkened even more. The wind, which had been favorable from the south at the beginning of the day, now battled against them. The sails were no longer billowing but were flapping as the wind had changed direction. The waves were flecked with whitecaps all around them, and The Emir was beginning to shudder slightly as it hit some of the bigger waves.

The captain bellowed out orders to trim the sails further as he also directed the helmsman. It became apparent it was a losing battle, however. Now the wind was blowing fiercely from the northeast, directing them further off course. The clouds were moving quickly and began to swirl around in a spiral. There were areas with noticeable lowering of the clouds, causing a funnel shape pointing toward the sea in the distance. In response, the water sent up sprays of water, and the surface was covered in whitecaps. The waves began to build into hills and valleys.

The older sailor with the bad knees was the first to say it, but soon the rest of the crew were passing it along. The word was repeated all over the deck. "Euroclydon!"

Gaius had been noticing the change in demeanor of the crew, and as they became more concerned, he felt a deep worry rising up in his own mind. One of the crew paused nearby gazing intently out to the north and east as the clouds began to move closer, and Gaius called out to him

"What is it everyone is saying? What is this 'Euroclydon'?"

The man answered without turning toward him, keeping his focus on the clouds. "It is a strong northeast wind, notorious in this part of the sea for blowing ships off their course. It comes up very quickly, with little or no warning. We have all heard stories of ships getting caught in a sudden storm and disappearing, never to be seen again!"

Another crew member nearby reprimanded him. "Don't say that. We only have two hours to our port. Surely we will not have trouble this close to Crete. There is no need to frighten the landlubbers with scary stories!" But as he said this, there were lines of worry etched on his forehead, and he, too, was watching the sky.

The men hurried on to continue their duties on the ship, as Gaius turned a worried gaze on Julius.

Julius' smile had faded. "Not to worry, Gaius!" He tried to sound reassuring, but the strained expression on his face belied his inner turmoil. "The captain has sailed these waters many times and we are very close to shore. If there is any problem, surely he can just head for the nearest shoreline to wait out the storm." He seemed to be trying to reassure himself as much as Gaius.

"I hope you're right!" Gaius muttered as he gripped the gunwales tighter.

Within a few minutes, even the soldiers who had never been on a ship could tell the storm was going to be a problem. The ship began to lean toward the port side as the wind strengthened and swung around to the northeast. The captain gave a constant stream of orders, and the crew fought valiantly to adjust the sails so they could tack to the north and west, but the battle was lost.

Finally the captain ordered them to set the sails at an angle to the wind and tied off the tiller in an effort to keep the rudder pointed roughly west, letting the storm drive them.

———

Down in the hold, the prisoners could feel a change in the ship and knew something was wrong. The soldiers had been milling around, talking in hushed tones, and some that had been on deck came down to report what had happened.

Aristarchus had developed a rapport with a few of the soldiers and was able to get their attention. He came back and reported to Paul that there was a fast-developing storm and the ship was not able to go toward the port. Instead they were being driven west and south, further away from Crete.

Immediately there was a wave of fear and anxiety that swept through the prisoners. The soldiers were already nervous, and now, unrest and panic began to affect those in the hold. Paul could sense what was happening.

"Listen to me!" he called out in a strong voice. "Listen!" he repeated. Those near him, who had been influenced by his teaching, turned and shushed the crowd, and slowly they began to quiet.

"We must trust God. He knows we are here and He has promised to never forsake us!"

The ship lurched and the deck slanted as it crashed into another wave. There was an audible gasp from those in the hold.

"What can he do? This storm will wreck us!" someone shouted.

"God is greater than the storm," Paul assured them.

"If he is so great, why did he send us into the storm to begin with?!" another joined in. "If you are his servant, and if he loves you, he would have made this a smooth journey!"

At this, Paul and Aristarchus laughed out loud.

"What's so funny?" The man said, now beginning to sound more annoyed than fearful.

"We were never promised smooth sailing," Paul said with a chuckle. "Our Lord, Jesus Himself, taught that in this world, we will have tribulations. In fact, He was caught in a storm with his disciples on the Sea of Galilee!"

A few more of the prisoners turned at this, interested. Although the ship continued its irregular movements in the rough seas, the fear seemed to be subsiding as they were listening to him speak.

"It must not have been much of a storm, if the Lord was caught in it. Surely God would not have put him in danger before his ministry was finished!" someone reasoned out loud.

"On the contrary," Paul said calmly, "His disciples, who had spent much of their lives in boats on the sea fishing, were actually panicking, fearful for their lives. And yet our Lord was at peace, sleeping in the back of the little boat."

The group around him looked incredulous at this. "So he was going to let his disciples perish?"

"Not at all!" Paul answered. "He was at peace because He has power over all of His creation. When His disciples came and woke Him, they were terrified, sure they were about to sink. Water was filling their boat. And yet, when they were most afraid, they turned to the Lord himself, telling him their fear."

"And what good did that do?" someone asked.

Paul and Aristarchus shared a smile as Paul answered. "He woke up and scolded the storm!"

The prisoners stared at him as though he had told them a bad joke. "Of course he did. Why don't we try yelling at the wind and see what happens!" they said sarcastically.

But a few were still paying close attention. "What happened?" they asked in anticipation.

Paul smiled reassuringly. "As soon as He spoke to the storm, it stopped."

The group around him gasped and murmured to each other. Even some of the soldiers nearby were listening closely.

Paul continued, "Then, He rebuked His disciples for their lack of faith. They were astonished that the wind and waves obeyed even just His voice."[7] He paused, looking around at the prisoners, and then continued with deep conviction in his voice. "We can be confident that our Lord will not leave us alone in the middle of this storm. The wind and waves still know His voice and His power. He may not choose to calm the storm, but I can assure you He is with us as we ride through it. We must keep our faith focused on Him rather than letting fear take us."

As he spoke, the soldiers could see there was a noticeable calm spreading through the prisoners. They breathed easier.

— — — — —

Deeper still, in the lowest hold, Demetrius also was aware of a change in the ship. The deck was rocking more and the creaking of the hull was magnified. Where he was sitting on the floor, leaning against the bulkhead, he was suddenly aware of water soaking into his clothes. He quickly jumped up and turned around. The wall was wet to touch, but so far nothing was accumulating in the deck below his feet. He knew it was only a

---

[7] Luke 8: 22–25

matter of time, however, and began to greatly regret his decision to stow away on this death trap.

Anger began to consume him. Not only did Paul take away his livelihood and his wife and son, now he was going to take his life as well. He could feel rage building and decided to find him before that happened.

He gathered his meager belongings and began to make his way toward the ladder. He reasoned that he could blend in with the crew and passengers, since there were so many. They would likely be distracted by the activity and their own fear. He thought about taking time to find the snake, in case he could use it to terrorize Paul, but he decided that was a lost cause. The snake was on its own.

# Chapter Sixteen

The wind had picked up and now was gusting strongly from the northeast. The ship had been pushed into a more western course, even with the sails set to correct their heading. The day had grown dark with the heavy storm clouds that had now overtaken them. The temperature had dropped considerably, and with the spray being thrown up from the rough waves, it was uncomfortably cool on the deck.

Gaius was torn, not sure whether it was better to be below deck where the wind was blocked and he could stay warmer and dryer than he was or to stay put where at least he could watch the horizon to ease his unsettled stomach. Julius seemed outwardly unaffected by the ship's movement, but Gaius could tell that much of this was a façade, his eyes tensing at times as his brow furrowed briefly.

After another thirty minutes of enduring this, the decision became much easier when the rain begin to fall. It was not just a gentle mist. These were fully formed raindrops, not so much falling as being hurled to earth by an unseen hand, stinging as they hit his exposed skin. Gaius was quickly soaked, and he and Julius turned as one to rush toward the hatch leading to the hold.

The crew members did not have that option. Each was attending to their assigned task with intense focus. They were securing everything that was loose on the deck and retrieving things that had already been blown about by the wind. Three of them had gone to the stern of the ship to attempt to haul in the small boat that was towed behind. After several attempts, the boat was still being tossed about in the waves, and the sailors had been rewarded with a variety of rope burns to their hands and forearms. Between the rain and the rough seas, it was beginning to take on water and becoming heavier by the minute.

Rayiz, the foreman, was stalking back and forth impervious to the heavy rain, bellowing out orders to the men, a scowl on his face. He helped tighten the sail rigging that was flapping in the wind and directed his crew to secure the foresail. He turned and saw the group laboring at the stern and made his way toward them as he braced against the tossing of the deck.

"What's the problem?!" he demanded. "Why is that boat not yet on the deck?"

The men looked quickly at each other. One of them spoke up.

"The waves and rain are filling it with water, and it is too heavy for us to pull it in with this wind and the ship moving so much! We need more help!"

Rayiz surveyed them, about to reprimand them for their laziness, but he could see the red welts of the rope burns on their arms. One of them had a deeper laceration that would require Dr. Luke's attention. Rayiz ordered him to go find the doctor and get his wounded hand treated. He turned to look out at the boat being towed behind them and could see that it was half full of water, riding lower in the waves, and the tow rope was stretched tight. If this went on much longer, they may lose the boat either by the rope snapping or the boat sinking below the waves. He muttered under his breath and turned to find more men to assign to this task.

As he was making his way forward, he saw the captain giving directions to the helmsman. Two men were struggling to direct the ship, pulling mightily at the tiller, but it appeared the storm was winning. The captain directed them to lash the rudder in a fixed position to keep the ship directed into the waves. The thought of the ship being broadsided by the waves was an unspoken fear they all shared, motivating them to greater effort.

The captain saw Rayiz approaching. "Has that boat been hauled aboard yet?"

Rayiz shook his head. "It is getting swamped by the waves and rain. We need calmer seas or more men. I'm going to get more crew to help work at it. What's our status?"

The captain shook his head, a frown on his face as he motioned him to step away from the helmsmen to continue the conversation. "Not good," he said in a lower tone. "This Euroclydon caught us all off guard. The wind is against us, so we have to give up our original course. I fear that if we force it too much, the rudder may break."

Rayiz' expression darkened at this as he nodded. "I was afraid that was the case. You and I have been at this a long time, but this is the worst storm we have had in many years. It came on us so suddenly and so intensely we had no time to prepare."

"We can't navigate right now, but with the direction of the wind and our position just before the storm, we may be near Cauda. If we can get on the leeward side of it, that may give us enough shelter to haul in the boat. We need to be ready to frap the ship as well. Tell the men to get the cables ready to pass around the hull when we have an opportunity."

"Aye, captain." Rayiz turned and headed to find his men as the captain turned back to the helm.

The rain lessened for a moment, giving a brief window of better visibility. The captain trained his eyes to the west and south. With a break in the rain, he was relieved to see an island rising above the sea in the distance. With their present trajectory, they had a good chance of making it to the southern side, giving them a brief respite from the wind. There may even be a chance of getting close enough to find a port to anchor in and ride out the storm, but he was not hopeful. Cauda was not known to have any suitable harbors for a ship of their size.

He called out orders to the helmsmen to continue steering toward Cauda as he went to his cabin to consult his charts. It took him a few minutes to find the proper one, and during that short time, the ship was once again being pelted by rain. The rocking of the ship in the waves was magnified by being in the small room with no way to see the horizon as a point of reference, but he was able to ignore the motion sickness as he examined the chart.

The island of Cauda was small, a speck in the sea about twenty-five miles to the south and west of Crete. It was roughly triangular in shape, with the point to the south. The southwest side, where they would find the best shelter from this wind, was only about five miles long and lined by cliffs. There was no suitable port anywhere. He briefly considered trying to anchor there and wait out the storm, but even on the leeward side, they would be exposed to the storm. They would not be able to get close enough to shore to be safe. They would only have a few minutes time to get the small boat secured and to pass cables under the hull to hold the ship together.

He studied the map closely to imprint it in his memory and then rolled it up and put it away. He made his way back to the helm as he peered through the rain to the southwest. The island was more visible now, and he gave orders to the helmsman to steer to the leeward side of the island.

It would be tricky to steer close enough to the island to be sheltered without being in danger of the rocks near the shore. He knew as soon as they passed the southern tip of Cauda they would need to quickly trim the sails and adjust the rudder to turn sharply north, and at the same time, the men at the stern would need to begin hauling in the small boat as the men at the bow would need to be ready to pass the cables over the front of the ship and pulling them back to the middle of the deck, tightening them to support the hull.

He called to Rayiz, who had returned from giving orders to his crew to help secure the boat. He quickly told him of the plans and all of the things that needed to be accomplished in a short period of time as they rounded the tip of Cauda. They would be there in a few minutes and much had to be prepared. Rayiz hurried to the bow to inform the crew members he had assigned to ready the frapping cables as the captain gave strict instructions to the helmsman on where to steer. The captain then moved to the stern of the ship to inform the crew there to be ready to haul in the boat when they reached the shelter of the island.

———

Luke and Temeros were still in his quarters securing his supplies as the room rocked back and forth. Temeros was already feeling queasy and Luke was giving him instructions on preparing the ginger root extract since they expected seasickness to be the order of the day.

After several minutes, a crew member appeared in the doorway holding a bloody piece of cloth to his left hand, blood dripping to the deck. Luke hurried to him as Temeros cleared a place for him to lay down. They worked together to inspect and clean the cut. It was fairly deep on his palm, but he was able to move his fingers and there appeared to be no major damage to the deeper structures. Luke bandaged it and gave him instructions to keep it covered and return the next day to have it redressed.

As the man thanked him and left, Julius and Gaius appeared. Gaius looked green and was holding his stomach. Temeros had the ginger extract prepared in a short time, and both he and Gaius took a dose, making a face at the bitter taste. However, in a few minutes, the nausea improved. Other passengers began to appear shortly after that requesting similar help.

After making sure Gaius was feeling better, Julius left him in Luke's care. He wanted to find the captain to get an update on the storm. He made his way toward the helm, knowing the captain would likely be there. The wind gusts and the slanting deck wet with rain made walking a challenge, and he nearly fell more than once.

He saw the captain returning from the stern of the ship, walking steadily even with the heaving deck. Julius could see he wore a troubled expression.

"Captain!" he called. "Do we know how long the storm will last? Are we getting close to Phoenix?"

The captain turned toward him, startled from his thoughts. "What!? No! We will not make it to Phoenix!" he said shortly.

"What do you mean!?" Julius asked, shock in his expression. "We were only a few hours from there and following the shore!"

"Do you see the shore anywhere?" The captain said, annoyed. "This storm came upon us so suddenly it is preventing us from following our course. Now we are being pushed out further into the sea."

He saw a passing sailor and brusquely ordered him to the stern to help the men there.

"Do we have a plan?" Julius persisted, worry in his tone.

"I'm pretty busy right now. We hope to reach the leeward side of the small island of Cauda in a few minutes, and I need my men to haul in the small boat so we don't lose it. Another crew will be passing cables under the hull to strengthen it so the ship does not begin to founder in these seas! Now I must get to my post to oversee this." He hurried to the helm calling out orders to the helmsman.

Julius paused, his heart racing as panic began to rise in his mind. Their short voyage to Phoenix was now a precarious trip through storm-tossed waves with their destination uncertain. He needed to inform his men to prepare for this change of plans. He turned back to Luke's infirmary to talk with Gaius.

He found Gaius looking much better, the green color of his skin back to normal. Luke and Temeros were tending to several people including passengers and soldiers. The crew were apparently unaffected by the movement of the waves.

Julius beckoned to Gaius and they huddled together as he passed along the captain's report. The relief Gaius had felt as his stomach settled down gave way to anxiety over the uncertainty now ahead of them.

"Did he say how long the storm may last?" Gaius asked, a hint of pleading in his voice.

"No, but surely it can't last more than a few hours, a day at the most," Julius responded hopefully. "We need to let the men know of the change of plans. For now, we can keep the prisoners gathered below decks but no need for shackles. There is no place for them to go. When we know more, I will let you know."

"Aye, Julius," Gaius responded, saluting. "Anything else I can do?"

Julius shook his head. "I don't think so. Just try to get comfortable. The next few hours may be more exciting than we anticipated!"

Gaius made his way to the lower hold to give the orders to his men. Julius remained, lost in thought as he tried to calm his unsettled nerves. He again told himself that this surely could only last a day at the most, right?

He would soon realize he had greatly underestimated this storm.

# Chapter Seventeen

Cauda was looming larger by the minute. The wind was strong and The Emir was scudding in the rough seas, crashing into waves and being tossed from side to side. The deck was wet from rain and sea spray. The crewmen were soaked, dripping with water. Many of them had tied lifelines around their waist as they attended to their assigned duties. All seemed ready for action as soon as they reached the leeward side of the small island.

The captain had his eyes trained on the approaching spit of land that was the southern tip of Cauda. He shouted orders to the helmsman, preparing to steer quickly to the north when the wind slackened. Rayiz was nearby ready to give the signal to the teams of men at both ends of the ship to be ready, one team to haul in the boat and the other to pass cables under the hull to strengthen it. They knew they may not have much time in the relative shelter of the island.

The gloom of the storm belied the fact that it was still early afternoon. The heavy cumulonimbus clouds blotted out the sun and flashes of lightning could be seen above them. The men could feel the booming thunder in their chests. The heavy rain caused a frothy appearance on the sea all around them, although the tossing waves and whitecaps made it difficult to see. The wind gusts at times caused the rain to blow sideways across the deck, and the men had to constantly wipe the rain from their eyes as they waited for the order to be given.

The ship rounded the southern point and there was a noticeable reduction in the intensity of the storm. The waves became much less violent and those gathered in the hold let out a collective sigh of relief. Luke and Temeros glanced up from their ministrations to the sick passengers as they noticed the changes, pausing to enjoy the relative calm. Even Demetrius relaxed a bit. He had found a place in the hold near a large group of passengers and kept to himself in the gloom near the bulkhead.

Captain Sahaq bellowed to the helmsman who quickly turned the rudders to steer the ship north along the leeward coast, pointing into the wind to try to reduce their drifting. At the same time, Rayiz turned and called out to the team at the stern to begin hauling in the boat.

As the ship turned into the wind, the rope slackened and the men were able to get into a rhythm of hauling the boat in bit by bit. When it finally was bobbing low in the water at the stern, the work became harder. It was much heavier now that it was more than half full of water. They did not have a way to tilt it over to the side to empty it, nor could they bail out the water. It was too dangerous to climb down to the boat for that. All they could do was dig in their heels, wrap cloth around their sore hands, and heave on the rope as best they could. They were afraid the rope would break or come loose from the boat and then they would not have a lifeboat to depend on, but the rope held. They were able to raise the front of the boat a few inches, and water sloshed over the sides and off the back of the small boat. They hauled again, and more water sloshed out. The third time, the rope slipped through their fingers and the boat fell back to the waves, but they quickly regained their grips and started again. Now the weight of the boat was lessened since they had been able to empty some of the water. They finally were rewarded with the bow of the boat rising up out of the water, reaching up toward them like a small child wanting to be carried.

The men paused to catch their breath and then turned again to their task. The designated leader of this taskforce called out the commands to "heave." Then they held the rope with one hand reaching quickly with the other hand to get another grip. Soon the full weight of the boat was dangling behind The Emir. Thankfully the wind was reduced in the lee of the island, and what remained was blocked by the bulk of the ship. There was still enough to cause the boat to sway behind them, however. The men had to time their pulling to coincide with the pendulum motion of the boat. The men knew they could not stop or it would fall back to the water. Slowly it rose closer.

Finally, the two front men were able to reach out and get a grip on the boat itself as the other men continued to pull. The rope was running through a pulley that extended a few feet above the deck, but it was still a difficult task to get the heavy boat to the deck. The men had to use grappling hooks to reach for the stern of the dangling boat to pull it to the side so more of the men could reach out for it. The weight of the boat threatened to pull them over the side, and others of the crew had to grab their lifelines to prevent that from happening. Soon the stern of the boat was resting on the railing. Several men grabbed it to pull it over the railing to the deck, while others kept the rope tight to keep the bow from falling back to the sea.

There was a shout of victory when the boat finally was on the ship. The men were exhausted, and their arms were cramping, but the job was completed. They turned the boat upside down and secured it with ropes and then hurried forward to see what needed to be done on the foredeck.

While they were struggling with the boat, another group was passing heavy cables around the hull. They had two groups, one on each side, holding each end of a heavy rope, while a third group took the middle section and tossed it over the front figurehead of the Lady and her Prince. The heavy rope sank slowly in the water as the two groups holding tight to the ends began to slowly walk back along the side to midship. The heavy rope grew heavier as it became saturated, and they had to walk slowly to let it pass through the water. When they reached the designated location just aft of the mast, near the back third of the deck, the groups began to pull the ends of the rope tight. When it was pulled as tight as they could get it, they tied each end to capstans. Another group of men was already repeating this procedure with a second cable, stopping just before the mast at the midpoint of the deck. Then a third cable was similarly deployed to the front third of the ship.

The men in the lower deck could tell there was a change in the amount of creaking they were hearing. This gave them a small degree of comfort, but only briefly since the ship was beginning to bob up and down more vigorously with each passing moment as it was slipping back into deeper, rougher water.

The ship was already being pushed further from shore by the winds, diminished though they were by the island. The captain was well aware of the sandbars at Syrtis to the south, and he feared being driven to them by the strong winds. If they were to run aground there, all would be lost.

As soon as the cables were secured around the hull, Rayiz gave the order to lower the sea anchor. They had no way to stop the ship from being blown back out to sea, but they hoped the sea anchor would give enough drag to keep them from getting crossways to the heavy waves. Being capsized by the waves would be worse than running aground on Syrtis.

The men heaved the heavy sea anchor over the stern of the ship, and within minutes, they were turned to the west once again and Cauda slipped slowly behind them. The crew helplessly watched it disappear in the darkness of the storm as they headed into the black unknown ahead of them. Each man silently prayed to his god for safety.

———————

In the hold, the prisoners and guards had been listening to the muffled shouts and bangs and clanks of the activity going on above them. Some of the guards had ventured to the deck to see what was happening and came back to report to their colleagues and word quickly spread. All were hopeful that they were anchoring near the small island to wait out the storm. However, the longer the frantic scurrying sounds went on, accompanied by the urgent shouts, their hope began to fade. Then there was a noticeable increase in the movement of the ship as it was once again buffeted by waves and wind.

Faces fell as the realization spread that it was not yet over. The storm was only a few hours old, and most were still expecting this to be an uncomfortable night and then a return to nicer weather. But Aristarchus could see by Paul's expression this was not likely the case. He leaned closer and spoke to him in a low voice so as to not alarm the others.

"Teacher, you appear to know something the rest of us do not know. Don't you think this will be over tomorrow?" he asked, hopefully.

Paul met his gaze and shook his head ever so slightly. "I'm afraid not. I don't want to cause more worry, but I warned the centurion to not venture out toward Phoenix."

"What?! Why?" Aristarchus could not completely hide the alarm in his voice. He quickly glanced around to be sure no one else was listening.

"In my prayers yesterday, God impressed upon me that if we left Fair Havens for Phoenix, our voyage would lead to disaster and loss, not only of the ship's cargo, but possibly of our lives as well. Unfortunately, the opinion of a prisoner does not hold much weight with a ship's captain and a centurion."

"What can we do?"

"At this point, all we can do is wait on the Lord and comfort those around us. It is even more imperative that the Gospel be preached if there is a chance we may not reach a safe harbor."

Aristarchus leaned back, closed his eyes, and began to pray, hoping maybe just this once Paul had misunderstood, but knowing that was unlikely.

———————

Demetrius remained in the shadows, his stomach lurching with the ship, as he strained to glean any information he could. Anger was rising in him. Once again, this devil, Paul, had caused him more trouble. If it wasn't for Paul, he would not have climbed aboard this cursed ship. He glared in the direction of the prisoners as he fumed and fantasized about ways to kill him. He could see all of the soldiers and knew it would be foolhardy to try anything now. This storm couldn't last forever, and once everyone relaxed and spread out around the ship, he would find a way. For now, he needed to get some fresh air to settle his stomach. The hold was really beginning to reek with the stench of fear and seasickness.

He pushed up from the floor where he sat, holding tightly to the bulkhead with his good right hand as the ship bobbed in the waves. He made his way to the ladder and climbed. The sudden cold wind took his breath and he had to squint against the driving raindrops. His stomach quickly calmed with the cool fresh air, but he grew more alarmed as he saw the lightning flashing in the clouds and the sails stowed.

He saw the crew working at securing any loose items on the deck. They hurried from one item to the next, seemingly unaffected by the movement of the deck. Seeing the ease with which they moved about, Demetrius stepped out from the ladder and immediately his foot slipped on the wet deck. He flailed his arms and narrowly avoided falling several feet back down the same hatch from which he had just emerged.

He cautiously got back to his feet and steadied himself as he tried to time his next steps. When the ship seemed to settle down into a valley between the waves, he quickly and gingerly made his way to the railing and grasped it firmly just as the ship began climbing up the next wave. Holding on tightly, he gulped in deep breaths of cool air, clearing the heavy stench of the hold from his nostrils. That many men below decks in a storm could quickly foul the air.

He gazed out into the darkness of the sea around him. There were still a few lanterns on the deck, and they cast a small halo of light but not much could be seen. The sea looked restless, covered in whitecaps and sending spray up onto the deck as the ship crashed into each wave with a shudder that caused his legs to wobble. He was overcome with the sense that he was but a speck in a vast, dark, chaotic world with no peace to be had—a fitting description of his life since the fire.

Even in this moment, tightening his grip on the railing, he felt abandoned. He had devoted himself to Artemis throughout his life and for what?! He had made it his life's work to create the silver shrines that were used in worship. He had visited the temple (and the temple prostitutes) regularly. To cover his bases, he had prayed to other gods as well, for safety, health, prosperity, and recognition. When Paul and his henchmen sought to spread their cult of following this Jesus, he had been the one to stand up against them, organizing his fellow silversmiths to protest and riot, expelling them from the city.

With all that he had done, the gods owed him! Yet where were they now, when he was alone, in a storm in the ocean, mere feet from his enemy, Paul. If they really existed, they would give him vengeance for the loss of his livelihood, his position of respect in the city, and especially for his burned wife and son! It was too much for him. He had long ago decided the gods were a farce! The only advantages you gained in this life were the ones you grasped with your own hands, and now he only had one good hand! If you did not place your own needs above everyone else's, no one would do it for you! Religion was for the weak and foolish. With these thoughts in his mind, he looked defiantly up into the storm and shook his fist.

Just then, with a high-pitched sizzling and a smell of ozone, a bolt of lightning crashed to the ocean just yards from where he stood. His vision was blinded by the brightness of the flash and his hearing dulled by the incredibly loud boom. The deck convulsed with the shock wave and he was lifted from his feet as he felt himself thrown forcefully into the railing!

His hands grabbed at anything he could touch but the railing was too smooth and wet to get a grip. His center of gravity caused him to topple headfirst over the railing toward the dark sea. He heard his own voice crying out "Oh God! Save me!" Just as he was beginning to plummet, his right hand grasped one of the cables that had been passed under the hull of the ship. There happened to be a knot just below where his hand gripped it, and he was able to halt his progress toward the certain death of the dark, stormy sea. He held tight with his right hand and flexed his feet over the top of the railing as he tried to push himself back up. His left hand, weak and scarred as it was, found a ridge on the outside of the ship's railing, and he was able to inch his way backward until his hips were able to flex over the railing and his feet found purchase on the deck.

He slumped to the deck as he tried to slow the hammering of his heart and catch his breath. His hands were shaking and his stomach lurched as he realized just how close he had been to dying. After a couple of minutes, he had calmed enough to regain his anger. Didn't this just prove his point!? The gods were not real or they would have kept this from happening! He carefully got to his feet and stumbled to the ladder, returning to the darkness and anonymity of the hold below.

———————

Luke had been busy with people coming to him for care since the storm started. Most were seasick, but there were a few crew members with various injuries. One had injured his arm hauling the boat up out of the sea, sustaining a nasty rope burn that needed bandaging. Another had slipped on the wet deck and broke two of his fingers as he fell. Through all of it, Temeros was observing and helping as the doctor directed him. He seemed to have a natural gift for evaluating various injuries and helping with the treatments.

Now, after a few hours, the passengers and crew had seemed to adjust to the storm, at least for the moment, and there was finally a lull in their duties. Luke saw Temeros stretching and looking worn out.

"Why don't you take a break? Go out and get some fresh air. I can finish up with these patients. I really appreciate your help."

At this, Temeros smiled, pleased at the praise. It was not something he had heard for most of his life and it was nice to be appreciated. "Thank you," he said. "I think I'll take you up on the offer. I won't be too long."

"Just be careful, and watch your step on the deck!" Luke warned. "You've seen what can happen!" he said with a wry smile, nodding in the direction of the two injured crewmen still recovering in the cabin.

He nodded and turned to the door leading out onto the deck. He could hear the whistling of the wind, and he steeled himself as he walked out into the cold rain. He made his way toward the back of the ship. The flashes of lightning in the clouds gave intermittent glimpses of the deck, and he was cautious to keep a firm hold on the railing.

He stopped at the stern of the ship as he steadied himself against the rocking of the boat. The wind was blowing in his face, pelting him with raindrops. It was not unpleasant, though. He had been perspiring as he cared for the sick and injured and the fresh air rejuvenated him. He peered out into the darkness behind the ship, seeing the wake and the whitecaps faintly in contrast to the blackness of the sea. From this vantage point, there was no recognizable landmark, and the sky was filled with black clouds that were seen in the bright flashes. There were no stars visible and the moon was nowhere to be seen either.

He thought over all that he had learned from Paul and Luke in the past few days. His opinion of Paul had completely changed, and he realized he had already begun to believe in this Jesus that Luke had been teaching him about. Just watching how Luke cared for the sick and wounded and sensing the peace he had within were new to Temeros. He seemed to have real compassion for these rough sailors and soldiers that he had never met.

He thought back to Paul's lesson from two days ago. He had talked about how the sailors could navigate by looking at the sun and stars. He wondered how they could do that now, with nothing to see. As he pondered this, he also recalled Paul saying that God can give guidance and a reference point in life. He thought about his life, how he had been drifting since his mother and father died in the fire. Now, here he was on a ship, far from anything he had ever known, the ship being tossed in the waves. Strangely, he did not feel fear, and this surprised him, even as he tightened his grip on the railing.

Looking out at the vast darkness and the roiling sea, he was overcome with the sense that he was but a speck in a vast, dark, chaotic world that would not provide him the peace he sought. And yet Luke was certain that God loved him, even to the point of taking the penalty for his sins. As he dwelt on this, he had a sudden peace that made no sense given his circumstances.

He raised his eyes to the sky, squinting against the raindrops. "Jesus,

I want to know you. I want to leave my old life behind and follow you. Please give light to my darkness. I need you!"

Suddenly, the sky was split with a huge bolt of lightning off to his right that seemed very near the ship. He jumped as the deck heaved and gripped the railing tighter. His first thought was just how powerful God really was. Then, he let out a laugh realizing this bright flash of light was a literal answer to his prayer of just seconds ago. He no longer felt isolated but knew that God heard him and knew exactly who he was and where he was. He was overcome by this thought.

After a few minutes of basking in this realization, he began to feel chilled and made his way back into Luke's quarters, excited to share with him what had just happened.

————

The lightning strike was very close, and Rayiz sent men to check for any damage. He himself took a lantern and descended into the hold to check on how much water they had taken on so far. This old ship had some leaks even in the calmest of seas. This was heavier weather than it had faced in a few years. He only hoped the storm would pass them by in a few hours.

Down in the hold, he saw water sloshing around but only deep enough to cover his foot. That was acceptable but they would need to continue monitoring. They had a small cargo of grain but it was stacked on pallets to keep it about a foot above the deck. There were small piles of loose grain that had accumulated through the years, and they were getting soggy but it could not be helped.

As he turned to go back up, he thought he saw some movement out of the corner of his eye. He turned, holding the lantern closer just in time to see the tail of a snake slithering into the grain. That was new! They always had rats to deal with, since their main cargo was grain. Somehow a snake must have made it into the ship. He hated snakes! Hopefully it would drown in the water. He shivered and quickly climbed up the ladder.

# Chapter Eighteen

The rest of the night, no one slept well. The constant rising and falling of the ship, the noise of the wind, the lightning flashes, and the sound of occasional retching were not conducive to rest. There was also an eager anticipation for daylight, with the hope that the storm would abate. They were all disappointed.

There was, indeed, a dusky light that was filtered through the clouds, giving witness to the fact that there really was still a sun somewhere up there. However, the morning brought ongoing rough seas, strong winds, and driving rain that seemed never-ending. There were a few times it let up considerably, but each time, their hopes for the end of the storm were dashed by a renewed frenzy of heavy downpours accompanied by thunder and lightning.

At least the light allowed them to see beyond the weak light of the ship's lanterns, but what they saw did not give them any peace. They could not see Cauda anywhere behind them, and despite searching every chart he had, Captain Sahaq could not find any other islands in their vicinity. Not that they would be able to reach them anyway with the storm driving them as it was. He had hoped to be able to see the edge of the storm clouds nearby so they would know how to steer out from under the storm, but the lowering clouds stretched on in every direction.

So far, the waves were not dangerous, despite what the landlubbers thought. What concerned him was the appearance of the cloud cover. He had rarely seen such a dense, dark sky. It diffused a greenish yellow light that was unsettling. The worst storm he had ever experienced had this type of clouds but he was safely on land at the time. That storm had sent a funnel descending from the sky that had reached down to carry away half of the village where he was staying as it pelted the other half with large hailstones. Devastation was everywhere. If that were to happen here, in the middle of the ocean, he did not know what to expect. But he could not show fear to his men. He must keep steering into the waves one at a time.

Partway through the morning, the soldiers tired of corralling the prisoners in the dank, close air of the hold, and Gaius and Julius agreed to let them roam freely with strict orders for the soldiers to watch them closely and make sure they did not have access to weapons. They reasoned that they had no place to go anyway, so escape was not an option.

Demetrius kept to himself but realized that on deck with everyone soaked with rain anyway, his rags did not look any different than most of the other passengers. He noticed a few quizzical glances, but he did not make eye contact and turned quickly away if anyone seemed ready to speak to him. The sullen angry look on his face was a natural deterrent to human contact anyway.

By midday, the waves were no lighter. There were more fearful expressions on the faces of those who had ventured out to the deck as they could see that even the crew members were apprehensive. The ship shuddered as it slammed into each wave with significant force. One of the soldiers had climbed down into the cargo hold and had seen the water sloshing around. This information had spread quickly causing a mild panic to the non-seafaring folk that they were taking on water. Once this talk was passed on to Rayiz, he knew he had to quell the panic that was setting in.

He went to the captain and they summoned Julius and Gaius. Being summoned to the captain's quarters in the midst of a storm was unsettling to say the least. They hurried to the meeting, faces etched with concern, as they speculated on how bad things had become. They had heard about the water in the lower hold.

They entered the small office and Captain Sahaq motioned for them to have a seat. They sat tensely, glancing at each other. Both had noticed the scowl etched on the captain's face.

"Thanks for coming," he began. "I need your help."

Both soldiers nodded. "What can we do?" Julius asked.

"It has come to my attention that many of the soldiers are concerned about seeing water in the hold. Rayiz has overheard several talking about this, and with each telling, the problem is becoming more exaggerated. I fear there will be panic, and panic on a ship is never good."

"Sure, I can talk to my men," Julius responded. "But captain, how bad is the water? That sounds like a problem."

"All ships get water in the hold," he responded with a dismissive wave. "Why do you think we put the cargo up off the floor? This is nothing. However, this ship is old and will take on more water as the storm continues. We can handle a lot more but will need to be watching closely."

Julius and Gaius sighed with relief. "I'm glad it is not as bad as people have been saying. We will give orders to the men to stop spreading unfounded rumors," Gaius said.

Julius still looked concerned. "Captain, is there any way to slow down the accumulation of water? It still sounds like it is only going to get worse."

Captain Sahaq and Rayiz looked at each other, and the captain gave a slight nod. Rayiz cleared his throat and spoke up. "The ship is riding lower through the waves because we have so many people as well as cargo on board. We were just discussing the fact that we will need to lighten the ship by throwing most of the cargo overboard. That will make the ship ride higher in the water and have less force battering the hull with each wave."

"I thought this storm would not last long. Is dumping the cargo necessary?"

Captain Sahaq took a deep breath. "I have been sailing these seas for many years. I have never seen storm clouds like this over the ocean. Most storms are small enough for us to see the lighter cloud cover in the distance, or they pass within twenty-four hours. So far, this storm seems to be growing in intensity. The lightning has continued, and there are portions of the clouds that appear to be forming funnels. That can be catastrophic if they come our way. And, unless I miss my guess, we are in for some heavy hail as well. It will get worse before it gets better."

Julius clenched his fists in his lap and drew a deep breath as he considered this. "How long do you expect before we get some relief?"

"I wish I could answer that. I am afraid this will last at least another five days the way this looks. The ship should be fine but it will not be a pleasant voyage. Once we dump the cargo, the ship will be lighter and subject to less impact from the waves, but it will also have more movement as it rides up and down each wave."

"Do you know where we are heading?" Gaius asked, a note of desperation in his voice.

The sailors shook their heads. "We are being pushed along with the storm, and so far we can't tell how large the storm coverage is. We have no visible stars to use for navigation, and even the sunlight is filtered so much by the clouds it is difficult to tell what direction it is coming from. All we can do is wait. Pray to whatever gods you honor that it will pass soon."

Julius and Gaius left to gather their officers and quell the anxiety that was spreading through the troops, but both felt a significant amount of their own anxiety after what they had been told. They knew they must not show fear before their men. As they walked through the driving rain on deck, they discussed the situation.

"Paul told me God had warned that we should not venture out of Fair Havens," Julius said. "Now I wish I would have listened to him."

"I remember him passing along that message to you, but both of us felt it was unfounded at the time. Besides, we have to trust the experience of the captain. He knows these waters better than any of us. So far, I am still undecided about Paul's teachings, but I must admit this seems to give credence to the message he claimed to have heard from God."

Julius grunted in reply. "Let's go talk to the men. I think I need to talk to Paul more about this, too."

Gaius inwardly was glad to hear that. He wanted to know more of Paul's teaching.

After the soldiers left Captain Sahaq's quarters, he and Rayiz remained, talking about the next steps they needed to take.

"We need to lighten the ship. Let's send men to the hold to get the grain and dump it," Rayiz said.

The captain nodded. "As much as I hate to do it, we have to. Just save ten or fifteen bags so we have something to eat if this does not end as soon as I told the soldiers."

Rayiz stiffened. "Do you really think it will last longer than five days?" he asked worriedly. "Can we survive a storm for that long?"

"I have seen this kind of storm over land and it was worse than anything you can imagine. I don't know what to expect from it over water. We have to trust that The Emir is strong enough to get through this. We don't have much choice. If dumping the cargo is not enough by tomorrow, we may be forced to throw the ships tackle overboard as well."

Rayiz cursed under his breath as he considered that. "Without the tackle, even the small amount of control we have now will be gone. We will be completely at the storm's mercy. Let's hope it doesn't come to that!"

Rayiz left to give orders to the crew. He gathered several men to form a line down to the hold so they could pass the bags of grain up and toss them into the sea. The damp bags were heavy enough to need two men to lift so it was a slow process, but over the next several hours, they were able to clear the hold. The men in the lowest hold were now in ankle-deep water and were well aware of the rats scurrying away from them as they removed the grain. The passed all of the bags up, and the crew members on the middle deck set aside fifteen of them for future rations should they be needed.

The crew gladly climbed up from the lowest hold, relieved to be out of that confined space. They did not notice the snake swimming toward the ladder as the last man climbed up.

———

With the dumping of the cargo, there was a noticeable increase in the movement of the ship as it climbed and fell with each wave. Those sequestered in the dark dank hold began to feel worse quickly. Many of the prisoners had tired of being confined and made their way out on deck as the soldiers kept a close watch, but it was only marginally more pleasant there. Yes, the cool air was refreshing and served to settle roiling stomachs, but the pelting rain and flashes of lightning were unsettling in their own right.

The heaving of the wet deck could be treacherous and several of the men, both soldiers and prisoners, found themselves sprawled on the wood nursing their bruises. The sailors found this amusing, but Rayiz could see that this would cause problems if any were washed overboard or more severely injured. He directed a few of his men to be sure there were lifelines tied around the waist of any non-seafaring men that ventured out on the deck.

Paul and Aristarchus were among those seeking fresh air. Aristarchus was closely attending to Paul, wanting to be sure he did not lose his footing on the constantly changing slope of the deck. They had hoped to see their friend Luke but they could see several people had gathered around his quarters seeking relief of their seasickness. Since they were feeling better in the cool rain, they turned aside to the ship's railing to watch the activity for a few minutes.

Several yards away, watching from the shadows, Porcius and Cassius were huddled together. They had continued to consider ways of eliminating Paul since their first discussion, although now it seemed more out of excitement of plotting than of actual hatred of the man. Now, with the storm and the lurching of the ship, it seemed a simple, although maybe less satisfying solution. They had their heads together discussing this and laughing quietly.

This caught the attention of another watcher. Demetrius had been following Paul and his friend from a short distance away. He paused to steady himself, still a bit tentative after almost going overboard the night before. A few feet to his left, he heard the men's voices and laughter and initially thought nothing of it, his focus on Paul. His ears perked up, however, when he heard them mention the name.

"There are too many other people around now," one of the soldiers had said. "We could toss him into the sea but we would be seen and severely punished by Julius."

"Yeah, you're right," the other had said. "We need to wait until we have a better chance of getting away with it."

Demetrius was about to speak to them, realizing he may have allies to help him get revenge, but then Paul and the other man had started walking back toward the hatch to the lower hold. The three observers remained on deck for a few minutes and then separated. Demetrius vowed to keep an eye on these soldiers in the next few days, wondering if they could be useful in his plot against Paul.

# CHAPTER NINETEEN

I t was another sleepless night, the motion of the ship worse than the night before. Some in the hold succumbed to physical exhaustion after a few hours and slept, but it was far from restful. By the next morning, almost all were achy and irritable, as well as queasy. Very few attempted to eat breakfast. The steady monotony of the rain drumming on the deck above became background noise that seemed never ending. Surely three days would be enough for this to pass!

In the midst of the groans and grumblings, Paul and Aristarchus along with a few of their followers were kneeling together in prayer. Luke and Temeros had come down to the hold to see them and be involved in the time of prayer as they began another day of uncertainty. After a moment, Paul said "Amen" and was echoed by the others murmuring the same.

This was all new to Temeros. He was pondering what he had seen, not sure what to think. He was still getting used to the idea that prayer was not just a duty he must do to please one of the gods, never expecting anything to really change in response. Now, he knew there was one all-powerful God, and his new friends appeared to believe wholeheartedly that He heard their prayers and actually cared about what they were going through. Luke noticed his pensive expression.

"What are you thinking about?" he asked quietly.

Temeros cleared his throat and turned away. "Oh, nothing. Just wondering when the storm will end," he responded, adjusting his expression quickly.

Luke paused, looking closely at him, but decided not to press the question. "Yes, it is unpleasant. I have been on a few voyages with Paul, and this time of year can be harsh out on the sea. I have not seen it last more than a few days, though, so I am holding out hope that it will be over in another day or two at the most."

"I hope you are right. My queasy stomach will be relieved when it ends!"

"You are not alone in that! I want you to know how grateful I am for your help in caring for the men. You seem to be learning quickly!"

Temeros smiled, pleased at the kind words. "Thank you for teaching me! It is fascinating to see how you are able to evaluate and treat all of the problems the men bring to you." His smile faded slightly as he said, "I am afraid I will be put back to work on the deck soon. My shoulder is not as stiff as it was a few days ago, and my headaches are improving. I know they must need help during the storm. I would much rather continue learning and helping you."

Luke considered this. "Well, it will be at least a few more days before I would consider letting you do the kind of work they need done. But I would love to have your continued help. I think I will talk to the captain about having you assigned to work with me for the rest of the voyage. I imagine he will accept that."

Temeros' expression brightened at this thought. "That would be great!"

Paul had approached as they were talking. He greeted Luke.

"Master Paul! Thank you for leading prayer! My day is always better when I spend time with the Lord. Oh, and you remember Temeros, of course."

"Hello, my young friend," he said, patting Temeros on the shoulder. "Are you feeling better?"

Temeros nodded. "Yes, thanks for asking."

Luke spoke up. "Paul, you will be happy to hear that Temeros has put his faith in Jesus. You are rubbing off on him!"

"That is wonderful to hear!" Paul's face beamed at the news. "Stay close to Dr. Luke and he can teach you much about our Lord! His research has been so helpful in our ministry. Luke, when will you have your book finished on the life of Jesus?"

"I am trying to organize it all. I hope to have it finished in a few months, if I ever reach a calm port!"

"All in good time. I believe this is of God, and when He begins a good work, He is able to complete it."

"I do feel He is leading me to write it. I will trust that He will do just that."

Aristarchus had joined them. "Luke! This crazy rocking of the ship is wreaking havoc on my stomach! Do you know any good doctors?"

Luke laughed. "I think you are a hopeless case! Your digestion is much too delicate for a voyage in a storm! Come up to my quarters and I'll see if I can help."

Aristarchus grinned. "I'll come with you but only if Temeros supervises what you are doing. I'm not so sure you have my best interest in mind! Help me Temeros. Surely you can do something for me!"

Temeros laughed. "I'm still recovering but I'll see what I can do."

Paul turned to speak to some of the others as the three men excused themselves to go to Luke's quarters.

Meanwhile, Demetrius had been observing the group gathered around Paul. He was disgusted by the respect and attention they were paying to this man. It was just too much to bear! He turned to go up on deck and get away. Even the storm was better than this!

As he made his way to the ladder, he noticed the two soldiers standing off to the side, sneers on their faces as they watched. Their disdain for this display of worship was plain to see. They turned and caught Demetrius' eyes before he could turn away. Their eyes briefly locked and Demetrius nodded to them slightly and then looked in Paul's direction and scowled. The two soldiers watched him climb up to the deck and then turned toward each other.

"What was that about?" Cassius asked, puzzled.

Porcius scratched his beard as he considered this. "I got the impression that guy was not too impressed with our troublemaking prisoner. He seemed a bit disgusted with him!"

"Hmm. We'll have to keep an eye on him. If something were to happen to Paul in the storm, he may be a likely suspect, wouldn't you say? That could leave us some interesting possibilities!" he said, a sly grin on his face.

Porcius sneered back. "Yes, this could provide a few opportunities that we could use!"

The men walked away, their heads together, as they talked in low tones.

———

Up on the deck, the storm continued unabated, with the rain blowing sideways, the thunder rumbling, and the ship laboring up one wave and crashing down the next. The sailors had found their rhythm as they braced against each change of pitch the ship provided.

Rayiz stalked the deck, bellowing orders to the men. He sent two of them to go check the level of water in the lower hold. Even with jettisoning the cargo, the ship was shuddering and laboring in the heavy seas. He was becoming more worried with each jarring wave. It was becoming more obvious that they would have to throw the ship's tackle and yard, the heavy crossbar of wood that held the sail, overboard to relieve more of the stresses on the hull. He hurried off to talk to the captain.

Captain Sahaq was in a foul mood, cursing under his breath as he surveyed the skies. No break in sight. This was already a financial disaster. With the loss of the cargo, his pay would be greatly reduced. Now his ship was being battered unmercifully. He turned as he heard Rayiz call to him over the sound of the wind.

"What is it?!" he said brusquely. "I hope you have some good news!"

"I'm afraid not, captain. This storm is really beating hard against the ship. I think we need to toss the yard and the tackle to lighten the load a little more."

The captain's expression hardened at these words and he scowled fiercely as he cursed their situation. "Can you think of any other way? Without that equipment we will not have control of the ship once this storm finally dies down. How is the water in the hold?"

"I sent men down to check it and they should be reporting any time. But captain, even with the frapping cables tightened around the hull, I've been doing this long enough that I can feel the ship's planks shifting. It's just a matter of time."

"Let's see what the water level is. If it is still just ankle deep, we can struggle along for a little while longer praying that the gods will turn this storm away. Maybe we need to talk to that prisoner, Paul, and see if he has any influence with his god."

Rayiz nodded reluctantly and was about to respond when the two sailors returned from the hold, breathless. They clutched at their lifelines as they braced themselves against a wooden capstan.

Rayiz turned to them. "Well? Out with it! What did you find?"

"Sir, the water is getting deeper. Now it is up above my knee! The hull is creaking and popping with every wave!" one of them said. The other just nodded, a frightened expression on his face.

This news was met with curses by both the captain and Rayiz. He dismissed the men and turned to the captain.

The captain hung his head for a moment and then took a deep breath as he looked up at his officer. "Give the word. We will need a lot of help to do that. See if any of the soldiers or even the strong prisoners are able to help get the ship's yard over the side into the sea."

Rayiz hurried away to gather his sailors and to talk to the centurion.

———————

Julius and Gaius had made their way up to the deck. Even with the cold wind and rain, the air was fresher and the rain served to wash away the sweat and grime that accumulated day by day. They had been holding tightly to the railing, enthralled by the size of the waves. Gaius had found that keeping his eyes on the horizon, stormy as it was, helped to lessen his nausea.

The howling of the wind made talking difficult and they had been mostly standing in silence. They had just about decided to return to the relative warmth of the hold when Rayiz approached.

"Centurion!" he called loudly, trying to be heard over the storm.

Julius turned to watch him approach. "What is it?"

"We need some men to help us. We are going to need to throw the tackle and yard overboard to lighten the ship and take the strain off the hull."

Gaius's eyes widened. "Don't we need that?" he asked, incredulously.

"We need our ship more! It is not doing us any good now anyway. We are simply at the mercy of this storm, and the sails will not help us. They just cause more stress on the mast. The ship is still too heavy for these waves. We need to take the strain off the hull before we take on too much water!"

Julius and Gaius were tense with worry. "We will send some of our men up to help. How many do you need?"

"Twenty or thirty should be enough. More than that will just be in the way. The stronger, the better! Even your prisoners may be helpful, as long as they can be trusted."

Julius nodded to Gaius and he made his way quickly to the hatch leading to the lower deck. Julius grabbed Rayiz by the arm before he turned away. "Just how bad is this?"

Rayiz looked him in the eye. "It is bad! The water in the hold is already knee deep. The ship is taking a beating from these waves. So far we don't see a break in the storm. We expect it has to begin to weaken in the next day or two, but we can't take the chance."

"Are there any ports in the area we can go to?"

Rayiz laughed bitterly. "We don't have any way to navigate. There are no stars to show us our position. We don't know how far we have been blown by this storm or even what direction. The charts don't show any ports in this section of the sea, but even if they did, we can't steer this ship against the wind. We go where it wants to push us. The sea gods will have their way with us whether we like it or not."

Julius' mouth hung open as he watched Rayiz hurry off to organize the task at hand. Suddenly he was more worried than at any point in his life. At least in battle, he had some measure of control in wielding his weapons, and the enemy could be slain by his own hand. If he was killed in the battle, it brought honor to his name. This, however, was a battle against an invisible foe. He had no weapon to fight with. To die at sea meant there could be no burial, no honor. His tradition had taught him that if he was not buried, he would be condemned to wander the earth as a spirit. He suddenly felt a level of dread he had not felt in many years.

As he considered their hopeless situation, he was reminded of Paul's teaching. Paul was in prison for two years and yet never seemed to lose his hope. He continued to teach that his God was powerful and in control, even though he remained in prison. Paul's teaching about Jesus had ignited in him a hunger to know more. There was a stark difference between the fear of those trusting in their own strength or trying to please their many bickering gods and the hope and peace of those who trusted in Christ.

As Julius pondered this, he felt a stirring in his soul. His fear was balanced against a longing for the peace that Paul taught. He turned toward the roiling seas as he spoke softly, so no one could hear. "Jesus, I have heard Paul teach about You and I see his confidence and contentment even in chains. I don't know You but I want to. I fear we will be destroyed by this storm. Paul claims You are more powerful than the storm. If that is true, I want to follow You. Save me!"

After saying that, he felt a little silly but at the same time was aware of a level of calmness that was not there before. He pondered this for a moment and then the wind picked up and the rain pounded harder. He turned to find the crew and see what he could do to help, resolving to talk to Paul about Jesus when there was time.

# CHAPTER TWENTY

After about twenty minutes, the group had gathered around the base of the mast, bracing themselves against the movement of the ship. Rayiz asked his sailors for a volunteers willing to go up into the rigging. It had to be cut loose and it could not be done from the deck. The sailors were the only ones experienced enough to do that job, but they tried to avoid eye contact as they hoped for someone else to step up. Rayiz was about to have them cast lots to make the decision when a voice called out from the middle of the group.

"I'll do it," Erastus said as he stepped forward. There was a collective sigh of relief as the men breathed easier. They had seen Erastus climbing the rigging and swinging on the ropes with ease and were confident he was the best one for this job.

Rayiz nodded in appreciation as Erastus approached. "You know what we need to do. Once you cut it loose, the men will have to support it with the cables that go through the tackle at the top of the mast. Signal us before you cut the ropes so we are ready. Just please use the lifeline and hold tight. None of your acrobatics this time!" he said with a slight smile.

"Don't worry. I know better than to tempt this storm!" he said with an air of cautious confidence.

Rayiz then turned to address the gathered men as Erastus began to get ready. "Listen closely!" he yelled loudly to be heard over the storm. "Erastus will cut loose the supports of the yard once he gets up there.

We cannot let it fall to the deck or we are all in trouble. We will need to support the weight of it with the cables that are running through the tackle. He will let us know when he is about to cut it loose, but we have to be ready to take the weight of it and let it be gradually lowered. We need several men on each rope. Be warned! It is very heavy!"

The men nodded in acknowledgment.

Erastus gathered a large knife and a spare as well as an axe and tied a lifeline around his waist. He wiped the rain off his face and shook the water off his hands as best as he could. Then he grasped the hand- and footholds on the mast as he started his precarious climb.

It was slow going, the mast swaying severely with the wind and waves. He focused on each step and paused frequently to let the ship settle back between waves. After a few minutes, he had reached the yard, the heavy wooden crossbar that supported the sail under better conditions. He paused to catch his breath, wiping his wet hands on his tunic, although it was soaking wet from the rain as well. He considered how to approach his task. He identified the four cables that ran through the tackle at the top of the mast and supported the yard at various intervals along its length. Whatever else he did, he did not want to cut those!!

The connection point to the mast was secured with a thick rope cable, about as big around as his wrist. A wooden dowel protruded perpendicular to the mast but aligned with the length of the ship. The yard was secured just above this, and the cable was wound securely around the dowel and the yard in a complex fashion to secure it. The cables to the deck were tied off securely as well, supporting the weight of the crossbar and keeping it level.

Erastus glanced down to the distant deck as he held tightly to the mast. The rain obscured his view somewhat, but he could see the group below, craning their necks as they watched him. He waved his arm (cautiously, holding tight with the other) and saw them wave in response. He then settled onto the yard with his legs tightly around it as he faced the heavy cable and began to saw through it with his knife.

As expected it was a slow process. The cable was weathered and tough. He had checked the large knife before he climbed and knew it was sharp, but it may as well have been a stick for all the good it seemed to do. He firmly sawed at the cable with the knife for a minute or two and finally was rewarded with a small cut in the fibers. He stopped to hold tightly as the ship rocked to starboard and then pitched forward. As that passed, he grabbed his axe and began to swing it against the cable. After several swings, the small cut had begun to deepen.

He alternated between the knife and the axe for several minutes, focused intently on his work as he instinctively adjusted his balance in response to the ship's movements. The storm faded into his subconscious. Even in the cold rain, he was soon perspiring. Slowly the cleft in the large rope cable widened. Finally, the thick cable separated. It did not immediately come loose, however, the loops of the connection having become fused together over time.

He pried the pieces of the cable apart bit by bit, and as they separated, he could see that there was more tension pulling them apart. He peeled the loop back and unwrapped it around the mast. He could feel the beginnings of movement in the crossbar he was sitting on, and he paused to look to the deck again. He waved one more time to be sure they were ready, and then he pried another segment of the fused cable apart.

Suddenly, with a loud tearing sound, the rope jumped and snapped around, narrowly missing his head. The yard he was sitting on lurched out from the mast and dropped a few feet as he scrambled to wrap his arms and legs tightly around it. The men below were ready, though, and quickly stopped it's fall as they gazed up intently to be sure he was ok. He was not about to loosen his grip to wave, however. This was too precarious. Now he was far enough out from the mast that it was too dangerous to get to the mast to climb down. His best option was to ride the yard all the way down.

Rayiz was barking orders to the men on each of the four cables as they found their rhythm. They began to work hand over hand to the cadence called out by Rayiz, and the heavy crossbar descended foot by foot with its human passenger riding it down. The ship's movement and the strong winds made it tough as they had to compensate for the swinging of the yard. Erastus held on for all he was worth, his breath coming in gasps. A few times, he felt his arms slip and immediately renewed his grip.

Finally the heavy crossbeam settled to the deck with a forceful thump that the men could feel. Rayiz hurried to Erastus as he sent a crew member to fetch Dr. Luke in case he was needed. When he reached Erastus, he feared the worst. He could not see any movement and his heart fell. He reached out to touch him and felt a gasp of breath.

"You're ok! You are back on the deck!" he called to him reassuringly.

Erastus slowly raised his head and looked around, finally slowing his breathing. He had to force his arms to release his grip on the wooden crossbar, and his hands trembled as he pushed himself to a sitting position as he was surrounded by the worried crewmen.

"Wow, that was quite a ride!" he said, his face breaking into a smile.

The men relaxed and laughed in relief, amazed that he had not been blown off his perch into the sea or crushed by the heavy beam as it settled to the deck. Luke and Temeros hurried over in time to see the men relaxing as Erastus was helped to his feet. He still appeared shaken but was appearing more comfortable by the moment. Luke approached and the men parted to allow him through.

"How are you feeling?" Luke asked, reaching out to take his arm. "Did you fall?"

Erastus shook his head. "No, but I sure thought I was going to. I was up on the crossbeam when it blew loose and I held on for dear life all the way down! I was sure I would slide off with all the wind and rain." He took a deep breath and closed his eyes for a moment.

Luke and Temeros helped guided him to a crate so he could sit down. Then Luke looked him over thoroughly as Temeros observed. "What do you think, Temeros?" he asked his young protégé.

Temeros was caught off guard. "Well, uh. I, uh," he stammered and then swallowed and collected himself. "I think he looks ok. He knows where he is and is able to walk. He does not appear in pain. I think he will be fine when he has time to rest a bit. I think he is very lucky!"

Luke nodded. "I think you are correct. But I would not say it is luck. I think God was watching over him and sent His angels to protect him!" He turned to the man who was appearing more relaxed and calm by the minute. "I don't think we need to do anything other than give you time to catch your breath!"

Erastus smiled at them. "Thank you! I am feeling better. I'm not so sure about the angels but someone was watching out for me, that's for sure!"

Seeing that he was going to be ok, Rayiz returned to the task at hand.

"Ok, men! We need to get this crossbeam overboard! We need everyone to help since it is so big. Find a place to get a hand on it!"

The men responded quickly and lined up along both sides of the huge wooden beam. Temeros and Luke pitched in as well. Rayiz called out to be prepared and then counted it down. When he shouted "Heave!", they all strained as one and at first the beam seemed like it would defy their collective strength, but then they put their backs into it and it rose from the deck.

"Ok everyone! To the starboard side! All together!"

They inched their way to the side of the ship, looking like a colony of ants carrying a large stick. The weight of the beam along with the weight of the men carrying it caused the ship to list to the right, and for a moment it seemed to be rolling over. The heavy seas were splashing over the side of the ship causing water to flow across the deck. The men feared they would lose their footing and fall under the crushing weight of the thing but then they were able to tip it over the side into the sea. A huge splash doused the men closest to the edge and took their breath away. The ship compensated by rolling sharply as several of the men lost their footing and were washed toward the port side by the flowing water. Then the ship righted itself and they were able to grab a lifeline or the port railing as the ship stabilized.

There were muted cheers as the rocking slowed and the men congratulated themselves on doing what was required. Then, the realization began to sink in that now they had no way to hoist a sail. The desperation of what they had done showed them all just how bad their situation had become. They turned to see the crossbeam fading behind them in the seas, and some of the sailors once again began to curse the Euroclydon that had them in its grasp.

# Chapter Twenty-One

T he next several days were a blur of chaos and terror. The storm continued but varied in intensity. The rain let up a few times, giving them a sense of fleeting hope, but then returned even fiercer than before. At times, hail sent the passengers and crew scurrying for shelter, leaving pockmarks on the deck. The waves were incredibly rough and often towered above the ship. Thankfully, the crew was able to keep the ship pointed into the waves, aided by the drag from the sea anchor. The sailors knew that if at any point the gargantuan waves were to hit them broadside, the ship would capsize and all would be lost.

The ship labored up each mountainous wave and then teetered at the top before nosing down into the trough between the waves. As it crashed, the seawater flowed freely across the deck, washing any loose items overboard. The men wore lifelines at all times but for the most part sought shelter in the hold. Those unfortunate enough to be on duty out on the deck were frequently sent sliding across the deck by the force of the water.

In the hold, they fell into a rhythm of climbing, leveling at the top, rocking right and left as the ship nosed downward, and then crashing into the water at the bottom. The water flowed through the hatch with each splash, no matter how tightly they tried to seal it. The constant movement with no horizon as a reference triggered seasickness in many of the men. Even if they were able to tolerate the motion of the ship, the smell of the vomit mixed with the salty water of the sea and the close quarters of the people huddled below deck caused many others to become sick. Several braved the elements on deck to visit Dr. Luke in his cabin. Many made their way cautiously forward to the small booth where they could relieve themselves but all returned drenched, and the smell of wet clothing added to the thick air in the hold.

Misery and fear can be endured for only so long before men lash out at each other. Their circumstances being so out of their control caused them to seek a way of forcing their will on those around them, giving them the illusion of control. But the others would not be controlled and the resulting clash of wills caused a few shouting matches. The soldiers were quick to quash any actual fights before they began but in return were the object of the wrath of many of the prisoners.

A few of the men in the hold turned inward, isolating themselves from the group, overcome by despair and resigning themselves to impending death. Others were trembling with anxiety, some in tears, as they begged for some reassurance.

In contrast, Paul and the other believers continued their routine of starting each day in prayer. Luke and Temeros joined the group each day, and Temeros found that he was looking forward to sharing in this time. It was a source of comfort to him in the midst of his fears. Although they were not overtly participating, Julius and Gaius were seen in the group daily as well. These times of prayer garnered more and more attention with each passing day. Even some of their harshest critics were drawn to the peace displayed by the believers. They wanted the reassurance of being around those who believed even if they were not ready to take that step personally.

One morning after the time of prayer, the storm seemed more intense, and the creaking and popping sounded as though the ship would be torn apart. After finishing his prayer, Paul looked around at the faces etched with fear. Suddenly he felt prompted by God.

"Brothers, we need to sing. Even in the midst of trouble, praise to God is needed. He will not leave us comfortless. As we sing psalms, hymns, and spiritual songs, we can lift the spirits of those around us, even if they don't yet believe!"

At Paul's words, Temeros looked at Luke incredulously, wondering if he had heard the teacher correctly. Some of the group shrugged half-heartedly but agreed to try. "What do you suggest we sing in such horrible circumstances as this?" one asked.

"I know just the Psalm!" Paul answered.

He began to sing, his voice a bit flat but not unpleasant. As they began to recognize David's psalm of thanksgiving to God for His deliverance, some joined him with quavering voices, stumbling over some of the less familiar words. Most listened, having never known the psalms to begin with.

> *Oh, give thanks to the Lord for He is good!*
> *For His mercy endures forever.*
> *Let the redeemed of the Lord say so,*
> *Whom He has redeemed from the hand of the enemy,*
> *And gathered out of the lands,*
> *From the east and from the west,*
> *From the north and from the south.*

As they continued, they together lifted their voices to sing:

> *Those who sat in darkness and in the shadow of death,*
> *Bound in affliction and irons-*
> *Because they rebelled against the words of God,*
> *And despised the counsel of the Most High...*
> *Then they cried out to the Lord in their trouble,*
> *And He saved them out of their distresses.*
> *He brought them out of darkness and the shadow of death,*
> *And broke their chains in pieces.*

At this, they glanced at the chains some of the prisoners still wore and smiled. Others began to gather and listen, thinking it strange at first for there to be singing in such circumstances, but the music had a calming effect on those in the hold. Even the soldiers leaned closer to listen.

> *Fools, because of their transgressions,*
> *And because of their iniquities, were afflicted.*
> *Their soul abhorred all manner of food,*
> *And they drew near to the gates of death.*
> *Then they cried out to the Lord in their trouble,*
> *And He saved them out of their distresses.*

Those gathered realized the truth of these words. Many were prisoners, here because of their transgressions. None desired food and most felt that they were near the gates of death.

> *Those who go down to the sea in ships,*
> *Who do business on great waters,*
> *They see the works of the Lord,*
> *And His wonders in the deep.*
> *For He commands and raises the stormy wind,*
> *Which lifts up the waves of the sea.*
> *They mount up to the heavens,*
> *They go down again to the depths;*
> *Their soul melts because of trouble.*
> *They reel to and fro, and stagger like a drunken man,*
> *And are at their wits' end.*

At these words, all in the hold were soberly considering the words that were written so long ago but yet so accurately describing their current situation. The song continued with its refrain that had been repeated three times already, but now they were eager to hear the words again:

*Then they cry out to the Lord in their trouble,*
*And He brings them out of their distresses.*

This time it was in the present tense, being even more pertinent to their time of need.

*He calms the storm,*
*So that its waves are still.*
*Then they are glad because they are quiet;*
*So He guides them to their desired haven.*

At these words, all those listening felt a glimmer of hope, longing for the storm to calm and the waves to be still.

*Oh, that men would give thanks to the Lord for His goodness,*
*And for His wonderful works to the children of men!*
*Let them exalt Him also in the assembly of the people,*
*And praise Him in the company of the elders.*

Paul finished, quietly quoting the end of the psalm:

*Whoever is wise will observe these things,*
*And they will understand the lovingkindness of the Lord.*[8]

It was quiet in the hold other than the sounds of the storm and the creaking and banging of the ship. There were tears in the eyes of some of the men around, and they sniffed and quickly turned aside to regain control of their emotions.

Paul cleared his throat and said, "Men, these words were written by King David almost a thousand years ago, and yet God has appointed them for us today. God is not ignorant of our circumstances, and He can bring

---

[8] Psalm 107 (NKJV)

us out of our distress whether the storms stop or not. I hope all of you will 'understand the lovingkindness of the Lord,' as the psalmist wrote."

There were a few murmurs of agreement and words of thanks as the group quietly turned back to their own activities, contemplating what they had heard.

Temeros stood quietly, lost in thought, amazed at what he had witnessed. Luke noticed his expression.

"What are you thinking about?" he asked him quietly.

Temeros looked around as he considered how to answer this. "I'm not sure how to say all that is on my mind. I am surprised at the singing when the situation is so bad, but somehow it has helped to relieve the worries I have been feeling. I am amazed that this song was written so long ago and yet seems to exactly describe what we are going through today. I am still new to this belief in God's power and goodness, and yet you and Paul and the others seem so sure He is good, even when this is happening. That gives peace but I wonder what will happen. Paul just said something about being rescued from our distress even if the storm continues. I am trying to figure out how that could be. And how could this show God's lovingkindness?"

Luke chuckled. "Wow, you have a lot going on in that head of yours!" He paused as he considered how to answer. "Paul has been in a lot of troubled spots and yet God has never forsaken him or any of us who believe. There was one time he and I were in Philippi together along with Silas, another one of our brothers in ministry. Paul and Silas were thrown in jail after casting out a demon. While they were in jail, they were singing and praying much like today. At that time, God showed his power in a mighty earthquake that caused the prisoners' chains to break and the prison doors to open."

"I imagine the jailer was severely punished at having his prisoners all escape!"

"Actually, they stayed put and ministered to the man, and he along with his entire family came to know the Lord that night!" Luke smiled at the memory.

Temeros considered this. "Do you mean that God will rescue us just like He opened the jail for Paul?"

Luke shook his head. "I'm afraid not. It just means that God is always aware of our troubles and He will not leave us. Even Paul has come close to death many times. In fact, he has been shipwrecked three times before, spending all night in deep water before someone rescued him. It really is amazing that he has survived to this day. God has never failed to rescue him but that does not mean life is not hard. God's goodness is not something we believe because life is easy. On the contrary, God's loving-kindness is seen in the way He is with us when we go through trials of many kinds. Our Lord promised never to leave us or forsake us. It is hard to see sometimes but our faith is strengthened by every one of the trials we face."

Temeros pondered this. "I have a lot to learn. I must admit, I would rather learn in a nice safe environment," he said with a smile.

Luke chuckled. "You and me both!"

———

About the time Paul started singing, Demetrius decided he had had enough. Being on deck in the storm would be better than being forced to hear more about how god was good. Surely they could see by now that there was no god! No one was helping them and they were going to die on the open ocean, never to be seen again! If there was a god, he was either too weak to do anything or did not know what was happening to them or, worse yet, wanted them to suffer. It was too much to bear!

He climbed up to the deck, tying the lifeline around his waist as he staggered aft. Shortly after him, two soldiers followed. They were the same two he had seen whispering and pointing at Paul. They also moved to the stern but kept a little distance from him.

There were three sailors on deck huddled together next to the ship's boat, holding the edge of the canvas covering over them for a little shelter. They appeared to be talking animatedly. As Demetrius and the soldiers came closer, they moved over to give them room to crouch under the canvas as well and then continued their discussion. The newcomers could hear one of the older sailors talking loudly over the storm. His weathered face and leathery skin gave witness to his many years of sailing experience.

"I tell you, the god's are angry! We need to figure out who has caused this curse on us and cast them into the sea!"

The other two sailors appeared appalled at this suggestion. "You're mad! That would be murder! Why would we do such a thing?"

"You are too young to know, but for hundreds of years, seagoing men have known that if there is a storm as deadly as this, and if you cast overboard the man who has angered the gods, the storm will cease. I've heard the stories all my life. In fact, one man *volunteered* to be thrown overboard, saying he knew he was the one that had brought catastrophe on them. As soon as they threw him in the sea, the waves became calm and the storm stopped!" he said. His conviction that this was true was evident to the men.

Demetrius had leaned nearer to hear what he was saying, and the two soldiers, Cassius and Porcius, were also listening intently.

"Who are you talking about!? That can't be true!" the other sailors responded.

"It *is* true, I tell you!" the older sailor responded. "In fact, I heard some Hebrews telling the exact same story once, saying it was written in their holy book! His name was Jonah! Of course they added some nonsense about him being eaten by a giant fish and then vomited up on shore alive. That can't be true, but I know the storm stopped when they did it. I heard the story from many different sailors!"

The two younger sailors looked at each other, considering this. "Even if it's true, how can we know who is the one that caused this?"

At this, Demetrius spoke up, surprising them. "I can tell you that!" he said. There is one of the prisoners in the hold spouting off about god all the time. If he was really such a god follower, I can tell you for sure he would not be a prisoner! He must have done something against god to be punished."

Porcius and Cassius glanced at each other, sensing an opportunity. "He's right!" said Porcius. At this, the sailors and Demetrius all turned toward them. "That man, Paul, has caused nothing but trouble. He must be the one!"

"Yes," Cassius joined in. "I hear he even told our centurion that if we left Fair Havens to go to Phoenix, disaster would strike! If that's not a curse on our ship, I don't know what is!"

Sailors tend to be a superstitious group by nature, and at this talk of curses, the issue was decided in their mind.

"It must be him! I say we grab him and take care of this now!" the old man said. The other sailors as well as Demetrius and the soldiers voiced agreement. "Let's go talk to the other men and figure out how to get to him!"

Porcius and Cassius suppressed smiles at this, and they could see Demetrius shared their satisfaction at the way this was going. The sailors made their way toward the hatch to the lower deck to talk to their crewmates.

Demetrius lingered by the boat as did Porcius and Cassius. The soldiers eyed him warily.

"Who are you? I don't remember seeing you around the ship when we left Myra. And why are you so eager to get rid of that rabble-rouser Paul?" Cassius asked him.

Demetrius glowered at them in return. "It doesn't matter who I am. The two of you seem just as eager. Why would two upstanding Roman soldiers want something to happen to a prisoner in their charge?"

They looked at each other trying to judge how much to say. "We have our reasons." Porcius paused as he considered his words. "Look. We seem to have a common aim. Let's not turn against each other. If we wanted to, we could report you as a stowaway, and we know that if you chose to, you could report us to our centurion. We won't say anything if you don't."

Demetrius considered this briefly and nodded, inwardly relieved. "Agreed."

"Really, though. What do you know of Paul?" they asked.

"You first," he said defiantly.

"He flaunts his Roman citizenship like he is someone important. We have been loyal soldiers for years but have yet to earn that title. Our centurion seems to be much too easily swayed by him, and for a prisoner to have that much power is never good. We are ready to put a stop to that."

At this, Demetrius' eyes narrowed. He had expected a much stronger reason than petty jealousy. What little respect he had for the soldiers' position diminished quickly to where he only saw them as weak and self-obsessed.

"What about you?" Porcius asked.

"I was the best silversmith in Ephesus when he came and started his preaching. After several months, people were turning away from the temple of the goddess Artemis. They stopped supporting the temple and, along with that, stopped buying my silver shrines. That man ruined my livelihood but would not stop there. He took my wife away from me when she started believing what he preached. Eventually, my house burned to the ground and my wife and boy died." At this his voice faltered, giving way to grief mixed with anger.

The soldiers were quiet for moment. "I'd say that is a good reason to want to toss him overboard."

"Do you really think that will happen?" Demetrius said with a skeptical tone.

Cassius laughed. "Not likely! No Roman soldier would let one of the prisoners be taken by someone unauthorized. He would be punished or perhaps even killed."

"So why bother suggesting it to the sailors?"

Porcius grinned slyly. "Because, if Paul goes missing later, who do you

THE LAST VOYAGE OF THE EMIR

think would be blamed? It takes the focus off of the three of us! Everyone would assume the sailors got to him after all!"

Demetrius realized he may have underestimated their cunning. That was a good plan to divert suspicion.

All three men shivered and decided it was time to return to the protection of the lower level.

# CHAPTER TWENTY-TWO

Porcius and Cassius were right. The plot to throw Paul overboard to calm the storm was quickly squelched by the soldiers guarding the prisoners. Surprisingly, many of the sailors had been in favor of the idea. Anything that would give hope of lessening the storm would be considered. After that, the soldiers were more watchful anytime the prisoners left the hold, making any attempt by Demetrius and his co-conspirators impossible.

Day after day, the storm seemed never ending. There were glimmers of hope when the rain decreased for an hour or so and the wind let up, but inevitably it returned full force. Hope was giving way to despair.

One day late in the afternoon during a lull in the storm, those on deck were suddenly shocked to see actual sunlight filtering through the clouds. It was only a short distance off their port side. Their shouts of excitement quickly brought others out to see what was going on and soon all the men of the ship were out on deck. All were hoping this signaled an end to the storm.

Captain Sahaq and Rayiz were as excited as everyone else to have even a short respite from the storm, but they also knew it was only temporary.

"It's just the eye of the storm, I'm sure of it," Rayiz said quietly to the captain.

"Aye, I know you are right," Captain Sahaq responded. "But if we can get far enough into the eye, we may have a glimpse of the stars in a few hours and be able to get some idea of where we are! All I can tell is that we are still heading west, now that I see the direction of the sun's rays."

"Yes, I wish we had a way to steer this cursed ship! Our rudders are no match for the wind and waves."

"One good thing about it, if the eye is to our south, that means the wind should be coming up from the south and east to circle around the center of the storm. Maybe they will keep us off the Syrtis sands. No telling how far south we have traveled with those terrible north and east winds, we had the first several days!"

For the next couple of hours, they were treated to lighter winds and rains, but they never got any closer to the sunlight. The deck was filled with people craning their necks and hoping by sheer force of will to make the ship move that direction but to no avail. The sunlight moved further to the south, and the clouds became steadily darker as the wind picked up and the rain intensified.

During this break, with the ship's company so focused on the port side, Demetrius, Porcius, and Cassius thought they may have their chance. They had been watching Paul as he made his way aft. He and his companions went toward the doctor's cabin and they followed at a distance. After a few minutes, Paul re-emerged with Aristarchus, followed by the doctor and his apprentice.

Demetrius had seen this apprentice a few times, always wearing a head scarf. Every time, he could not shake the feeling he had met the man somewhere, but he was not able to place him. He thought it may be the same man that was talking in his sleep the night he had come aboard and crept down to the hold. After a moment of consideration, he shook his head and focused on Paul. The men moved toward the port side at the aft of the ship.

Demetrius pulled his accomplices aside. "I have a plan." He said. "You two call for the doctor. That should at least get two of them occupied elsewhere. I may be able to sneak up behind Paul and get him over the side before anyone else notices. If one of his other friends is there too, well he may just have to join him in the water."

The two soldiers liked this plan and moved further away before implementing it. Demetrius took a circuitous path to station himself behind Paul a little further to the starboard side. No one was looking aft since the eye of the storm was the other direction. Demetrius nodded to the soldiers and they approached Paul and the others.

"Doctor Luke, they are calling for you on the forward deck. They wanted you to check on someone," Cassius said, feigning concern.

Luke turned to respond. "Certainly! Any idea what the trouble is? Do I need to get some of my instruments?"

This caught them off guard. Porcius spoke up. "Uh, I don't think so. They just wanted to have you check on someone who slipped on the wet deck."

"Ok, I'll head that way." He turned to Temeros. "Would you like to come help me?"

"Sure!" Temeros responded, eager for more experience.

The two headed toward the other end of the ship as the soldiers withdrew. Paul and Aristarchus watched them walk away and then turned back to the railing.

Porcius and Cassius waited until Luke and Temeros were out of sight and then turned to come up behind Paul and help Demetrius finish him off. Just then, Gaius called out to them from the other side of the deck.

"Hey! You two, Porcius and Cassius. Get over here. I need you to help watch these prisoners!"

The two soldiers glanced at each other, disappointed, but hurried to obey their commanding officer. They figured Demetrius could handle this.

Demetrius watched them go, in some ways relieved they were gone. He did not feel he could fully trust them and felt more confident doing it himself. He walked slowly toward the two men leaning on the railing. He caught snatches of their conversation over the increasing wind as he got closer but was not really paying much attention to what they were saying. He was preoccupied with making sure no one was watching. He was considering the best way to subdue both of them quickly but knew he did not have much time.

He took a deep breath, steeling his resolve and preparing to make his move. Just as he started to rush them, there was a lull in the wind and their voices became clearer. What he heard stopped him in his tracks, stunned.

Aristarchus said, "I'm glad Luke has some help. He appears to be learning quickly and seems to have a gift for treating the sick and injured."

Paul nodded. "Yes, I think young Temeros was placed here by God. He seems to be growing in his faith as he also learns this new trade with Dr. Luke."

It was only a few words but it shook Demetrius to his core. Temeros! Suddenly it was clear to him. The man with the head scarf that looked so familiar was his own son, now grown! How could this be? He was sure the boy had died in the fire. As glad as he was to discover that he had survived, he was overcome with a mix of guilt and anger—guilt at the painful memory of the fire, realizing it occurred as a result of his own rage, guilt at the memory of the look on his son's face when he lashed out at his wife, and guilt at not being more diligent to search for his son after the fire, but also anger at Temeros. Why did he not come to search for him? Why did his own son abandon him when he was recovering from his injuries?

Then Paul's words sunk in. Growing in his faith? No! How could Paul have beguiled his son also?! How could his Temeros be following this man who had destroyed his livelihood and torn apart his family? He felt a quick rush of rage and his good right hand closed over the hilt of his silver dagger. He was about to rush them both, but just at that time, the men had turned to see him standing there.

In the blink of an eye, Aristarchus saw the man with a wild look in his eyes, a cry of rage on his lips, and a silver dagger raised as he advanced quickly toward them. He cried out and pushed Paul aside as he jumped in front of him. As the man hesitated and adjusted his angle of attack toward him, Aristarchus raised his hands in defense and closed his eyes in anticipation of the blow to come.

Just as Demetrius started the downward motion of his hand wielding the dagger, someone grabbed him from behind pushing him aside. The death blow he had planned failed, only catching the man on the forearm as he was thrown to the deck. As he fell, he saw the Roman soldier, Gaius, pouncing on him, a firm grip on his right forearm. He twisted severely, causing a sharp pain as his grip loosened letting his dagger fall to the deck. He was no match for the strength and training of the soldier, and after a few feeble struggles, he gave up, panting for breath and crying out in pain.

Chaos followed as the rain began pouring down again, water washing across the deck. Several more soldiers arrived, summoned by Gaius' shouts. Two of them grabbed the attacker as Gaius turned to check on Aristarchus. Seeing the deep cut on his arm and the pale look on his face, Gaius ordered two other soldiers to quickly take him to Luke's quarters and fetch the physician. He saw the silver dagger glinting on the deck, the blood being washed away by the heavy rain that had just started. He picked it up and tucked it in his belt.

Paul was standing nearby, a look of shock and concern on his face. Gaius assured him the attack was over, and he took his arm and led him to Luke's quarters to be checked out. Then, with the deck starting to heave up and down again with the resurgence of the storm, the soldiers made their way below with their new prisoner in their grasp. It was all done in a matter of a few minutes.

Down in the hold, the soldiers roughly tied Demetrius' arms behind him as they isolated him from the others in a corner of the room. Once he was secured and disarmed, three soldiers were posted over him until the commander and the centurion could decide what to do with him. He sat slumped on the floor, head down, his mind churning and a look of torment on his face.

Up on the deck, Luke and Temeros quickly returned to his quarters. They had realized the initial report of someone on deck needing their attention was a false alarm. Just as they were turning to return to Paul, the soldiers rushed up with a report that someone had tried to attack the teacher and he was hurt. Immediate worry and concern for Pauls' welfare lent speed to them on the slick water-washed deck. Just as they arrived, they saw Paul being led there by Gaius and were relieved to see that he appeared to be ok.

"Paul!" Luke called over the noise of the storm. "Are you ok? They told me you were hurt! What happened?"

Paul responded breathlessly. "No! I'm fine, I'm fine. It's Aristarchus! Someone had a knife and tried to stab him! I saw a lot of blood but I don't know how bad it is. Please go in and check on him!" he said, standing back to allow the doctor into the room.

The first thing they saw was blood. It had dripped on the floor of the room causing a sticky mess. Aristarchus was lying on the table, appearing very pale. One of the soldiers had found a piece of cloth and put it loosely around his arm, but it was saturated and had not yet slowed the bleeding. The soldier did not look too well himself, appearing very pale as he turned away from the sight (he had yet to see any combat and was not used to seeing that much blood).

Luke quickly crossed over and put pressure on the wound as he directed Temeros to get a fresh cloth. As he held pressure to the area on the left forearm, he quickly assessed Aristarchus for any other signs of trauma. The blood on his tunic appeared to all be from this wound on his arm.

"Aristarchus! Can you hear me?" Aristarchus opened his eyes, a dazed look on his face as he turned toward Luke's voice. "Are you hurt anywhere else other than your arm?"

He looked down at his bloody arm, appearing almost surprised to see the blood there. As he struggled to remember all that had happened, he slowly shook his head. "I—I don't think so. I don't really know. Right now, just my arm hurts."

"Just relax. We'll take care of you." Temeros returned with a fresh bandage as well as a leather thong to use as a tourniquet around the upper arm.

"Ok. But Luke…" Luke leaned closer to hear what he wanted to say.

"I don't want you taking out any revenge on me for my earlier comments! Temeros better watch what you do to me! I'd like to still have both arms when you are done!" he said with a slight smile. Luke laughed, caught off guard. It was a good sign if he was still joking around.

He turned his attention to the bloody dressing. After the tourniquet was applied around the upper arm (with a cry of pain from Aristarchus), the bleeding was slowed greatly. Luke removed the dressing and washed the wound with clean water and a cloth. It appeared to be about five inches long, just below the elbow running down his forearm. Although the slice was clean and straight, it was gaping open and the muscle tissue could be seen partially severed. More concerning was the continued bleeding, which was much reduced but not yet stopped by the tourniquet.

"Temeros, can you see that spot where the blood is coming from? I want you to put your finger there and press it down firmly to stop the bleeding."

Temeros leaned closer, seeing what Luke had indicated. He quickly put his index finger on the spot and pressed down (with another cry of pain from the patient), feeling the flow of blood stop. Luke quickly wiped away the blood from the wound to get a better view. "Good! That is the right place. Now just hold it until I tell you to let it go!"

They worked together, bracing themselves against the rocking of the ship. Exploring the wound, Luke was able to see that the majority of the muscle was intact so he would not need to sew it back together. Aristarchus was able to move his wrist and fingers (although with a lot of pain) so his function appeared to be maintained. The biggest problems appeared to be the bleeding and the wound itself. After a few minutes of inspection, Luke asked Temeros to slowly let up the pressure on the bleeding vessel. As he did, there was once again fresh blood pouring into the wound, but this time it was much slower. Luke was pleased by this, knowing it was a good sign the bleeding should stop with longer compression. Temeros applied pressure again as Luke got more supplies to wrap the wound.

"How does it look?" Aristarchus asked. He appeared to have regained some of his color as he was lying down on the bed.

"I don't think there is any major damage. It's just a deep cut that should heal. You'll be sore and we need to watch for any infection, but you should just have a nice scar for all of your trouble."

Aristarchus smiled at that. "Scars will make me look fiercer. I'll have to think up a good story about how I got it."

"What *did* happen?" Luke asked him. "They told me somebody tried to stab you! Did you make jokes about the wrong person?"

"I really don't know who that man was. I haven't seen him before. I think he was actually aiming for Paul but I got in his way. I did not hear him say why."

"Hmm. Well, Paul has made a few enemies through the years." He turned toward Paul, leaning against the wall to steady himself. "Paul, did you see who did this? Do you know why he attacked you?"

Paul shook his head. "No, I could not see. You know how my eyes are these days, and with the rain, and shadows of the storm, all I could see was a flash of movement before Aristarchus pushed me out of the way. I think he saved my life!"

Aristarchus frowned at this. "No, I did not do anything quite that brave. I was hoping he would miss us both, but I did not move fast enough."

Luke smiled at him. "I am impressed!"

Aristarchus blushed at the attention from those in the room and tried to change the subject.

"Well, anyway, neither of us knew the man who did this. Maybe the soldiers can find out more."

After a few more minutes of continuous pressure on the wound, Luke asked Temeros to once again release the pressure. This time, there was no significant bleeding. It stayed dry as they continued to watch.

Luke prepared the dressing. Since it was such a straight cut, just wrapping it securely should approximate the edges of the wound to allow it to heal. He placed a clean cloth over the wound being sure the edges of the wound met. Then he wound a strip of cloth around the area several times, being sure it was firm but not too tight. After tying it securely, it was time for the moment of truth.

"Ok, let's let the tourniquet loose slowly." Temeros complied as they watched the dressing closely. The fingers once again turned a healthy color of pink. After a minute or two, there was a small stain of blood visible on the dressing, but it did not expand. Luke checked the function of his hand and finger movement once again and made sure the flingers stayed pink.

"I think that will be ok," he declared. "But, we will need to keep you here to watch it closely. You will need to limit how much you do with your left arm for a few days. Try to keep it raised over your chest or on a pillow."

"Whatever you say, doctor. I'll be your best patient," Aristarchus declared.

Luke turned to Paul. "Ok, now it's your turn. How are you feeling? Did you have any injuries during the attack?" he asked with concern as he directed him to the adjacent cot to sit down.

"No, I seem to be fine. I was shocked when it happened and anxious, but that has passed. I know the Lord has protected us once again."

Luke examined him quickly. There were no obvious wounds other than a superficial scrape on one knee from when he was knocked to the deck. He was able to move all of his extremities and seemed oriented. His heart rate seemed normal and steady.

"I agree, you seem to be doing well. If you start to have any problems, be sure to let me or Temeros know!"

Temeros brightened at being included in the care.

"Well, let's get some rest if we can. The storm is picking up again. Be careful going back to the lower deck," Luke said as the men made their way toward the door.

# CHAPTER TWENTY-THREE

Paul returned to the lower level and was greeted by several of the other prisoners in the hold asking what had happened. They had seen the attacker roughly hauled to the other end of the hold and could see the soldiers guarding him closely.

He recounted the story two or three times until their curiosity had been satisfied. Some of the believers gathered around him and placed their hands on him for a time of prayer, thanking God for His safekeeping and praying for a quick recovery for Aristarchus and wisdom in his treatment by Dr. Luke and Temeros. Paul joined in briefly, asking God to forgive the attacker and bring him to knowledge of the love and grace and sacrifice provided by Jesus, the Christ.

Gaius, standing nearby, was surprised by this compassion for someone that wanted him dead. After all of the teaching he had heard from Paul, though, he knew it was consistent with everything he had heard about Jesus so far. As he reflected on this, he was flooded with a deep desire for this same spirit he had seen demonstrated by Paul and the other believers.

Porcius and Cassius also observed this as they stood in the shadows a short distance away. They shared a quick glance and sneered at the idea of asking this shadowy god to forgive, whispering to each other about how weak this prisoner must be to so quickly give up on any desire for revenge. They walked away, planning to get a glimpse of Demetrius and make sure he did not implicate them in any of his actions.

———————

The shadows descended in the hold, and the noise of the storm and the heaving of the ship worsened. The mood in the hold became drearier with each passing hour. The few who had kept their spirits up the best were faltering, giving in to hopelessness and fear. Even Paul seemed more quiet and somber than he had been.

Paul sat on the floor, his back to the bulkhead. He could feel the throbbing of the ship with each wave. His mood darkened as he thought of the hardships he had faced. Yes, God had brought him through each one, but couldn't he be spared, just once?! Surely he had sacrificed enough. Here he was, once again a prisoner, alone in the dark. His closest companions on this voyage were occupied elsewhere. He was tired, hungry, and sick to his stomach from the never-ending movement of the ship. He felt pressure from those around him to show no fear or weakness, but he was only human!

He had been so sure God had directed him to appeal to Caesar, and he saw how God could use this to impact Rome, the center of the known world! He had started off with excitement and anticipation, but now, it had been thirteen days of storms, rain, rocking of the ship, uncertainty, and fear. He had maintained his faith that God would rescue them, and he did not doubt God's power or His goodness. But he had expected to have respite several days ago.

As he thought about Rome, he remembered his correspondence to the church there. He had written to them a few years before, hoping to someday see them in person, and he had such hopes that this would be the way he could accomplish this. As he thought of that letter, he remembered the words he had written to them, encouraging them in their faith.

"What can separate us from God's love? Nothing." He had listed many hardships, including tribulations, distress, and persecution. He had asked the rhetorical question, "If God is for us, who can be against us?" Now the word "If" was dancing in his mind, teasing him. "Are you sure God is for you?" Didn't he in the same letter write "For Your sake we are killed all day long; We are accounted as sheep for the slaughter"?[9]

He was overcome with discouragement. Even feeling as low as he did, he recognized the truth of God's love. He was convinced that God really was for him. He remembered his own words, inspired by the Spirit of God himself. "In all these things, we are more than conquerors through Him who loved us."[10] It was only through Jesus himself that this would be conquered. It is strange how God sometimes used the very same words he had preached to others to confront his own doubts.

He tried to sleep, but rest was hard to come by. After a couple of hours, the pressure in his bladder and his own restlessness made the decision for him. He signaled to the guard indicating he planned to go to relieve himself up on deck. The soldier grumbled but agreed to escort him to be sure he was safe. After the earlier attack, they had orders to not leave him unaccompanied.

As they made their way to the ladder, Gaius saw what was happening and offered to take him since he also felt the same bodily needs. He had been tossing and turning, dozing a few minutes at a time, but not able to sleep.

He led Paul up the ladder, steadying him. On deck, they each secured themselves with a lifeline as they steadied themselves against the heaving deck and the heavy rain. Intermittent flashes of lightning gave them glimpses of the deck but in turn took away their night vision briefly after each flash. They felt their way together toward the prow of the ship to the small room designated for waste. It was at the very front of the ship, and there was a small open window for ventilation. The main view was of the

---

[9] See Romans 8:31ff.

[10] Romans 8:37

figurehead adjacent to it. The sailors had taken to calling it the "head" because of its location.

Gaius went in first, quickly taking care of his needs, and then exited for Paul to take his turn. As Gaius waited outside the door, holding tightly to the rope, he could see the massive, mountainous waves with each flash of lightning. Some loomed higher than the ship, and it seemed impossible that they could survive much more of this.

As he was overcome by the dread and fear of dying in this storm, he became aware of what sounded like voices. He looked around but no one else was near. He glanced at the door to the head and was startled to see what looked like a bright shining light in the crack at the bottom of the door. There was no lightning at the time. He started to knock on the wooden door, but as he reached out his hand, he realized the voices he heard were coming from inside. How could this be? No one else was there when he left just moments before. Was Paul losing his mind and talking to himself?

He leaned his ear to the door and could hear Paul but he also heard another voice. The voice was difficult to describe. It sounded like a mixture of a rushing wind and a flowing river, but he could tell there were words in the sound. It was so hard to decipher what was being said. It seemed as though it was in a different tongue. He gripped the handle of his sword with his right hand as he grabbed the door handle with his left, determined to find out what was happening.

He yanked open the door and saw a flash of silver light quickly fading away. It appeared it had come from outside the window, and he had the odd impression it was the figurehead itself that had been glowing a moment before. He wiped his eyes and shook his head to clear it. Maybe he had dozed off while he was waiting and was still dreaming. Now, all he saw was Paul standing alone, head bowed, tears on his face with an expression of overwhelming contentment and peace now visible where before he had looked so discouraged.

"Paul, are you ok?" he asked. "What happened?"

Paul looked up, seemingly startled to see him standing there. "What? Oh, everything is just fine now. I know we will be safe."

Gaius looked at him dubiously. They both stumbled as a large wave poured over the railing drenching them. "How can you say that? What makes you so sure?"

Paul looked at him smiling, seemingly oblivious to the danger of the storm now. "The angel of God told me."

"What are you talking about!? Did you bump your head? Are you delirious?"

"No, I am sure of it."

Gaius was dumbfounded, not sure what to say. "Let's take you to Dr. Luke. I think he needs to check on you."

Paul nodded in agreement. "Yes, I think I need to share this with him and Aristarchus. Let's go there now, please."

Gaius grabbed Paul's arm, now concerned that he had some problem with his head, and they made their treacherous way back to Luke's quarters. Gaius was aware of the danger with each wave and was in a state of fear the whole way, but Paul was smiling and appeared content as if he did not notice the danger around them.

Gaius pounded on Luke's door and opened, not waiting for an answer.

"What? What is it?" Luke cried out, startled by the sudden entrance. He saw Gaius and Paul and sat up. "Come in. What's going on? Is everything ok? Did someone attack him again?" he asked alarmed.

"No, nothing like that, but he is definitely not ok!" Gaius reported. "He claims to have spoken to angels. I'm afraid he is losing his mind!"

Paul actually laughed at this. "Gaius, I am fine. I am not going crazy. But yes, I did speak with an angel just a few moments ago, and I truly needed the encouragement he brought!"

Luke was now wide awake, and Temeros, who had not been able to sleep, heard this as well. Both were sitting up in bed. Aristarchus was also awake but lying down with his arm wrapped and resting across his chest. Luke stood and motioned to a chair. "Sit! I need to know what happened!"

Paul sat and was quiet for a moment as he considered what had happened. Luke, Temeros, and Gaius waited in anticipation, as Aristarchus rolled over to listen as well.

"After the attack, I found myself discouraged and losing hope," he began. "I am ashamed to say I was doubting God's goodness in spite of all He has done for me. I knew I was slipping into despair, and even while feeling the fear and hopelessness welling up in me, I knew God was good and that He had a plan. In my head, I knew whatever His plan was, it was for His glory and kingdom, but in my selfishness, I wanted to be relieved of my doubts and fears, for the storm to cease. Finally, after wrestling with this, I got up to relieve myself. While I was in the "head," looking out the small window at the bow, I was praying. All of a sudden, I saw..." he paused considering how to describe what happened.

"What? What did you see?" Luke prompted, eager for more information.

"Well, I saw the face of the lady in the figurehead come alive!"

The others gasped at this, and Gaius' look of concern deepened.

"I know it sounds strange. I know it was not really the figurehead but an angel sent from God. I was startled and fell back against the wall, but then she spoke. I did not understand the spoken words, but I know in my heart what she was saying, as clear as I am speaking to you. She told me not to be afraid. God knows our circumstances and has not left us alone in the storm. She spoke words of encouragement for my despair, reminding me that I belong to God and he is aware of my service." As he spoke, Paul looked embarrassed to be saying this. "She rebuked my doubts, reminding me that God has ordained that we be on this ship at this time. His plan is for me to reach Rome and appear before Caesar. I confessed my fear that the storm was too much for the ship and that it had lasted for so many days, but she assured me that God has granted me the lives of all aboard."

At these words, the men in the room felt a great sense of hope return. All had been fearful, wondering when the ship would finally succumb to the waves leaving them to drown. Now with these words, and Paul's absolute assurance of their truth, their faith was strengthened. Even Gaius felt peace for the first time in a few days.

"Did she say anything else? How long the storm will continue, or when we will reach shore?" Temeros asked hopefully.

"She did not tell me those specifics but she did tell me we will run aground on an island somewhere. And she again assured me that all will survive if we just trust God."

"Thanks be to God," Luke said. "I am running low on supplies, and the sooner we reach land, the better. I am so glad to have reassurance that God will see us ashore. I hope there are not many injuries in the process! Master Paul, will you pray for us?"

Paul led them in prayer, thanking God for the reassurance and encouragement of their sure salvation both bodily from the storm and spiritually from their sins.

As they prepared to return to the hold for the remainder of the night, Gaius considered these events. He could see that Paul was not insane, and the others had no doubt that his story was true. Even his own doubts diminished as he observed Paul's conviction that this was what really happened. He knew he had to talk to Julius about this since it involved the safety of the ship and those on board but decided there was no reason to wake him (although he doubted whether he was sleeping). He planned to go to him early in the morning, a few hours away. Knowing the fantastic nature of this tale, he decided it may be best to have Paul there to confirm the truth of the story.

Before leaving the relative quiet of the room, he grasped Paul's arm and, in a low voice, spoke to him. "Paul, I need to pass this information to Julius, and if he agrees, the captain will need to know this as well. I think you should be with me to relay your story to them directly. I will escort you to Julius early in the morning."

Paul nodded in affirmation. "Of course. I will be happy to speak to them."

They exited into the storm, which somehow seemed less menacing, though no less fierce, and made their way carefully below decks. Both of them felt more relaxed now, and after settling to the floor in the hold, they both dozed off quickly.

# CHAPTER TWENTY-FOUR

Gaius slept more restfully than he had for several days and woke early in the morning to his own internal clock. He sat up, looking around the dark hold. He had dreamed of angels and solid ground and dry weather, and although the ship was still rocking wildly on the waves, and water was still dripping through the hatch from the rain-washed deck above, his heart was at peace. He found it strange he felt so assured by this fantastic story Paul had related. He seemed to be so far from where he started three weeks ago, not just in distance physically but spiritually as well. He shook his head with a smile, imagining what his father would think of him in this situation. Guarding prisoners and spending time with people who follow Jesus: two things his father would never in a million years condone.

He got up and straightened his uniform as he made his way to where Paul was sleeping. He, too, appeared to be enjoying deep sleep unlike all of the other prisoners in the hold. The soldiers standing watch over the prisoners snapped to attention as he approached, and Gaius saluted as he made a quick inspection. He informed them that he was taking Paul to see Julius and they nodded in understanding. One of them went to where Paul slept and nudged him with the toe of his sandal, careful to not appear too rough under the watchful eye of his commander.

Paul woke quickly and sat up.

"You are being summoned to see the centurion," The soldier informed him. "Get up!"

Paul complied, brushing the dirt off his damp robe. He had long ago grown weary of being constantly wet but was in a much better frame of mind to tolerate it today than before. External circumstances may not have changed, but communication with angels always seemed to have a positive effect on his outlook. He smiled slightly as he nodded a greeting to Gaius.

"Good morning," Gaius said. "Did anything else happen during the night?"

"Well, I slept better than I have in days! But no more visions. I believe God has already given us His message for now."

"Fair enough. I have not talked to Julius yet. I think we need to speak to him first about your, um, vision. Then, he can decide if we need to talk to the Captain about it," Gaius explained as they walked together.

Julius had claimed a somewhat private space for himself in the hold. As they approached, they found him awake, a scowl on his unshaven face. He glanced up at their approach and nodded at Gaius's salute. "What is it now?" he asked wearily.

"Sorry to disturb you, Centurion," Gaius said formally. "Something happened last night that I think you need to hear." He motioned for Paul to step forward. "Tell him what you told us last night."

Paul cleared his throat. "I was given a message from God most high. He assured me that all on board will survive but that we will run aground on an island somewhere."

Julius stared at him slack-jawed for a moment as he processed this straightforward declaration. He shook his head briefly and then looked at Gaius to see if this was some sort of joke, but Gaius surprisingly showed every sign of believing this tale. "Uh, *ok*, um." He paused considering his response. "When did this happen?"

Paul showed no hesitation or embarrassment with this tale. "During the night. I had gone up on deck to relieve myself, accompanied by Gaius."

Julius turned to Gaius. "Did you see this happen? Did you also talk to God?" he asked, a hint of sarcasm in his voice.

Gaius dropped his gaze briefly, feeling more doubt now than before this conversation started. "No sir, but I heard more than one voice through the door of the "head." There was a bright light shining under the door, and I am sure it was not lightning playing tricks on me. When I opened the door to check on Paul, I caught a glimpse of the light fading quickly through the little porthole. Julius, I know it sounds incredible, but I felt I had to bring this to you. You know of Paul's reputation for signs and wonders and miraculous doings before he was imprisoned." Julius nodded as he considered the truth of these words. "I admit I thought he had lost his sanity when he told me what happened. I took him to the doctor, Luke, to be checked out. I was surprised that all three of the men there had no doubt this really happened."

"Three?" Julius asked, trying to hide his interest in this tall tale. He had known Gaius to be as skeptical as he was, and for him to believe a story such as this deserved his consideration.

"There was Dr. Luke, his apprentice, and then the other prisoner that was injured in the attack last evening. All three seem to be followers of Jesus and they truly believe what Paul says happened. All of them can't be insane, can they?" Gaius had become more excited and hopeful as he recounted what happened.

"So do you know any details? Did God tell you when we will run aground? Or where we are?"

"No, I'm afraid not," Paul answered. "Sometimes God does not give us all of the details, but in all of my years of serving Him, his word has never been shown to be false. I believe it will be soon, but I don't know when or where."

Julius considered this thoughtfully as he studied Paul. "Well, you were correct when you said we should stay at Fair Havens. I think you even told us if we tried to go to the next port, it would end in disaster and much loss. Maybe you can foretell the future."

Paul shook his head, "No, that is not the case. I claim no magical ability. I am not a fortune-teller. I am a servant of God, and He is merciful enough in our distress to give us a word of encouragement through His message to me. It has nothing to do with me and is all from Him."

Julius observed him silently for a moment and then seemed to come to a decision. Pushing himself up from the deck, he said "Well, regardless, this impacts all of us as well as the ship. I think we should go talk to Captain Sahaq. Maybe he will know where this island is that you referred to."

The three men climbed up to the deck. The wind and rain continued unabated, and they braced against the heaving of the deck now without much thought. The last fourteen days of the storm had given them plenty of time to adapt to the constantly changing footing. They supported each other as they held onto the lifelines strung out across the deck. They made unsteady progress to the captain's quarters aft. When they arrived, Julius pounded firmly on the wooden door.

"What is it?! What do you want?" was the grumpy reply from inside.

"It's Julius, the centurion. I have some information I think you need to hear!" Julius called out loud enough to be heard over the wind and rain.

"Come in, then."

They opened the door and hurried into the relative shelter of the cabin, hastily closing the door against the wind and rain. They turned to see Captain Sahaq sitting at his table with Rayiz. Both men were unshaven, with bags under their eyes and scowls on their faces that had become permanent. They sat with their elbows on the table, shoulders slumped. They looked up at the three men.

"Oof, there's a whole group of you!" the captain exclaimed. "Well, out with it. What do you want?"

Julius paused. Now that he was faced with relaying this fantastic story, he was hesitant. But he took a deep breath and plunged ahead.

"Gaius and the prisoner Paul came to me this morning with some, uh, information that I think you need to hear. It will sound strange and maybe even crazy but please hear him before passing judgment."

Captain Sahaq and Rayiz looked at each other with raised eyebrows and then turned to the men with wary, skeptical expressions.

"Ok. Lets' get this over with. What do you have to tell me?" the captain said gruffly.

Julius and Gaius gestured to Paul to tell his story.

"Gentlemen, we have been caught in this storm for fourteen days now. I had told you before we left Fair Havens that we should remain there instead of leaving for Phoenix, and I told you we would meet disaster if we left. I wish you had listened to me!" Paul said in the oratorical style he had developed over the past few years of preaching.

The Captain's countenance darkened at these words. He took a breath and was about to speak when Paul continued.

"However, I tell you now to take courage! There will be no loss of life but only the ship."

He definitely had their attention now. Captain Sahaq and Rayiz both stood to their feet, their eyes blazing.

"What do you mean by this?" Rayiz demanded. "How can you know such a thing?"

"All of us have been in fear of our lives, even me. Days without sun or food or hope have brought us despair. Last night, as I was crying out to God for rescue, an Angel of the God to whom I belong and whom I serve stood before me. He said 'Do not be afraid, Paul; you must be brought before Caesar. But God has granted you the lives of all who sail with you.' So I tell you, Captain, to take heart! I believe God that it will be just as I was told! However, we must run aground on some island."

The Captain and his first officer were silent for a moment, dumbfounded.

Captain Sahaq found his voice. "You come to me speaking of Angels and God speaking to you, telling me we will run aground somewhere! How am I supposed to believe that? Did God tell you where we are or when this will happen?"

"No," Paul said. "But as I told these soldiers, God has never been wrong in all of my years of serving Him."

Julius cleared his throat. "Captain, I know this is an amazing story, and I too had trouble believing it, but keep in mind sir. Paul was accurate in predicting our current troubles. And in addition to that, he has traveled around Greece and the eastern Empire preaching. Everywhere he goes, there are stories of the incredible deeds he has done. There are witnesses to these deeds that are credible beyond reproach. Whether you believe in his God or not, I believe we cannot ignore this. Since it involves the safety of the ship and running aground, I needed to bring this to you."

Rayiz and the Captain considered this. They could not deny the truth of what Julius had said. The fact that a Roman centurion and his first officer were here bearing witness to what their prisoner had to say was, in itself, reason to consider this information rather than dismissing it out of hand. They settled back to their seats at the table, contemplating what they had heard.

"Let's say this is true," Captain Sahaq began. "And I'm not saying I believe it all, mind you!! But let's pretend it is true. We have been in this storm for fourteen days now, no landmarks and no way to navigate. And even if we knew where we were, there is no way we can direct our ship even if we saw an island. If we are to run aground somewhere, then I would have to believe this God of yours must be real because no man on earth can say with certainty what you have told me."

Gaius spoke up for the first time. "But captain, are there any islands in this area of the sea that you know of?" he asked hopefully.

Both sailors shook their head. "No. After we passed Cauda on the first day of the storm, the rest of the sea is empty. If we go too far south, we may run aground on the Syrtis sands, but we passed the eye of the storm yesterday to our port side. The winds would be blowing us more to the north and west now. Maybe we are getting close to Italy but we have no idea. We are at the mercy of the sea gods, hoping to find any port anywhere. Is your God greater than the storm and the sea?" The captain's question to Paul was said in defiance, but there was also a pleading, hopeful expression on his face.

"Captain, I can assure you my God is the God above all gods. He created the world and all we see. This storm is nothing to His mighty power. When He became a man, Jesus the Christ, and walked on this earth, He was able to calm storms with just His voice. I can guarantee you He is stronger than this or any other storm. I know that the wind and the waves you see around us still know His mighty name. If He says we will live, I guarantee it to be true."

Paul declared this with such authority that all in the small room were comforted, even as the wind and rain continued to roar and the ship to bob in the water. All were quiet and introspective for a moment.

The Captain cleared his throat gruffly as he surreptitiously wiped his hand across his eyes. "Well, uh, thank you for bringing this to our attention. I'm not sure what we need to do but we will be on the lookout for any land close by."

"Thank you, Captain Sahaq," Julius said as the three turned to return to the hold.

There was no indication of a break in the weather, but the men were buoyed with optimism as they braced themselves against the rain and wind while the ship continued to rise and fall.

# CHAPTER TWENTY-FIVE

D own in the hold, Demetrius fumed. He has been tied up and guarded like one of the prisoners for two days now. If they knew who he was, they would treat him differently! He used to be rich and famous, a leader in Ephesus. The town leaders consulted him, and the other silversmiths looked to him for direction. He was not some lowly criminal! It was Paul's fault all of this had happened to him, and yet Paul was free, even appearing to be friends with the soldiers guarding him! Only those two soldiers, Porcius and Cassius, seemed to see through him. Their motives were weak and they did not have the hunger for revenge that drove Demetrius, but still they did not fawn at the feet of their prisoner the way the centurion and the other officer seemed to.

Now to find out his son, Temeros, was alive?! It was almost too much to bear! He wanted to go to him, to find out why he had run off and abandoned his father when he was injured and alone. But they tied him up and threw him in the dark, wet hold, away from anyone who could help him. He needed to find a way to reach Temeros! Surely he would help his father, wouldn't he?

When it was time for his guard's shift to end, he was replaced by Porcius. Maybe now they would help him to get loose. When the others were occupied elsewhere in the hold, he gestured to Porcius.

"Hey, what is going on? Can you let me out of here?" he asked quietly.

Porcius shook his head. "No, we are being watched all the time. Our commander, Gaius, won't let us have any freedom. There are too many soldiers that are loyal to Paul for us to help you right now. But just hold on. Maybe an opportunity will present itself."

"Well can you at least get a message to someone for me?" He pleaded.

"Who do you want to give a message to? I didn't think you knew anyone on board!"

"The guy working with the doctor. The young one that always wears a scarf on his head. I want to talk to him!"

Porcius looked puzzled. "Why in the world would you want to talk to a young guy like him? You're not planning to do something scandalous, are you?" he asked with a sneer and a wink.

"No! Of course not!" he responded indignantly. "I have my own reasons for needing to talk to him."

Porcius studied him for a moment and slowly nodded. "Ok, I'll see if we can get a message to him somehow. Is there anything I can tell him that will help convince him to come see you?"

"No, I need to see him and talk to him privately. I can't share anything else with you yet."

The rest of his shift passed slowly. Not much more was said between them.

————

After all of this time in the storm, the ship was barely holding together. Time was running out for all of them, and they were keenly aware of it. The water in the hold that had been knee deep twelve days ago had continued to rise. For the past ten days, there had been a line of sailors passing buckets of water up from the lowest hold to the deck to bail out the water. Although they had been able to keep the water from flooding over into the middle deck where everyone was huddled, they were not able to gain the upper hand and see it diminish, either. The most progress they had made was during the few hours of relative calm when they had passed near the eye of the storm, but once they were back into the heavy seas and rain, they were back to where they had started.

The planks making up the hull groaned with each heavy wave. The men bailing water out of the hold had been fearful with each thud, expecting the hull to breach and water to come flooding in. If that happened, there was no hope. Thankfully, the frapping cables they had placed on the first day of the storm were still holding, and the crew were diligent about checking them and tightening them each day.

The exhaustion of working round the clock to bail water, and inspect the frapping cables, as well as monitoring all of the other structures of the ship was matched equally by the mental fatigue of constant unrelenting stress and fear. The level of anxiety had built up quickly in the first three days of the storm and had never subsided. Some of the men had grown numb to it, walking through each day with tense nervous looks on their faces, eyes staring widely, jumping slightly with each shudder of the ship. Others had lashed out at anyone for anything, and the rough men who made up the ship's crew were constantly striking out both verbally and physically, only to call a truce several times a day, with their version of a quick apology.

The steady line of crewmen with buckets became part of the monotonous rhythm of the ship during the storm. Most of this occurred in the hatch to the stern, not the one they were used to using for their biological breaks or respite from the funk of the hold. The soldiers and prisoners and passengers quickly lost interest. There were rare intrusions into their awareness of this ongoing battle against the accumulating bilge water. Once or twice a sailor slipped on the wet deck falling down the ladder and crying out in pain. And once, oddly enough, a crewman passing a full bucket to the man on the ladder above him happened to catch a glimpse in the murky light of something moving in his bucket. He paused to look closer and was shocked by the sudden appearance of a snake lunging over the side of the wooden bucket toward his arm. He had cried out in fear and dropped the entire bucket of water as he jumped back quickly, narrowly escaping its fangs. The snake, briefly glimpsed on the floor of the hold, slithered out of sight in the shadows. Of course all were on high alert after that for any reappearance but the snake remained in hiding.

Now, fourteen days into the storm, hope had long since dissolved into despair. But then, there was a breath of hope. Throughout the day, rumors had begun to spread that Paul had spoken to God. Some had heard that Paul had magic powers and would rescue them. Others had heard that there was an army of angels headed their way to carry them out of the storm. Someone else heard that they would be transported to an island paradise full of beautiful angels. Nobody seemed to know the real story, but all felt a sense of hope that something may finally change with this accursed storm.

As this information was passed through the dark, wet hold, people began congregating around Paul, asking him to confirm what they had heard. Several were talking at once, and finally Gaius and Julius directed the guards to intervene and control the crowd. Julius approached Paul and asked him to share his vision with the crowd so the wild rumors would be quelled.

Paul stood up, braced against the bulkhead, as he raised one hand to get their attention.

"Brothers, it is true. God, to whom I belong and whom I serve, spoke to me through His angel last night. The angel's words are for all of us. 'Do not be afraid.' He confirmed to me that I will be brought before Caesar and that not just I but all of you also will survive this storm. God has granted me that all who are on board will survive. So take courage! I believe God that it will be just like He said. However, the ship will not survive. We will have to run aground on an island. I do not know where or when, but I believe the storm will be over soon. Trust in God that he will save us from the storm, but also trust in the Son of God, Jesus the risen Christ, that he will save us from our sins to give us eternal life."

Several of those around nodded and murmured in agreement. Someone asked Paul to pray for them and he led them in prayer of thanksgiving to God for his coming deliverance, even as the rain and wind roared around them and the creaking of the ship continued.

The rest of the day, there was a definite air of relief and hope, but as the day wore into night, the hope began to slip away again, and doubts and fears returned.

Paul and Gaius went up to Luke's quarters for a visit in the evening as darkness descended on the deck. Paul was pleased that Aristarchus seemed to be recovering. His arm was still in pain but he was moving it easier, a fresh, clean bandage in place. His spirits seemed to have returned and he carried on a constant good-natured ribbing of his friend, Luke.

"Despite Luke's best efforts, my arm is improving. I'm really glad Temeros is taking care of me. I was sure Luke was going to amputate. Now I just have to get my function back. Didn't the Lord teach something about the right hand not knowing how to do what the left hand does?"

They laughed as Luke responded. "You are going to confuse poor Temeros if you keep misquoting our Lord's teaching! I don't think that is what He said when He was talking about charitable giving! Temeros, don't pay any attention to him or he will lead you astray!"

Temeros laughed as well, although he still had much to learn about the teachings of Jesus. He glanced at Luke's collection of scrolls once again, hoping to read them sometime soon.

Temeros was busy caring for the crew who were injured and those still suffering from seasickness. A few were weakened from prolonged time with no food, and he was helping to give them sips of water and small bites of gruel to strengthen them.

Thankfully they were not called out into the storm, although there was one soldier who had come up searching for Temeros. Evidently one of the prisoners in the hold had asked to see him. In fact, it was Aristarchus' attacker. The soldier was not able to tell him why the man wanted to see him, and Luke intervened saying they were much too busy to leave the patients they were attending for something like that. The man grudgingly turned and left, and after he left, they both agreed there was something unsettling about his demeanor. They quickly returned to their duties and put it out of their mind.

Gaius escorted Paul back to the hold. All those below prepared once again for another night of dark, damp despair. The ship continued to rise and fall against the heavy waves, but as the night wore on, there was a subtle change. There seemed to be more side-to-side rolling of the ship, and the waves crashed against the hull in a different rhythm than before. They did not think much about this, assuming it was one more aspect of the deadly storm. Many still held out hope that they would be saved soon, holding on to God's promise delivered to Paul.

# CHAPTER TWENTY-SIX

U p on the deck, Captain Sahaq also noticed the change in the ship's rhythm. He summoned Rayiz and ordered the crew to be on sharp lookout. This could mean that they were approaching land somewhere, although he could not imagine where.

Rayiz assigned several of his crew to start taking soundings. If they were nearing shore, they needed to know and take precautions. They couldn't see anything in the stormy darkness.

After giving orders, Rayiz returned to Captain Sahaq, looking astounded. "Captain, you don't suppose the prisoner, Paul, was right, do you? How could he know that we would run aground?"

The captain mulled this over, puzzled. He shrugged. "I don't know how he could predict the future. If he really saw an angel, like he claims he did, I don't know whether to trust him or be scared of him. The only good thing is that if he is right about us running aground, maybe he's right about everyone surviving."

Rayiz nodded. "I hope so!" he said as he went to supervise the crew.

The men went to the prow of the ship with the sounding lines. The lines were ropes with a heavy lead weight at the end. At measured lengths along the rope, there were leather thongs of various shapes to designate the depth. The men gathered the sounding line carefully to be sure it was not tangled or knotted and then dropped the lead weight overboard.

The ship continued to rise and fall with the heavy waves, and the seawater washed over the deck frequently. The men steadied themselves and held fast to their lifelines as they watched the sounding line drop into the sea segment by segment. Finally it went slack in the ever-changing sea, and the crew quickly took up the slack watching closely for the marker closest to the surface.

"We are at twenty fathoms, sir," the lead crewman called out to Rayiz.

Rayiz made a quick note of this. "Ok, haul up the line and we will check again in a little while."

As he watched the men hauling up the line, there was a brief lull in the heavy downpour. With the decreased noise of the storm, Rayiz became aware of another sound. He looked sharply out to the sea ahead of them but it was too dark. He was sure he heard surf breaking on a rocky shore. He had been sailing long enough to recognize that sound anywhere. Usually it was a welcome sound indicating they were approaching a port where they would have time to relax, but this time it brought only foreboding of danger. If there truly were rocks nearby, and the ship ran against them in this weakened state, there was danger of sinking in the night in rough seas.

He caught his breath and turned to make his way back to Captain Sahaq. He needed to report this right away. When he reached the captain's quarters, he was hunched over his table poring over his navigational charts.

"Captain!" he called out, breathless.

"What is it?" the captain said gruffly, not looking up. "What was the sounding depth?"

"We are at twenty fathoms, but there is something else!"

The tone of his voice got the captain's attention, and he looked up from the charts, eyebrows raised. "What? What's the trouble?"

"I heard surf breaking over rocks off in the distance ahead!"

The captain's eyes widened and his breath caught. "How far away? Could you see anything?"

"No, but by the sound, it is not very far off. What would you like me to do?"

Captain Sahaq considered this, his eyes shifting back and forth as he thought. "First, let's get another sounding right away. We are still making fast progress with this wind, even with no sail. If the next sounding is any less, we need to cast out every anchor we have from the stern until we have enough light to see what is ahead!"

"Aye, captain!" Rayiz responded. "I'll have some of the men move the anchors to the stern and prepare to drop them on my signal. The men are getting the sounding line hauled up now and trying to lay it out for the next sounding. We should be ready for another reading soon."

He hurried out to give the orders. Captain Sahaq returned to his charts, now searching more urgently for any sign of a coast or an island. Where could they be? North? South? Surely not all the way to Italy! He had no way of knowing if they had lost their heading in the shifting winds. Briefly, he considered summoning the prisoner, Paul, to see if he had any more information but he dismissed that thought quickly. He was a sea captain in the Imperial Grain Fleet! If word got out that he was getting messages from God through a Roman prisoner, his sailing days would be over!

———————

In the hold, one of the guards brought news of the crew using the sounding line. Yes, it was true! Yes, he had seen it with his own eyes! Of course he knew it was a sounding line; he was not an idiot!

With that news, there was a sudden return of hope. If they were sounding the depth, the ship must be getting near land! Just the word "land" was like a magical incantation! They could barely remember what it was like to be on a solid surface that was not constantly changing. And all remembered Paul's report of what he believed to be a message from God. They were about to be saved!

Several of the guards and prisoners wanted to go up on deck right away. Julius and Gaius had to quiet them and remind them that there was a storm raging and the crew was fighting the elements trying to keep them safe. They must remain below until further orders, but Julius and Gaius would go up to get more news from the Captain.

Julius and Gaius made their way up to the deck. While Julius went to the Captain's quarters, Gaius went forward to talk to the crew. When Gaius approached them, Rayiz was just ordering them to drop the sounding line again.

They all watched apprehensively as each depth marker disappeared under the surface. Ten, twelve, fourteen fathoms all submerged, but then, the sixteen fathom mark floated on the surface! They all strained their eyes and leaned over, careful to hold tight against the movement of the ship, hoping to see it drop below the surface, but it did not. They quickly took up the slack and it was suspended above the surface of the water.

"Fifteen fathoms, sir!" the leader of the crew called out.

Rayiz hurried over. "Are you sure?"

"No doubt. You can see the sixteen fathom marker still above the waves."

Without a word, Rayiz wheeled and rushed toward the stern of the ship. Gaius, observing all of this, hurried after him unsteadily.

"Wait!" he called.

Rayiz called over his shoulder. "What do you need? I have to get to the stern of the ship."

"Why?" Gaius called out. "What is going on?" He was barely keeping up with Rayiz on the slippery deck.

"The sounding shows the water is shallower than just a few minutes ago. I heard waves breaking on rocks not too far away. We need to drop anchor now! We can't risk running aground in the dark. We have to make it through until morning light so we can see what we are dealing with!"

That stopped Gaius in his tracks and he watched Rayiz hurry off. He turned to go find Julius at the Captain's quarters.

Julius and Captain Sahaq were huddled tensely over the charts when Gaius arrived. He quickly wiped off his face as he went over to the table. They both glanced up, surprised to see him instead of Rayiz.

"What's going on?" Julius asked. "Did you find out anything from the crew?"

"Yes!" he said breathlessly. "They just finished their sounding measurement and Rayiz took off for the back of the boat. I tried to catch up with him and he would only tell me the water is getting shallower and we have to drop anchors to keep from breaking up on the rocks ahead!"

Julius stood up quickly, alarmed, while the captain put his head in his hands. "Captain, what do we need to do? What is going on?" Julius asked.

Captain Sahaq raised his head and met Julius's eyes, his face lined with the mounting stress he felt. "We are doing everything I know that can be done. For now, we drop our anchors hoping to keep us from getting closer to a rocky shore we can't see. Once daybreak comes, then we may have a better idea of what's ahead."

The soldiers gulped as they considered what this could mean. "This must be what Paul was telling us about! Surely if he was right about running aground, he must be right about us surviving, too!" There was hope in Gaius's voice.

"I can't let myself trust the word of a prisoner who claims to see angels and talks to God!" Captain Sahaq spat out. "We will just have to see what the morning brings! Whatever God you believe in, pray that our anchors will take hold and keep us still until morning!"

With that, the soldiers returned to the hold. Both of them hoped to speak to Paul about this. Maybe he had another vision or more information to tell them. As they crossed the undulating deck to the hatch, there was a sudden lurch of the ship, throwing them forward to the deck. Thankfully they both had their lifelines securely tied. The picked themselves up and crouched low to the deck as they made their way to the hatch.

Lifting the hatch sent the usual cascade of water to the hold below. As they descended the ladder, all were eagerly watching. As soon as they stepped to the floor of the hold, the soldiers began asking questions. The prisoners and passengers nearby leaned in closer straining to hear any information. There was a mixture of apprehension and hope in all their faces.

Julius raised his hands calling for order and quiet, and gradually the babbling died to a murmur. "The sounding of the depth of the sea shows we are reaching shallower water." This was met with muted cheers of those in the hold. "The crew has heard waves crashing against a shore somewhere ahead, but it is too dark to see how close we are. The captain has ordered anchors to be dropped from the stern to halt our progress toward the shore until we can see what is out there. There may be rocks that could destroy the ship before we can tell where we are." The cheers quickly turned to worried murmurs at this.

"For now, we can do nothing but wait for morning. Those of you who believe in God, pray that we will be safe!"

Julius turned away as the crowd broke into smaller groups discussing what they had heard. He and Gaius made their way to Paul, who was already surrounded by other believers, plying him with questions, seeking reassurance, asking again to hear his promise that they would all live.

Gaius pushed through the small crowd, telling them he needed to speak with the prisoner privately. They grudgingly withdrew and Gaius helped Paul to his feet and led him a short distance to where Julius was standing.

"Julius, how can I help you?" Paul said as the three huddled close together for privacy.

"It appears that your vision may have been true. We are close to land but we don't know where. We are asking you once more if you have any further information we can use."

Paul remained calm and confident but shook his head. "No, I'm afraid not. I told you all of the message I was given."

"Are you certain your vision said all will survive? Do you believe that to be true?" Gaius asked.

Paul paused before speaking. "I believe God that this will happen just as He said it will. I have served Him for many years, and I have been in some bad situations that threatened my life. And yet, God has been faithful. He seldom will tell us the details of what to expect. I imagine you, Julius, as a Centurion of Rome, do not expect your lowliest soldiers to know all that you plan in battle, but you do expect them to follow orders and trust that you know the battle ahead. It is the same with God. He knows the plan, and He will tell us what we need to do, but not always why. It is a walk of faith."

Julius nodded as he considered this. "I can understand what you mean. But please, if you hear anything else, let us know!"

Paul nodded in agreement. As the soldiers turned to go, he spoke up again. "I would like to go up to Luke's quarters if you would allow it. I feel one of my headaches coming on."

Julius nodded. "Actually, I would like to go back up to see if the Captain has further information. Gaius can take you to the doctor while I see the captain."

As they made their way to the deck, Julius, Gaius, and Paul could see a flurry of activity involving several crew members toward the bow of the ship as well as a few soldiers. They knew the crew had dropped anchors from the stern of the ship, but this seemed like a lot of activity at the bow. Julius wanted to see what was happening and started in that direction with Gaius and Paul following. As they got closer, there was something in the furtive manner of the men that piqued their interest. Gaius and Julius looked at each other silently but both knew there was something subversive going on.

As they approached, several of the men straightened quickly and turned away, trying too hard to appear innocent. Gaius recognized Porcius and Cassius among them and called out to them.

"You two, soldiers of Rome! What are you doing?"

The guilt in their demeanor was obvious, even in the darkness. "Commander!" they saluted. "We are helping the crew. They were getting ready to drop a heavy anchor from the bow and saw us on deck and asked us to help!" Cassius replied.

The crew dropped their gaze and turned away at this. Julius, Gaius, and Paul drew closer. As they did, it was apparent that there were no anchors on the deck. The men were huddled around the ship's boat that had been hauled aboard at the beginning of the storm. It had been moved from the stern when they were dropping the anchors since it was in the way. It appeared this group had dragged it to the forward deck and now had it suspended by ropes ready to swing it out over the water at the prow.

"What is the meaning of this?" Julius demanded. "The anchors are already in the water. Are you trying to get away in the boat? Is this desertion?"

"No, no sir!" Porcius and Cassius stammered, fearful of immediate execution if they were guilty of desertion. "These crewmen were trying to escape and we came up and found them. We were trying to stop them when you arrived!"

Paul pulled Gaius and Julius aside. "Julius, I must tell you that unless these men stay on the ship, you cannot be saved!"

Julius and Gaius shared a puzzled look at this statement. "Why do you say that?"

"I know they must remain on board. The message from the angel was that all of us together would be saved. I know in my heart that if these men leave on the small boat, none of us will survive."

This was good enough for the centurion and his first officer after all that had transpired so far. Both of them advance and pulled their swords as the crewmen scattered. Porcius and Cassius, trying to repair their reputations, followed suit, although the look in their eyes as they looked at each other and then at Paul betrayed their desire to use the sword in another way.

The four soldiers each began attacking the ropes holding the skiff and were quickly rewarded by the sight of the small boat plunging into to the rough waves below and quickly being lost in the darkness. After this, Gaius wheeled on Porcius and Cassius.

"Get below and stay there with the prisoners!" he ordered angrily. "And don't think for a moment that I believe your story of trying to stop the crew from escaping! I'll deal with you after this crisis is over!"

The two quickly saluted and hurried away, glad to be dismissed. The other crewmen had dispersed, not wanting to be identified.

Julius turned to Gaius. "We need to punish those two!"

"I agree, Centurion! Once we are ashore, I will see to it!"

Julius nodded at that. "I will go inform the captain of what just happened. I imagine he may not be too thrilled that we cut lose his boat. We may wish we had it to reach whatever shore is ahead!"

He walked away as Gaius and Paul turned to go to Luke's quarters. By the time they arrived, the headache Paul had felt building was fading away. He wondered if God had allowed him to have a headache so he would be on deck going to Luke's quarters at just the right time to see the men trying to escape and thwart their plan. He smiled slightly at the thought of God directing their impending rescue even with something like a headache!

They informed Luke, Aristarchus, and Temeros of all that had happened. All were excited, anticipating the possibility that they would be saved once the daylight came but also began considering all that they should do as they prepared for leaving the ship. After a brief visit and time of prayer (which Gaius silently participated in), Gaius and Paul returned to the hold to await what the coming dawn may bring.

After they left, Luke told Temeros he needed to gather all of his parchments and secure them in waterproof pots with wax seals so they would survive if they had to swim to shore. He had gathered a lot of written information over the past few years and did not want to lose it. They began to gather them and also any medical supplies they may need on shore, planning to work the rest of the night.

Meanwhile, Julius met with Captain Sahaq. His expectation that the captain would not be happy they had jettisoned his small boat turned out to be an understatement. The captain spewed a tirade of angry profanity at the situation, much of it in another language, the general theme of which was the soldier's ignorance of safety on the ship and how vital it was to have a small boat to rescue people, especially if they were about to run aground!

Julius stood his ground, reminding the captain that as a Roman Centurion, he outranked the captain on this ship and regardless what was done was done. There was no way to recover the skiff after it had been dumped in the sea.

After a few minutes, the anger faded slightly and they were able to communicate in a more civil manner. He eventually learned that the anchors seemed to be holding and that there was hope of daylight in just a few short hours. Julius remained there for the rest of the night to monitor any changes.

# CHAPTER TWENTY-SEVEN

Paul and Gaius returned to the hold. As Paul settled in, he looked around in the gloom at the prisoners, passengers, and soldiers. Most still wore fearful and anxious expressions, although news of the approaching shore brought a wave of hope. They all knew there were still trials ahead in the next several hours, but for most, any change in their circumstances was welcome, even if it brought dangers. All were eager for this stormy voyage to be over.

At the beginning of the voyage, Julius had made arrangements with Captain Sahaq for provisions for his soldiers as well as the prisoners in their care. There was a cooking hut on the forward part of the deck where one of the crew had been responsible for making bread and stew and cooking any fish that were caught.

This had worked well until the storm hit, at which point there was no cooking to be done. Their stores of bread and fish had quickly dwindled. The soldiers had some reserves of jerky and hard, crusty pieces of unleavened bread that would keep for long periods of time, but these also began to give out. All that seemed to be left were several large bags of the grain cargo that were not dumped early in the storm. They had taken to supplying a ration of this grain to all who wanted it, but as the storm wore on, there were few takers.

Fortunately, there was plenty of fresh water. They just had to collect the rain in any containers available. Hydration was not a problem, as long as they were able to keep it in their stomachs. The epidemic of seasickness at the beginning of the storm had diminished as the passengers became accustomed to the motion of the ship in the storm. They still did not like it, but at least they were no longer vomiting as often as they did at the beginning.

As Paul surveyed the men around him, he could see that they were weak and pale-appearing. Most had dried lips and sunken cheeks. All appeared much thinner than when they left port two weeks prior. Everyone on board was struggling with nutrition, due to a combination of lack of appetite and seasickness. Fear and uncertainty had taken away most of their desire for food of any kind.

Paul stood up and called out in a loud voice to be heard over the storm. "Men, we all need to eat something." This was met with a few groans. "It has been fourteen days that we have been in this storm, and for many days now, we have not had steady nourishment. We are all feeling weak but I believe our voyage is about to end. This day, we will need our strength to get to shore. I urge you to eat to regain your strength for what we will face. This is for your survival! Not a hair will fall from your heads. God will protect us all!"

"But what can we eat?" someone called out. "Even if we wanted to, the stores of food are mostly depleted."

"I have a small loaf of bread still in my bag," one of the soldiers called out. "I think it is pretty stale and may be moldy by now."

"We still have the grain sacks," one of the crew offered.

Paul responded, "See! We are not out of options. Can you bring me the bread you have? And also the bag of grain?"

The soldier rummaged in his damp rucksack, pulling out a parcel wrapped in cloth. He brought it to Paul as two of the crew members carried a heavy bag of grain.

"It's not much!" the men said.

Paul took the bread loaf. It was indeed hard, and there were a few spots on the surface that appeared dark with mold, but it was still bread. "During His ministry, our Lord Jesus was able to multiply bread to feed a large multitude of people that were following Him. I think God can provide for us with the provisions we have. Let's thank Him for what He has provided."

He bowed his head, holding the bread in his hands. The others in the hold bowed as well, although some were watching closely as they did so, wondering what was going to happen.

"Our Father in heaven, we thank you for this bread that we have to share. You know every need even before we bring it to You, and You know we are weak and need strength for the day to come. We thank You already that You have provided rescue, saving us from this storm. Now we ask You to bless these humble provisions to give us what we need. We pray in the name of Jesus Christ our Lord, amen."

Paul took the bread and broke it, and as he did, he saw that inside the crust, the bread appeared fresh and soft. He took a portion and passed it around and there were gasps of surprise in seeing the state of the bread after so long in the musty wet hold.

They cut open the sack of grain and were happy to see than instead of wheat kernels, there was corn. All were able to scoop a handful to munch on and after such a long time of fasting, they savored the flavor and sweetness of this corn as much as the finest meal they could remember.

Others found spare pieces of jerky they were willing to share, and one passenger even found a small bag of oranges that he had thought lost early in the storm. They shared this as well.

After this humble meal, none were full but all were strengthened. The act of sharing food was an encouragement to each of them, and as their spirits were lifted, so was their energy. The general mood of anger and despair lessened noticeably and there were even some smiles.

————

With the anchors restraining its forward progress, the ship was tossed roughly in the waves, groaning and creaking with each battering blow.

The weight of the water in the hold and what remained of the cargo was not helping matters.

Captain Sahaq and Rayiz became more concerned with each passing moment. They desperately needed to make it until morning when they would have enough daylight to see what was ahead. Thankfully the rain seemed to be lighter and the thunder and lightning had passed.

"Captain, I think we need to dump all of the cargo that remains. It isn't much but every bit of weight we can remove could help."

Captain Sahaq scowled at this, thinking of the last of his income disappearing making this voyage a heavy loss. But at least he was alive, and he knew that was the only logical recourse. He nodded. "Aye, you're right. As much as I hate to, we better do it. Send the men down to the hold to get the last of the grain sacks overboard. And double the men on the buckets to get more water out of the lowest hold. Maybe we can catch up with it enough to increase our chances. It's only a few more hours until daylight and then we can see what we are up against."

"I'll get the men on it right away. I hope Paul's god was telling the truth and that we will all survive! Now that we have no skiff to use for ferrying people to shore, it is going to be rough!" He turned to go.

"And Rayiz!" He stopped and turned. "We need a final head count. I want to account for everyone under my care!"

Rayiz hurried out to give the orders. When he arrived in the hold, he found many of the crewmen participating in the makeshift meal orchestrated by Paul. He could sense that all were in better spirits. He marveled, not for the first time, about the power Paul seemed to have over the level of optimism of those on board.

He called his crew over and gave the orders to dump all remaining bags of grain as well as to double the bucket brigade to get as much water out of the hold as possible. Upon hearing the order to dump all remaining bags of grain, those listening shared a mixture of fear and excitement. If they were dumping the grain, they must feel they were not going to be needing it, which must mean they were close to landfall! But at the same time, they sensed the urgency of the order and the concern about the water in the hull in these rough, pounding waves.

Rayiz also tasked three of his most trusted men to make a head count, two to count those on the lower levels and the other to count those on deck. They were ordered to bring him the counts so he could report to the captain and the centurion.

As the crew moved to follow orders, the prisoners and soldiers watched warily, sensitive to any change in the motion of the ship or any new groan or creak or pop that could signal a breach of the hull. Since the rain had let up, many of them went up on deck, straining in the pre-dawn darkness for any sight or sound of land. Julius and Gaius were among them.

Shortly, the crewmen found Rayiz with their count. "142 men below!" "131 on deck including you and the Captain, sir!"

"Did you check the doctor's quarters?" Rayiz prompted.

He turned sheepishly, without a word, as he hurried to Luke's quarters. He was back in a moment with the report. "Just three, sir!"

Rayiz added these numbers quickly. "That makes 276 on board. Do you agree?" he asked the men to double check. All three men agreed.

Slowly, almost imperceptibly, the sky changed from inky black to regular blackness and then to various shades of slowly lighter gray. They remained aware of the heavy clouds overhead, but as light increased on the eastern horizon abaft, there was a wave of elation bordering on euphoria as they saw actual sunlight at the tail end of the storm.

As many of them were turned to the east basking in the sight of the rays of sunlight breaking through the cloud cover, the eyes of the crew and Captain Sahaq were strained forward, willing themselves to sharper vision and hoping against hope to see a welcoming shore rather than rocky cliffs with no place to land a ship.

Erastus, the good-natured sailor that had climbed up and loosened the yardarm, was the first to cry out. "Land ahead! There in front and a little starboard! I can see the surf breaking!"

All rushed to his side, leaning forward and straining to see. There was a general cry of agreement, and Captain Sahaq and Rayiz pushed their way through the crew to Erastus' side. Slowly, inexorably, the breaking waves were more visible with each passing minute. As they continued their watch, they began to make out the rocks on which the waves were beating, but soon they could see the welcome sight of what appeared to be a bay with a beach area.

"There!" Captain Sahaq shouted. "That's our goal! Let's prepare everyone and get ready to cut the anchors loose on my command! Rayiz, have some of the men hoist the small foresail to give us some momentum and direction. This is our chance to finally reach safety!"

There was a shout of excitement from the crew and Rayiz delegated several of the men to various tasks. Some prepared the foresail to be hoisted on the small mast at the prow. Others made their way to the stern ready to cut lose the anchors. Two men were sent to the rudder lines to loosen them so the ship would not fight against the direction of the waves flowing ashore. Rayiz called Julius over and told him to ready those in the hold. Running the ship aground could be very rough, and they needed to brace against the crash to come. Then Rayiz himself went below to order the men bailing out the bilgewater to stop their labors since it was no longer needed.

Within a few minutes, all was prepared and they could see more clearly what was ahead. Captain Sahaq, not wanting to chance waiting a minute longer in the rough surf, gave the order.

"Now! Hoist the foresail, cut the anchors, and loosen the rudders! Prepare to run aground! Everyone, brace yourselves!"

The orders were relayed to the various groups assigned to each task and the replies came one by one.

"Foresail hoisted, Captain"

"Rudders loosened."

And then, the final task before their rush ashore. "Anchor lines cut!" and with a sudden lurch, The Emir was making its last rush for land.

All were holding tight, a thrill of exhilaration mixed with a tinge of terror, as they focused all of their attention on the beach ahead. The rain was falling, but not a torrent anymore, just a steady soaking rain that was almost pleasant in contrast to what it was for the past two weeks. The wind was blowing steadily and strongly from behind, and the foresail billowed quickly, snapping as it fully bowed out as if reaching for the shore.

Their excitement rose by the second and they were audibly cheering on the ship as it bounded with the waves toward shore. All of the worries were dropping away as they drew closer, closer to the beach.

But suddenly the ship stopped in its tracks, ramming into a sandbar about seventy-five yards from shore.

# Chapter Twenty-Eight

In the hold, the prisoners and guards were bracing themselves. They had all heard the plan and were getting regular updates shouted from the main deck as the preparations were underway. When the anchors were cut loose, the surge of excitement in the hold matched the sudden surge forward of the ship. They expected to run up on the sandy beach and knew it could be a little rough, but they were ready to be on solid ground.

But the sudden stop when The Emir grounded on the sandbar caught everyone off guard. There was a tremendous upheaval of everything around them, and the ship seemed to almost stand on its head for a moment before slamming back to the water, the stern suddenly lower in the crashing waves as it rolled slightly starboard. The figurehead of the young maiden holding her child partially separated from the front of the ship and leaned crazily out over the sandbar as the foresail fell into the sea below. The front of the ship now had a narrow gap exposing the hold. The frapping cables supporting the hull were no match for the force of the crash into the sandbar. All three of the heavy ropes snapped, whipping through the air as they fell into the water. The force of the collision was enough to separate the planking of the hull allowing the seawater to flood the lowest level unabated.

The men in the hold rolled around violently, ending in a heap along the starboard bulkhead. Surprisingly, none were injured seriously but they would definitely be sore and stiff the next day. They clambered to their feet with some difficulty as the deck canted in a crazy slant. They were immediately aware of the opening of the forward bulkhead allowing the muted light of growing day into the previously dark hold. All were squinting as they adjusted to the relative brightness. Those furthest aft began to cry out as the water finally rose above the hatchway to the lowest hold and began to rise steadily.

At the same time, those on the main deck were tossed around and several of the crew were thrown over the railing. Rayiz quickly regained his feet and rushed to the edge to check on them. He counted eight men in the water as well as four others hanging precariously from the railing. He watched them drop into the sea one by one and was relieved to see that all were moving with purpose and appeared alert and uninjured. They were standing on the sandbar in shoulder-deep water.

Rayiz waved to catch their attention. "Are you ok?" They waved reassuringly, looks of amazement on their faces. "Head to shore! We will all follow as soon as we are able!"

The men turned and after taking a deep breath plunged ahead toward shore, being pushed along by the advancing waves.

Rayiz watched only long enough to be sure they were making progress and then turned to the others sprawled on the listing deck. Incredibly, all seemed to be conscious and no serious injuries were evident, although several had terrified looks on their faces. Rayiz hurried to Captain Sahaq and helped him to his feet.

"Get someone below to check the hull. I fear we may have breached and we may not have much time to abandon the ship!" the captain ordered.

"Aye, captain!" Rayiz turned to climb the slanted deck to the hatch.

Julius and Gaius likewise found each other and surveyed their men. The soldiers were all regaining their feet.

"Gaius, we need to go check on the prisoners and those guarding them." He turned to the hatch as Gaius followed.

Back in the hold, Cassius and Porcius found themselves next to Demetrius, still securely tied.

"Hey!" he shouted to them. "Cut me loose! I don't want to drown here!"

They looked at each other and shrugged. Porcius took out his dagger as he sliced through the ropes around Demetrius' ankles and wrists. Once he was free of his bonds, Demetrius looked around quickly.

"Where is that devil, Paul?" he asked them. "Now I intend to finish him!"

The two soldiers looked at each other. "You know, we can't let our prisoners escape!" Cassius said with a raised eyebrow. "I think we need to do the right thing as Roman soldiers and finish them off!"

Porcius had a slight smirk at this. "I agree! It is only our duty!"

Both drew their swords as they turned toward the jumble of prisoners still surveying their surroundings.

Just then, Julius and Gaius climbed down into the hold. The daylight from the forward bulkhead breach was enough to illuminate the scene, and they immediately saw the two soldiers with their swords drawn advancing toward the prisoners.

Paul had climbed to his feet and was braced against the starboard bulkhead. He turned to see Demetrius advancing toward him followed closely by Cassius and Porcius, the glint of their swords reflecting the filtered daylight.

Gaius, acting on instinct, drew his own sword and leapt in their direction. "Halt! You two, what are you doing? Lower your swords!" he shouted.

They turned, startled, and stopped in their tracks. Demetrius continue to advance toward Paul, but his fellow prisoners saw him and blocked his way as Julius approached and grabbed his arms.

"Centurion!" Porcius said. "These are prisoners of Rome. We can't allow them to escape to shore and out of our custody! Our orders dictate that we execute them! We are just doing our duties as soldiers of the Empire!"

The other soldiers in the hold watched closely, unsure whether they should draw their swords or not.

"I am your centurion and I am ordering you to put away your swords!" Julius shouted. "These prisoners are not to be harmed!"

Reluctantly, Cassius and Porcius sheathed their swords. They turned slightly to hide their scowls, but both complied and saluted. "Yes sir!"

"Listen everyone!" Julius shouted. "The ship has run aground on a sandbar, but we are still many yards from shore. Everyone that can swim needs to make their way to shore. The rest of you, I suggest you hang on to pieces of wood from the ship and float to shore that way!"

There was a moment of stunned silence while those in the hold absorbed this information and then there was a rush of activity as they made their way to the ladder.

Gaius was glaring at Porcius and Cassius, making sure they did not attempt to do anything sneaky, but they turned to rush to the exit. After watching them climb, along with Demetrius, he turned to be sure Paul was ok.

Julius was already at the teacher's side. "Can you swim?" he was asking, as Gaius approached.

"Yes, I'll be fine! Thank you for checking!" Paul replied.

"I am concerned for your safety, not from the sea but from these men who have tried to attack!"

"Julius, you go ahead with him!" Gaius interjected. "You need to be ashore anyway, watching as the others arrive. I can't swim but I'll find something to float on after I make sure the men are off the ship safely!"

Julius frowned at this, wanting to disagree, but his logic was sound. He nodded in response. "You make a good point. I hate to leave you, but of the two of us, I am better suited to get ashore quicker. Please be careful, my friend!"

"I'll see you ashore!" he called as they turned to go. He hoped he sounded more confident than he felt.

———

When Demetrius climbed up from the hold, he scanned the forward deck. He could not see Temeros anywhere and assumed he had already headed to shore. He was eager to find the boy and talk to him, almost as eager as he was to find Paul and exact his revenge!

He forced his way through the crowd as he found a spot along the railing. He hated water but he could swim. He jumped over the side and started making his way to land, pushing some of the slower people out of his way in the process.

———————

Luke, Temeros, and Aristarchus picked themselves up shakily after the ship crashed. There were no other patients in Luke's quarters at that time. Temeros quickly checked on Aristarchus' dressing as Luke checked to make sure his supplies were still secured in bags ready for moving to the shore.

"I'm fine, I'm fine!" Aristarchus protested as Temeros tightened the dressing on his arm. He winced briefly and waved him off, flexing and extending his arm as he clenched his teeth against the pain. "Don't worry about me! I think we have arrived. We need to get ready to get off this ship!"

The three men hurried to the bow, moving carefully on the sloped deck. Luke quickly surveyed the men to be sure there were no major injuries. He was pleased to see that Paul's vision so far was correct. No one appeared injured on the deck. They went forward and were surprised at the damage, with the figurehead sagging off the prow exposing a rift in the hull.

Several of the men were jumping over the side into the water. They were jumping from the starboard side since it was lower, closer to the surface of the water. From their vantage point, Luke, Temeros, and Aristarchus could see a large number of people in the water already, some almost to shore.

The rain was still falling steadily but much lighter than it was the day before. It felt like a reprieve to those on board, but it still made the deck slippery. And even though the storm was abating, the waves continued to roll in steadily and with much force. Now, the ship was immobile on the sandbar and absorbing each blow with lurching and rolling accompanied by loud crashes and groans. There were already many planks floating in the water, and some of the men were holding on to them as they made their way to land.

"I need to check on Paul!" Luke said.

The three turned toward the hatch below, but it was clogged with men erupting from the hold one after the other. Luke saw Julius climbing up and was about to ask him about Paul when he saw his teacher and friend pop up from the hatch.

"Paul!" he called out. "Are you ok? Any problems with the crash?"

Paul smiled, pleased to see them there. "I am fine, just as God promised!"

Julius held Paul's arm. "I'll see him to the shore. Gaius is waiting to clear the lower level, but you should also get to land as quickly as you can!"

Luke and his friends agreed as they watched them turn toward the starboard railing. "I need to gather my parchments and supplies. I already have them in a bag. You go on and I'll meet you ashore!" Luke said.

Temeros and Aristarchus protested. "No, you'll need help with the bags. Let us help!"

Luke hesitated but it was true that he had more than he could take on his own. "Ok but let's hurry. The ship is breaking apart with every wave!" They rushed away to Luke's quarters.

Within minutes, Luke and his companions returned from his quarters, each one holding a bag. Luke made sure he was the one to hold the clay jar holding his writings, sealed against the water. He wanted to be sure it was not broken or ruined as they made their way to shore.

As they approached the prow of the ship, there were very few men still remaining. Captain Sahaq and Rayiz were making one last survey of the deck and saw no one else other than Luke and his friends. The hatch to the lower level was now empty, with no one else climbing up.

"Ok! That's it! We are the last on board. All of us need to get off the ship now! It won't survive much longer!" the captain shouted.

As if on cue, a large wave crashed against the stern causing the ship to lurch suddenly. The main mast had survived two weeks of severe wind, hail, lightning, and pounding waves, but now in its weakened state, it gave up. The mast snapped about a third of the way above the deck, and the top portion crashed downward causing a large crack to appear in the deck around the hatch and blocking access to the lower level.

The five remaining men quickly jumped over the side into the chilly water.

But they were not the last on the ship. Gaius was still below.

# CHAPTER TWENTY-NINE

Julius and Paul had made it to shore without incident. Several had already arrived and were crawling out of the water onto the beach, catching their breath. The rain was becoming lighter and there were actual sunbeams filtering through the clouds.

Julius called one of his trusted soldiers and ordered that he watch Paul to be sure no one harassed him. Then he began organizing the prisoners and soldiers that were arriving, being sure each was accounted for. He saw Porcius and Cassius and made a note to keep track of their whereabouts.

He assigned another of his men to make a tally of those arriving on the beach. He had heard Rayiz' report that the head count on the ship was 276 and was eager to be sure all had survived. By this time, though, his confidence in Paul's angelic vision had grown and he was expecting no loss of life.

Erastus was one of the early arrivals as well and was tracking his fellow crewmen and helping people out of the water. Several were clinging to wooden planks or other flotsam, and they needed help getting to solid ground.

Slowly the numbers grew and the beach filled with people. As they reached the sandy beach, most were suddenly dizzy. Their bodies had grown accustomed to constant movement of the ship, heaving up and down in the rough seas. Now that the ground was still, their brains struggled to adjust, leaving them vertiginous and nauseated. Those who rose to their feet were staggering and quickly settled back to the ground.

The crowd watched the ship being battered by heavy waves. Suddenly there was a gasp as those on the beach saw a large wave toss the ship and then the main mast succumbed to crash to the deck. They were glad to see the last few people jumping into the water at that point and hoped no one else remained on board.

As they watched the ship, they could see it appeared to be breaking apart at the stern under the pounding waves. Those with sharper eyes saw the figurehead finally fall to the water below.

Captain Sahaq and Rayiz dragged themselves onto the beach and quickly stood to survey the crowd. Without being ordered, Rayiz hurried off to check on the crew as the captain settled back to the sand gazing out sadly at his broken ship.

Luke, Aristarchus, and Temeros crawled out of the surf to the wet sandy shore. They laid down breathing heavily as they recovered from their swim. After a couple of minutes, Luke sat up and checked his bag. He was pleased to see the container holding his parchments seemed intact. The bags containing the medical supplies seemed to be fine as well.

Luke checked the bandage on Aristarchus' arm. The saltwater had soaked through causing him a lot of pain, but when the bandage was removed, the laceration appeared clean and was showing good signs of healing. Temeros rewrapped it for him as Luke supervised.

"I better go check to see if anyone needs my help," Luke said as he looked around at the crowded beach.

"I'll go with you," Temeros volunteered. He was still eager to get as much experience and training as he could from Luke.

"You two go ahead. I'm just going to sit here and rest. If you run across any problems you can't solve on your own, you know where to find me!" Aristarchus grinned and settled back to the sand as they got up and began to circulate unsteadily through the throng of people scattered across the area.

The survivors nearest the tree line were startled to hear voices approaching. Soon there was a sizeable group of people, evidently inhabitants of this area, emerging from the trees. Several were carrying blankets and a few had torches. All had worried looks on their faces.

"Hello! Are you all right? Does anyone need assistance?" they began calling out as they divided up and hurried to various groups.

A babble of conversations ensued, and it became apparent they had landed on the island of Malta. The Maltese natives were relieved to hear that there was no major injury or loss of life. They distributed blankets and sent a few of their group to gather wood to light a fire. The rain was not heavy but still enough to cause a chill to those who had just washed up on the beach.

Within a few minutes, four bonfires were blazing and the passengers were warming up. Spirits were rising by the minute as the realization spread that the nightmare voyage was ended. As the fear and anxiety subsided, they were acutely aware of their hunger. The citizens of the island quickly sent runners to gather food to bring to the survivors.

Julius steadied himself against a tree as he surveyed the activity on the beach. One of his men approached and cleared his throat.

"Excuse me, Centurion," he said with a salute

Julius returned the salute. "What is it?"

"We have the head count you requested, sir. We have 275 people from the ship accounted for."

"Are you sure?" Julius asked, concerned. "There should be 276!"

"Yes, sir. We checked it three times to make sure we did not miss someone, and each time we came up with the same number."

Julius turned to find Gaius to inform him of this but stopped cold with the sudden realization that he had not seen him anywhere since he arrived. He had left him in the hold to be sure all got out safely. He whipped around to stare out at the sea, now seeing that the ship was disintegrating, the water filled with wooden planks and pieces of the ship.

Gaius had become more than just his second-in-command. He was his best friend. Julius knew of his fear of the water and that he was not able to swim. He strode quickly to the water's edge, oblivious of the soldier's voice calling after him as he scanned the wreckage hoping to see Gaius clinging to the flotsam.

There was no sign of him in the water.

———————

Gaius had been in the hold directing the men up the ladder. After the last one climbed up, he wanted to make one more pass in the murky hold to be sure he had not missed anyone. He made his way back to the stern where the water was above his knees and looked closely to be sure none remained. No one was visible.

The climb back forward was more difficult than he anticipated as the ship was constantly buffeted by the waves, bucking and twisting with each. He slipped more than once but finally was almost to the ladder. He looked forward to the hole where the figurehead was sagging off the prow, appearing to be barely attached now. In the filtered light, he could see no one there either.

He took a deep breath as he prepared to climb the ladder and vacate the ship. Just as he placed his foot on the lowest rung and reached up with his hand, there was suddenly a heaving of the ship under a powerful wave that knocked him to the floor. He cursed under his breath but he was not hurt. He was just about to climb to his feet again when there was a horrible crash above his head and the ceiling of the hold caved in to within two feet of his head.

His heart stopped with the realization that if he had been standing or on the ladder, it would have caved in his skull. His first thought was that God had protected him. He breathed a quick "Thank you!", something he had never done before.

He caught his breath as he looked around. The floor of the hold was now littered with pieces of wood large and small and he could no longer climb up. He was trapped! What was he going to do?! He crawled forward to get out from under the broken ceiling that was sagging further with each passing moment. The stern was steadily sinking deeper into the water, and as a result, the hold was quickly being claimed by the rising water levels. All the hatches were blocked.

As he contemplated his predicament, he was faced with the real possibility that this was the end of his life. In a flash, he thought of all he had heard from Paul's teachings and of the assurance and peace he had seen in him even under dire circumstances. He now knew he wanted that same peace.

He cleared his throat and said, "Jesus, I have heard Paul talk about You. He is convinced You are present with him and in control of all the circumstances we face. I want that same assurance. I have heard him teach that You were crucified for the sins of each of us. I know my sins are great. I can never pay for them on my own, but Paul said You died to pay the penalty for me. I believe based on his example and teaching. Save me from my sins! Help me now as I am about to die."

Somehow, although his surroundings did not change, he felt a change within. There was a definite sense of calm that flooded his soul. He felt that his death was approaching but he was surprisingly not afraid. He almost smiled at that.

The water was getting closer to his feet and he turned to the prow, looking at the hole in the bulkhead. It was just large enough that he could put his head through it. He crawled closer to look out and was surprised to see that the water was not too far below him. The figurehead of the lady and her child was now leaning out over the water and moved easily as he rested against it.

Suddenly he heard a voice. "Go!"

He looked around quickly but saw no one. He felt a chill go up his spine. "Who said that?!" he called out.

He turned back to the opening and leaned out to see if there was someone hanging on below him that he did not see before. No one.

As he was leaning out, his hand resting on the figurehead, he felt a hand on his back pushing him with some force out of the opening. He lost his balance falling directly onto the figurehead, and under his weight, the whole thing separated, falling to the water. He braced himself, expecting the worst, but the landing was surprisingly gentle.

He found himself floating on the wooden figurehead, the lady and her child upright ahead of him in the water. The waves caught him and pushed him steadily toward shore. He was rescued! He glanced back at the ship seeing the waves washing over the top of the deck, knowing that he escaped just in time.

He was struck by the immediate conviction that the voice he heard and the hand he felt on his back were God, saving him and answering his prayer. Tears came to his eyes at this thought, and he quickly wiped them away, not wanting to be seen crying when he arrived on shore.

# CHAPTER THIRTY

Julius saw Captain Sahaq sitting on the sand looking out at the broken hulk of his ship, shoulders slumped. He hurried over to him.

"Captain! Have you seen Gaius? My second-in-command?" he called out breathlessly.

The captain looked up at him. "What? No, I haven't, but I haven't really been up looking. Why?"

Julius continued to scan the wreckage approaching shore. "He has not made it to shore! He was staying behind in the hold to be sure everyone got out safely. Did you see him evacuate?"

An alarmed look spread over the captain's face. "No! I thought everyone was gone! No one else was coming up the ladder so I thought it was empty! Then when the mast collapsed and crashed onto the deck, we jumped!" He rubbed his face dejectedly. "If he was still down in the hold, I'm afraid there is not much hope for him. The deck was crumbling under the mast and the hatch was blocked."

Julius sank to the sand, sadness and guilt enveloping him at the loss of his friend. He should have been the one to remain behind evacuating the ship! He was in command. How could he have left Gaius there alone? He held his head in his hands, his heart heavy.

He and captain Sahaq sat in silence, dimly aware of wreckage washing up on shore around them. The figurehead rolled onto the beach nearby, but they did not notice the human figure that scooted awkwardly from it onto the sand.

Gaius stood up but immediately fell to his knees. He knelt there for a moment as the ground stopped moving and then saw the two men nearby, recognizing Julius and the captain. Rather than risking falling again, he crawled to them approaching from behind.

"Julius!" he called. "Everyone was out of the hold. Did they all make it to shore?"

Both Julius and the captain jumped and whirled around. "Gaius! You're alive!" Julius called out reaching out for him. "Where did you come from?"

Gaius was taken aback at the greeting. "Yes, I'm fine. Had a little rough time getting off the ship but I got here. I floated to shore on the ship's figurehead."

Julius hugged him. "I thought you were dead!" he said with a laugh.

Gaius smiled. "No, I'm alive. I don't think I can stand up yet, but thank God for solid ground!"

"Sit here and rest. I need to tell the men you made it. I'll have someone bring you a blanket and something to eat!" Julius said. He hurried off, leaving Gaius and the captain sitting on the sand.

After the joy of seeing Gaius alive on shore, reality set in again. Captain Sahaq slumped forward and brooded as he watched the ship sinking lower in the water with each wave.

Gaius watched as well, but with relief and joy as he considered what they had come through.

"Captain, you did an amazing job of keeping us afloat for the past two weeks. I am grateful to you for everything you did."

The captain grunted in response as he slowly turned to look at Gaius. "I'm not sure I did much. Our cargo is lost, the ship is being battered to pieces as we speak, and we are stranded on this island. I don't see this as my finest hour!"

"You are forgetting that we just came through a storm that did not end for fourteen days! The ship held together and the people survived, all with no way to navigate or steer. I don't know of anyone else on earth that could have accomplished that."

Captain Sahaq turned toward the water again, his eyes watering at these words of praise. After a moment, he cleared his throat. "Thank you for your kind words." He waved his arm out toward the ship. "I just wish the ship had made it to port. It was a fine ship."

They both were silent as they watched flotsam washing up on the beach. Gaius turned to see the figurehead nearby, bobbing in the surf. The carved lady and child had been his salvation, carrying him to shore.

"Captain, I've been meaning to ask you about the ship's name. The Emir? I thought that meant prince but the figurehead is of a woman. Why is it called The Emir?"

Captain Sahaq smiled at the question. "The woman is not the Emir, but she is holding a child. The child is the Emir. My father told me the story as I was growing up. He was a shipbuilder and was the foreman of the shipyard where this ship was built some sixty years ago. When they were working on this ship, one day a man showed up looking for work. My father was a good boss, always looking to help those who needed an opportunity and were willing to work for it. Turns out the man was a carpenter by training but had never worked on ships. He and his wife and young child had fled to Egypt from Canaan to escape some threat, I don't remember what. Well, he turned out to be a hard worker and my father quickly developed a friendship and deep respect for him." He paused.

"Was he the Emir? The Prince?" Gaius asked.

"No, not him. His wife and young son began coming to visit him at work. My father remembers the boy being something special. He was only about two or three years old but seemed somehow to make an impression on all the men working. One day, my father called him a little prince. The boy's father said that he had been called that before but did not volunteer more details. Of course this piqued my father's curiosity and he pressed him for more information. My father is not much of a superstitious or religious man, but the story this carpenter told him amazed him and left quite an impression that lasted for the rest of his life." He gazed into the distance as he remembered the story. He had not thought much about it for years.

"What did he say?" Gaius said, eager for more of the story.

The captain blinked and sighed as he turned to Gaius. "Well, it turns out, when this boy was born, there was an angelic vision that declared he was a savior sent from God himself. Even wise men from the east traveled to seek him out as a King. The Roman ruler in the area became jealous and issued some threat to any young children in order to wipe out any rivals to his own throne, and that is why they fled the country and came to Egypt. The carpenter told my father that this boy had been prophesied hundreds of years ago by a Jewish prophet that had referred to him the Prince of Peace. My father christened this ship Emir Al Salaam, which means Prince of Peace in our language, after that little boy. The figurehead is his mother holding him. I never heard what happened to him."

Gaius' heart jumped at this as he considered the captain's words. Could it really be the same child his grandfather was ordered to find, the reason for slaughtering the children of Canaan?

"Captain, do you remember the boy's name?" he asked, almost holding his breath.

The captain looked at him quizzically. "I haven't thought of this story in a long time. When my father used to tell me about it, he usually called him the Emir, the Prince. I do remember him saying that the angels had given the boy his name. They called him Yeshua, or something like that."

Gaius leaned back on the sand, a smile on his face as he considered this. It had to be Jesus. From his grandfather, to his father, and now to him on this voyage with Paul, it was as if Jesus had been following him, pursuing him all of his life. Now, He had saved him from certain death on the ship, but more than that, Gaius had a certainty that He had also saved his soul leading him to eternal life. He shook his head in amazement, knowing that God had orchestrated all that had happened.

As he laid there contemplating these revelations, he heard someone approaching. He turned to see Luke and Temeros making their way toward him. He waved in greeting.

"How are you feeling?" Luke asked as he knelt by him in the sand. He watched him closely as he sat up and was pleased to see that he seemed to be fairly strong. He even had a smile on his face.

"I actually am feeling better by the minute. I think the ground finally stopped moving!"

"Any cuts or injuries?" Luke quickly surveyed him physically, feeling his arms and legs. There were no apparent injuries or painful areas.

"No, surprisingly I feel good. I guess I should not be surprised since Paul said God would protect us!"

At this, Luke smiled. "Yes, praise God. It appears you have come to believe that Paul's teaching is true!"

Gaius smiled and nodded. "Yes, there are too many things that have happened through my life to be coincidences. And I know God saved me from the ship."

Temeros was standing nearby observing, pleased to hear of Gaius' new faith. Suddenly, a glint of metal on Gaius' belt caught his eye. He glanced at it, expecting it was just his sword, but was stunned to see a small silver dagger with a figure of Artemis on the handle.

"Where did you get that?" he blurted out, interrupting their conversation. He pointed a shaking finger at the dagger. "Where did that come from?" he repeated, an urgent tone in his voice.

Gaius and Luke looked up, puzzled by his reaction.

Gaius glanced at his belt, following the direction Temeros was pointing. He was almost surprised to see the dagger was still there. He had forgotten it after all that had happened.

"Oh, that is the knife from Paul's attacker. When we grabbed him, I stuck it in my belt and forgot about it." He pulled it from his belt as he held it out for a better view.

Temeros was staring wide eyed at the knife. He reached out and picked it up, turning it over and over in his hands, his breathing shallow. There it was. The mark. "It can't be!"

Luke was concerned. "What is it?" he asked, his hand on Temeros' shoulder. "Are you ok?"

Temeros licked his lips and gulped. "How...? What...?" He looked up at Gaius. "Tell me about the man that had this! Where is he? What did he look like?"

Gaius looked bewildered. "Well, he was angry and arrogant. He kept his left arm close to him like it was damaged or something. Now that I think about it, he may have been the same guy that brought me back to the ship after we had stopped in Fair Havens, but it was pretty dark. Why, what's going on?"

Temeros held up the silver dagger. "This is my father's knife. It has his mark on it right there," he said pointing. "I'd know it anywhere. It is the same mark that is on this silver pendant that was my mother's. See?" he pulled the pendant from where it hung under his shirt. "I was sure he had died in the fire. I saw the burning roof fall directly on him and I barely escaped." He grimaced. "I don't understand! How is he here?"

# CHAPTER THIRTY-ONE

After pushing his way through the slower swimmers advancing to shore, Demetrius was one of the first to arrive. He dragged himself up on the sand and rested for a few minutes. As the number of survivors arriving on the shore increased, he decided it was time to find a more private place where he could survey the crowd. He was wanting to find both Paul and Temeros. With any luck, maybe Paul drowned!

He stood and immediately found himself staggering in a circle trying to regain his balance. Someone nearby snickered as they watched and he glared at them as he steadied himself. He was able to make it to the tree line and leaned against one of the trees. Slowly his vertigo subsided and his stomach settled.

He saw a few soldiers circulating, evidently counting the people. They passed by him preoccupied with their chore, and once he was tallied, he moved along the trees until he was at the far end of the beach.

The water closest to him was cluttered with boards, planks, boxes, and other varied detritus of the ship. There were a few wooden boxes that had floated to the beach, and as he glanced at them, he was surprised to see the snake, his snake, slithering onto the sand. He hurried over and snatched it up, grabbing it carefully behind its head to avoid being bitten. Since he no longer had his silver dagger, the snake may come in handy when he tracked down Paul. Maybe it would provide a way of escape since it would be hard to blame a snakebite on him.

He saw a piece of cloth nearby and with his clumsy left hand smoothed it out on the sand. He held the snake down on it as he carefully folded the corners up to form a pouch and quickly grabbed them together securely. He picked this up and faded back into the trees to continue watching the survivors.

He saw the Centurion, Julius, and knew that he had been with Paul. He must have dragged Paul to shore with him. Finally he spotted him sitting on the sand surrounded by other survivors. There seemed to be a steady stream of people coming over to talk to him. Probably they all felt like he was some kind of hero for saying they would survive. Big deal! He could have said anything and they would have fawned all over him. Demetrius muttered and cursed under his breath as he glared at him.

One of the islanders walked by carrying a basket of bread and fruit.

"Hey, you!" Demetrius called out gruffly. "Bring me some of that! I'm starving! I've been waiting for you. It's about time!"

The young man frowned briefly but walked over to offer him something. Demetrius roughly grabbed a handful of fruit and a piece of bread and turned away without a word of thanks. The man watched him go with a shake of his head before turning back to the other needy souls on the beach.

Demetrius settled down to sit at the base of tree where he could still keep an eye on the beach and the general location of Paul. Eventually there would be a chance.

————

At Temeros' revelation that his father was Paul's attacker, Luke and Gaius were shocked.

"If he came all this way to attack Paul, he probably won't give up now. We better find him! Let's go see if anyone has seen him!" Luke suggested.

Gaius agreed. "I am feeling well enough to get up. I'll help. If he's walking around unguarded, he may still be causing trouble. We need to make sure Paul is safe and warn him."

The three men made their way quickly up the beach where they saw Julius walking in their direction with a blanket.

"What's going on?" he called out. "Are you sure you should be up walking around? You better eat something." He held out a piece of fruit and a cup of water.

Gaius realized how famished he was as he took the food and ate it greedily. As he did so, Luke informed Julius of the need to find Paul's attacker and of Temeros' discovery that the man was his father.

Julius looked around. "I left Paul in the group right over there. I don't see him now. We better check on him!"

The men picked their way through the scattered survivors to where Paul had been and asked those seated there where he was.

"He said he wanted to help and was going to gather some firewood. I think he went into the trees there at that pathway," one of the prisoners said.

With a growing sense of concern, the men quickened their pace as they made their way to the path and plunged into the trees. There were several people on the path, their arms loaded with sticks and small branches as they were returning to the beach. The searchers scurried past them as they went deeper into the trees.

Soon they saw Paul up ahead in the distance. He was alone but appeared to be fine. They all breathed a sigh of relief and slowed their pace.

"You three go on to help him and I'll head back to the beach to look for his attacker," Julius said.

Gaius, Luke, and Temeros nodded assent as Julius turned back. As they walked more slowly toward Paul, another movement caught their attention off to the left. The trees obscured the view. Gaius told Luke and Temeros to go on and he would investigate. They heard him crashing through the underbrush as he searched.

As they approached the bend in the path where Paul was gathering sticks and brush, suddenly another figure appeared, rushing toward him with a guttural cry. Luke quickly jumped to Paul's side, knocking the sticks from his arms as he barred the path. Temeros ran to intercept the attacker.

"Paul, you killed my wife and destroyed my life!" the man was shouting. "I have been waiting a long time to find you and make you pay!" He reached to his belt where a cloth pouch was hanging and jerked it free.

Temeros jumped in his direction, tackling him and knocking the bag to the ground. As Temeros was scrambling back to his feet, the man already had the bag and was hurrying to open it, but his clumsy left hand was slowing him down. Just as the bag opened, the man screamed out in pain, jerking back his left arm. Blood was beginning to drip from a gash on the side of his hand. Temeros reached him in time to see a snake slithering away.

"He had a snake!" he called out to Luke. "I think it bit him! What do I do?"

Luke rushed over. "Do you still have the knife?"

Temeros had almost forgotten but quickly pulled it from his belt.

"Cut across the fang marks and let the blood wash it out. It may be the only thing we can do!"

Demetrius looked up to see Temeros approaching with a small silver knife and immediately grabbed at it with his good right hand.

"Temeros! My son! What are you doing? Where have you been the past few years?" he cried out angrily. "I'm your father! How could you abandon me and join up with people like this! You should know better!"

Temeros tried to wrench his hand free of his father's vise-like grip. "Let go! I need to do this or you may die!" he said with tears in his eyes.

But Demetrius would not yield. Within minutes the fire in his eyes began to fade and his breathing became ragged as his grip finally relaxed. By then, Luke and Temeros knew it was too late. The venom had already spread through his system.

Temeros wept as he knelt by his father. "Where have you been? Why did you attack us the night of the fire? I thought you were dead and I have been on my own for the past three years now."

Demetrius looked at Temeros sadly. "I thought you had died too. I have been searching for this devil, Paul, to make him pay for what he did to us. I can't believe you are here. Why are you with him?"

"These men saved me. I have learned the truth from them and I know that Jesus is the son of God. Let Paul pray for you and maybe God will still heal you," Temeros pleaded.

At this, he scowled and drew back, crying out "Never! That man will never have a part in my life!" He shook his fist at Paul, and with a shuddering breath, he collapsed back to the ground, his breathing irregular and shallow. His left arm was now swollen up to twice its normal size and there was blood from his nose. Suddenly he convulsed and in a moment sagged back to the dirt path, limp and no longer breathing.

Temeros stared at him, tears running down his face. Luke approached and put an arm around his shoulders. Paul stood nearby as well.

"I'm so sorry. There was nothing you could do," Luke said. "You can only help someone if they are willing to be helped."

Paul nodded. "It is the same with our spiritual life. God has provided everything as a free gift to us in Jesus, through his death and resurrection, but unless we accept that gift and admit our needs, we cannot be saved. We can only trust in the mercy and grace of our Lord to watch over his soul."

Temeros nodded sadly. "I understand. He made his own choice." He wiped his eyes on his tunic. "I never had a good relationship with him. The beatings and punishments and the attacks verbally and physically on my mother caused me to hate him. Now, I just pity him. I hoped he would change when he knew his life was ending."

Gaius had arrived just in time to see Demetrius breathe his last. After a moment, he cleared his throat.

"Let's go back to find Julius and report what happened. I'll send someone to gather his body and we can discuss what to do."

They stood and helped Paul gather the sticks that had been scattered. They walked slowly back down the path to the beach, supporting each other. They walked over to the nearest bonfire and stood there for a moment.

Paul began placing the armload of wood on the fire, and suddenly he cried out in pain, dropping the sticks. As he raised his arm, the same snake was hanging, having bitten him on the arm. It evidently had slith-ered to a hollow stick and Paul had gathered it up with the other firewood.

Luke and Temeros panicked, having just witnessed the deadly nature of the snake's venomous bite, but Paul just shook his arm, actually smil-ing, and the snake fell into the fire. He wiped his arm on the tunic and the blood disappeared.

Luke rushed over to examine him. "Where is the bite? We need to cut it to get the venom out!" But there was no bite mark to be seen.

Paul chuckled softly. "Don't worry. God has already told me I will stand before Caesar. You don't think this serpent will be able to stand in the way of His plan, do you?"

The people that had witnessed this were staring openmouthed. Some of the islanders that were tending the fire were whispering to themselves that this must be one of the Roman prisoners. He seemed to always be guarded. Now, he was bitten by a snake so the gods must be punishing him for his crimes. They watched, waiting for him to fall into the fire or to at least scream in tortured pain.

But nothing happened! They watched him for the next few hours, expecting symptoms to start at any moment, but he seemed to have not suffered any ill effects. They had heard the rumors circulating among the soldiers of the man who had died from a bite from this very snake, succumbing within minutes. But this man was not affected at all! They began whispering that he must be a god and this word spread all the way to town.

# CHAPTER THIRTY-TWO

The weather on Malta had been turbulent for the past two days as the storm made landfall. Storms were not uncommon at this time of year, but this storm was memorable. It came in suddenly with heavy downpours, strong winds, and a few hailstones. The villagers had huddled in their houses as the walls and roofs rattled. Then, as quickly as it had arrived, the storm departed, moving west out to sea.

The people emerged to the chaos left behind. There were branches down everywhere, and even a few taller trees uprooted. Thankfully the houses stood triumphant through the storm, a little worse for the wear but still standing. Anything that was not secured had blown about, and the children were assigned the task of gathering the scattered items. The rain continued but much gentler than the day before.

The islanders felt fortunate to have come through such a strong storm with minimal damage after a full day of strong winds and rain. Little did they know of the ship that had been carried along by the same storm for a full fourteen days with no way of escape.

There was a small town a short distance inland from the beach. The leader of the island, Publius, lived there with his elderly father as well as his daughter, Alexandra. His wife had died when she was a toddler, succumbing to dysentery as the accompanying fever spread through her system. The first several years after her death were difficult, but the towns-people rallied around him and supported him and his daughter, helping to raise her. As the years passed, she was beloved by all of the islanders, who considered her part of their families as well. Now, she was nineteen and was a great help to her father.

They lived in one of the nicer houses, suitable to his status as the chief man of the island. It was large enough for each of them to have their own room as well as an extra room for any visiting dignitaries from the mainland. Alexandra helped to manage the household, cooking and cleaning and mending for her father and grandfather.

Lately, her duties had expanded to caring for her ailing grandfather. He had come down with dysentery, suffering a lot of distress in his stomach and having trouble maintaining his nutrition. He seemed to be getting worse, and she and her father grew more concerned as each day passed without improvement. Publius did not say it, but he was well aware of the similarity of his symptoms to those his wife had suffered at the time of her death.

The day the storm broke, a few of the townspeople had gone to the beach and hurried back spreading word of a ship that had foundered on the sandbar at the entrance to the bay. They rallied several to gather blankets and food to share with the survivors and shuttled back and forth the half mile to the beach.

Alexandra was eager to go see the excitement, but her grandfather was particularly ill that day, beginning to spike a fever and looking flushed. She needed to stay by his side. Her father was busy meeting with the ruling counsel as they considered how to recover from the storm damage in addition to providing for the sudden influx of people that had washed up from the wreckage with nothing.

As the day wore on, some returned from the beach talking excitedly about one of the men that seemed to have some magic power. They told the story of a large poisonous snake that had somehow jumped out of the fire and bitten him on the arm. All expected him to fall to the ground with convulsions as he died an agonizing death, but he merely smiled as he dropped the snake back into the fire and watched it burn. They swore there was not any visible bite on his arm where the snake had fastened itself securely.

As more people took up this tale, word was passed along to Publius of this powerful visitor. The counsel urged him to invite the man and his traveling companions to the town so they could meet him. Although Publius knew that stories could get easily exaggerated, he wanted to appease the counsel, so he sent a messenger to find this man and bring him to the town.

Soon a small delegation arrived, led by a few of the townspeople. They were ushered into the house, and Publius was surprised to see two Roman soldiers, one of whom was a centurion, flanking the man Paul. He appeared to be a prisoner but Publius noticed the respect and deference the soldiers seemed to pay to him.

"Welcome!" he said, motioning for them to be seated. "I'm sure you must be starving after your ordeal. I'm anxious to hear all about it but first let's get you something to eat." He gave orders to his servants who were waiting at the door with trays of food. They quickly entered and served them plates of bread and fruit as well as hot stew.

Publius and the soldiers immediately began to eat, but Paul paused as he bowed his head in thanks to God. Publius noticed this and looked at his guests quizzically but said nothing. Soon, all were enjoying the meal. It was the first hot food Julius, Gaius, and Paul had had for many days, and they could not remember a meal that was more satisfying.

Soon, they were finished and the dishes were cleared away. Publius sat back and looked at his guests. "Now, please tell me about your journey!"

Julius, being the senior officer present, started the tale, providing the background and purpose of the trip but soon Paul joined in. His skill as an orator was unmistakable, and all of the men present were captivated by the tale. Even Julius and Gaius found themselves caught up in the story, though they knew what had happened.

When Paul shared his angelic vision and the message from God, Publius began to chuckle assuming it was a joke. He was surprised to see that the soldiers did not show any evidence of disbelieving this implausible account. Their apparent belief and Paul's conviction that this was true caused him to wonder.

"And so, most excellent Publius, here we are. We were saved just as God promised, none even injured in the evacuation from the ship. I praise God that He has once again proven Himself to be faithful to me as His servant. And we are truly grateful to you for your hospitality to us in our time of need." Paul finished his report and sat down.

Publius looked at the soldiers as he considered what he had heard. "Centurion, do you agree with this summation? Is this true that you survived for fourteen days in one of the worst storms any of us have seen? And that you were saved by the hand of God?"

Julius looked down at his hands as he mulled this over. Clearing his throat he looked up and met Publius' gaze. "I must admit I have not believed such things before, but I can tell you we were hopelessly lost, about to die, and Someone or Something intervened. Our ship should have long ago been swamped by the waves in the storm, and yet here we stand, alive to tell the tale. Having heard Paul's teaching on the ship and his report that God spoke to him..." He paused, realizing what he had come to believe. "Yes, the God that Paul serves saved us."

Gaius nodded in agreement. "I must agree. I was trapped in the hold of the ship alone, sure of my impending death, and I felt the hand of God as I was rescued."

Paul bowed his head and briefly closed his eyes as he heard these men testify to God's intervention.

Publius had a sober look on his face as he considered this. "And what about the snake? I heard you were bitten by a deadly snake and yet survived. The people who reported this to me claimed you have magic powers."

Paul smiled at that as he shook his head. "No, your excellency. I have no power of my own. Only what God works in and through me. Yes, the snake bit me, and yes, it was a deadly snake. We had ample evidence of that just a few minutes before. But God, who made the earth and all that live on it, is greater than any snake. He chose to protect me. He has already promised I will go to Rome and stand before Caesar. If He promised it, there is nothing that will stop it from happening."

The door to the room suddenly opened and a young lady appeared.

"Gentlemen, this is my daughter, Alexandra," Publius said, turning to her with a smile. "What is it, my dear?"

"I'm sorry to interrupt, father," she said, concern etching her face. "It's grandfather. He is worse and his fever is climbing. I don't know what to do! I'm worried about him."

Publius immediately stood with a look of foreboding spreading across his face. He turned to his guests. "I'm sorry. I need to go check on him. He has been sick for several days. Please excuse me." He turned toward the door as Alexandra also wheeled and left the room.

Paul spoke up. "Publius, let me come with you. I will pray for him that God will heal him."

Publius stopped and turned to look at him. He clenched his jaw, stifling his first retort. But his expression softened as his brow furrowed. "I would welcome that after what I have heard from you. Please come." He turned back to the door.

Paul stood and quickly spoke to Gaius. "We need to find Luke. He may be needed. Tell him to bring his supplies." Gaius nodded in agreement as he hurried to the door.

Paul and Julius followed Publius through the door to the adjoining bedroom. Despite the open window, the stench of disease hung in the room. The frail figure lying on the soiled bedclothes moaned with each breath as he clasped his hands across his distended abdomen.

Alexandra was at his side, a cool cloth in her hand as she dabbed his forehead. She leaned to his ear as she whispered to him. "Papa, it will be ok. Just rest. Take a deep breath." She looked up surprised to see Paul and Julius accompanying her father.

Publius rushed to the bedside as he leaned down. "Dad! It's me, Publius. I'm here. What can I do to help you?"

His father did not respond. His moaning became a wail as he started to writhe on the bed, his legs thrashing as he tried to relieve his pain.

Tears welled up in his eyes and Alexandra also wept softly as they realized their helplessness.

Paul approached and Publius looked up with a pleading expression. "Can you do anything?" he asked.

"I can't but God can. My Lord said, 'All things are possible if you believe.'" Paul placed his hand on the sick man's forehead. He was obviously feverish, his face flushed and his mouth dry. His eyes were staring unaware of his surroundings as he panted with open mouth.

Paul bowed his head. "Father in heaven, You know this man and his illness. You made him and You love him. We don't know what to do for him but our trust is in You. I ask that You heal him with Your mighty power. I pray this in the name of Jesus my Lord. Amen"

Publius looked at him disconcerted. "That's it? No incantation or magic words? Surely you can do more than that!"

Paul shook his head. "Publius, God is all powerful. We don't control Him with our words. We bring our concerns to Him and He will answer according to His will. We just need to believe."

Suddenly, Alexandra gasped. Publius whirled to see his father shudder as he took a deep breath and then relax. His eyes cleared as he looked up at those in the room. He smiled as he patted Alexandra's arm and then reached out his hand for his son. Julius looked on amazed. Only Paul did not appear at all surprised by what happened.

Publius was astounded at this transformation. "Dad! Are you ok? You were so sick just a moment ago. How do you feel?" He felt his father's forehead and the fever was gone.

His father struggled to sit up. He spoke with a weak raspy voice. "I feel better than I have in days! I'm thirsty, though. Do we have anything to drink?"

Alexandra quickly reached for the pitcher of water by the bed and with shaking hands poured it into a cup and helped him drink.

Publius looked at Paul in astonishment, a smile on his face. "Your God did this? I need to hear more about Him!"

They spent a few minutes at the bedside making sure he was really ok and then excused themselves to let him rest. Alexandra remained at his side.

They returned to the room where they had been, and in a few minutes, Luke and Temeros arrived trailing Gaius. Luke had his bag of supplies with him

Gaius introduced him and Temeros to Publius. "This is Luke. He is the doctor from our ship, and Temeros is his assistant."

"How can I help?" Luke asked.

Publius smiled as he looked at Paul. "Well, I'm not sure we need you now. A few minutes ago, my father was close to death. But this man here," he gestured at Paul, "touched him and talked to his God and now he is fine! I'm still trying to figure that out!"

Luke laughed. "I have seen this happen many times! It seems to be how God works when Paul is around! If you don't mind, I'd still like to look in on him."

Publius agreed and led him to the bedroom as Temeros followed. Luke went to the bedside to see the man sitting up, drinking from a cup. He spoke to him and checked his eyes and his stomach, feeling his pulse. Other than needing nourishment and fluid, he could find nothing wrong.

Temeros stood at the bedside as well, focused on the patient. After a moment he heard a noise and looked up to see a young lady entering the room carrying a tray with a bowl of porridge. Suddenly he felt dizzy and his heart rate increased as he stared at her. She looked at him and smiled before she bashfully looked away. Luke observed this exchange with a slight smile.

"Well, he certainly looks healed!" Luke proclaimed. "God does nothing halfway, so I imagine he will be up on his feet before you know it. If you have any concerns, feel free to send someone to summon me." He glanced at Temeros who still looked spellbound. "What do you think, Temeros?"

Temeros jumped as if shocked. "Uh. Um. Yes! I agree. He should be fine! But please call for us," he glanced at the young lady and caught himself. "I mean, if you need us for anything!"

Luke suppressed a smile as he turned to her. "I'm Luke, the doctor from the ship, and this is Temeros, my partner. Who are you?"

She looked at Temeros and quickly looked back to Luke. "I'm Alexandra. This is my grandfather. So you are both doctors?" she asked, surprised.

Temeros had been caught off guard to be introduced as Luke's partner. "Well, he is the doctor. I'm learning from him."

She smiled at this and met his gaze briefly. "It's nice to meet you! I mean both of you!"

As they turned to leave, Temeros glanced back at her and was pleasantly surprised to see her quickly looking away as she had been watching him leave.

Luke reported to Paul and the others that all was in order and he was doing well. "I think I better return to the beach, in case anyone there needs me. Temeros do you want to stay here?" he asked with a playful smile.

Temeros blushed and shook his head. "No. I'll come with you." He turned quickly to the door, eager to escape their scrutiny.

Luke laughed lightly as he followed him outside. They headed down the path to the beach and Luke put a friendly arm around Temeros' shoulder. "So, is there anything we need to talk about?" he asked playfully.

Temeros' ears turned red. "What are you talking about?"

"I saw how you looked at Alexandra. She is a beautiful girl! And I think she's about your age."

Temeros turned away, his shoulders tense. "I suppose. I don't think I can do anything about that. She must already have a boyfriend or be pledged to someone."

"I'm not so sure! From what I saw, she had eyes only for you! I think she may be just as interested in you as you are in her!"

Temeros had a sudden hopeful look on his face. "Really!"

Luke laughed at this but before he could respond, one of Publius' servants caught up with them breathlessly.

"Excuse me, doctors!" he called out. "The centurion said I should come get you."

Luke was immediately concerned. "Is Publius' father getting sick again? What happened?"

"No, nothing like that. There are many of the townspeople who heard what happened and rushed over. Many of them are sick and wanting to be healed. The man who healed him wanted us to get you to help heal the sick of the island."

Luke and Temeros looked at each other. "I guess we better go back! I'm sure you won't mind that, will you Temeros?"

Temeros tried to hide his grin as they turned to follow the man back to the house.

# Chapter Thirty-Three

T he first few days after the shipwreck were filled with activity. Word of Paul's miraculous survival from the snakebite and the healing of Publius' father spread through the people of the island. Many of them who had been sick came to the house. Luke and Temeros were kept busy for several days evaluating and treating the sick and injured. Many were disappointed that Paul did not work a miracle to fix their problems, but when they saw the skill and compassion of Luke and Temeros, there were no complaints. God healed many of them through the care offered by the men, and some were healed even beyond their abilities as God established His name on the island.

As for Porcius and Cassius, they were apprehended by a squadron of soldiers under orders from Gaius. A general muster of the regiment was called and their transgressions were publicly proclaimed. They were then flogged and assigned a work detail assisting with cleanup of the storm debris on the island. Two days later, they disappeared. After a thorough search, it was discovered that a small fishing boat was missing from the seaport on the other side of the island. Gaius and Julius were livid at this until a supply ship anchored in port later that week. The captain of this ship reported a sudden squall with severe winds that lasted only two hours. Following this, his ship had happened upon the hull of a capsized boat matching the description of the one that had been stolen. No survivors were found.

A team of the ship's crew, led by Erastus, made several trips to the wreckage of The Emir. They were able to salvage some of the belongings of the survivors, but the ship itself continued to disintegrate day by day. Finally, all that remained was the skeleton of the wooden hull visible above the waves.

Over time, the people settled into a routine. The islanders generously shared food and supplies with the new arrivals, and the newcomers in turn found ways to contribute in the daily work. All were required to sacrifice to some degree.

The next three months passed quickly. Paul began teaching all who wanted to listen, as was his usual custom on his missionary journeys. Initially, there were a few that came merely out of curiosity, but word quickly spread and soon there was a thriving church on the island, meeting weekly. Many were saved. Paul and Luke baptized the new believers, among them Temeros, Gaius, and Julius. Several of the survivors as well as the islanders became believers through the ministry of Paul.

Under Luke's ongoing tutelage, Temeros became more and more proficient at treating those who needed care. He became steadily more involved in the growing church on the island as well. And of course, he began to spend more time with Alexandra. They quickly became friends although both could tell it was more than that. Their relationship slowly strengthened, but they were hesitant to pursue more than friendship as they anticipated that Temeros would likely be leaving soon.

After the gruesome death of his father, Demetrius, Temeros had struggled with his feelings. His father had been abusive, not showing much love to him or his mother. His father's rage was a frequent part of his life growing up and of course had triggered the fire that set him on his course here. Over time, with support from his friends and with his growing faith, the wounds healed.

The winter was mild, with warm sunny days and cool nights. Many continued to sleep on the beach. Some built makeshift shelters out of tree branches but some slept under the stars. Although they kept the fires burning for warmth at night, there were no more snakes found on the island.

Captain Sahaq began attending the church regularly, interested in learning more about Paul's God, although he was not ready to make a commitment. He was intrigued to find that The Emir's namesake, the little prince that had so impressed his father, was the same Jesus worshipped by Paul.

After learning of the port on the north shore of the island, Captain Sahaq and Rayiz made frequent visits there to explore options for reaching the mainland. Small supply boats frequently arrived with food for the island dwellers, braving the winter seas, but larger ships would not ply these waters until the winter storm season had passed. They were pleasantly surprised to find another grain ship from the Alexandrian fleet was wintering there. It was called the Twin Brothers, and the figurehead had the likeness of Castor and Pollux. Captain Sahaq knew the captain of this ship and was able to arrange passage with him for those from his ship once the winter had ended.

A few nights before their planned departure, Luke and Temeros were together talking. Their friendship had strengthened as they worked side by side and Luke was pleased to see his skills growing steadily. Their conversation naturally turned to spiritual discussions.

"Luke, I find myself wondering why God would allow us to go through such a horrible storm for so long. I trust Him and His power and love, but I wish sometimes He would tell us why He allows such things to happen."

Luke smiled at this. "I think every believer has those thoughts. God rarely tells us every detail of His plans for our lives. As we take steps of faith, He may reveal more when the time is right, but as our faith matures, we usually require fewer details, learning to leave all of that in His strong hands."

"I suppose you are right. I know good things have come from this."

"Absolutely! God has impacted so many lives through this voyage. Just think, Publius' father was healed by Paul on the day we arrived. If we had not arrived when we did, he likely would be dead. And I doubt we would have arrived this quickly without being driven by the storm. Many have come to faith in Jesus through Paul's teaching, and God has been working through us in treating the sick and hurting as well."

Temeros nodded in agreement. "I know God has changed me through meeting you and Paul. And I feel He has led me to a new path in learning medical treatments from you. I wish I knew what the future holds."

"How are you feeling about leaving?" Luke asked him

Temeros lowered his eyes, a pained expression flashing across his face. "Ok I guess."

Luke studied him for a moment. "Temeros, look. I know how you feel about Alexandra. She is a beautiful young lady and her involvement in the church and her growing faith in Jesus are a joy to behold." Temeros studied his hands, listening. "I also have seen how much you have learned in treating the sick and injured. I am so happy to see how God has used you here on the island."

"I feel like I have found a calling for my life." Temeros responded, not looking up. "I want to continue to treat the sick, but I'm not sure how that will go once I am in such a big city like Rome. It frightens me a little bit."

Luke watched him closely as he spoke. "I have been considering this for a couple of days, and I think it is something you may want to pray about. What would you think about staying here? The people on the island need someone who can treat their illnesses. And I know Alexandra would love to have you stay. Even her father, Publius, has told me how much he admires you as you have been treating his friends."

Temeros looked up, his face brighter as he considered this. "Do you really think I'm ready for that?" he asked hopefully.

Luke smiled as he looked at him. "Temeros, you are ready to do anything God calls you to do. Pray about it, but I think it could be a good decision for you."

Temeros did not sleep much that night. He spent much time in prayer as he considered Luke's words. The next day, he made his way to Publius' house. He knew he had to speak to him about what Luke had suggested.

He knocked nervously on the door and requested to see Publius. He was ushered into his office and spent an hour talking with him. Temeros was pleasantly surprised to find that Publius actually seemed excited about the prospect of him staying on Malta. By the end of the visit, it was decided, and he went from there to find Alexandra and share the news with her.

Two days later, the ship was packed and ready. The prisoners boarded under the watchful eyes of the soldiers and Temeros said farewell to his friends. His future seemed brighter than it had ever been, and he breathed a prayer of thanks to God for bringing him to this place.

# Epilogue

It had been warm so far this spring, and there was a gentle breeze. Temeros sat leaning against a tree, watching the hubbub of activity in the bay. A ship had anchored and the small boats were ferrying people back and forth to the dock. He had been enjoying the view most of the morning, lost in his thoughts.

He could scarcely believe it had been over a year since they had arrived in Malta. So much had changed. The church Paul had started was thriving as more had put their faith in Christ. The medical knowledge Temeros had gained by working with Luke had been put to good use as he ministered to the people of Malta. He had become a part of the community, developing friendships with the people here. And of course there was Alexandra. Their relationship had grown stronger in the past year and he felt they were becoming more than just friends. He smiled to himself just thinking about her.

His reverie was interrupted by the sound of footsteps on the path and someone calling his name.

"I'm over here," he responded. His face brightened to see Alex appearing at the edge of the tree line.

"There you are! I wondered where you had been hiding all morning!" she said, as her expression brightened.

"I came up here to pray and to think," he said. "I love this place with the view of the bay. I guess I lost track of time. What have you been up to?"

"I was busy cleaning for most of the morning. Dad finally let me escape to enjoy the sunshine. I was down at the dock watching all of the activity."

"I was surprised to see a ship entering port. Do you know where they came from?"

"Actually, that's why I was looking for you," she said with an excited gleam in her eye. "They came from Rome and there was a package of messages. One of them is addressed to you!" She held out a leather parcel, barely able to contain her anticipation.

He grinned at her enthusiasm as he reached out to take it. His hand brushed against hers and his heart skipped a beat as he blushed. They had been spending a lot of time together over the past few months, but he still felt nervous at times, worried she did not share his same feelings. She didn't seem to mind the contact, however. She seemed to let her hand linger against his as she loosened her grip on the parcel. There was an awkward pause as their eyes met, but then he cleared his throat and pulled the parcel onto his lap.

"Uh, ahem, thanks. I mean…" He fumbled for words for a moment as she giggled at his discomfort.

She settled into the grass beside him and put her arm through his, leaning against him. "You know I like being with you, don't you?" She could be very direct when she had a mind to.

He gulped, his mouth dry and a silly grin spreading across his face. "Yes, I kind of got that idea. And I…" he paused, taking a deep breath. "I love spending time with you. I am so thankful God brought us together." He could feel his cheeks flush even more, but now that he had said it, he felt better. He laughed and tightened his arm against hers. She smiled, her teeth flashing white and a twinkle in her eyes.

"Well, don't keep me in suspense! What is it?"

For a moment he did not know what she was asking about. Then, his eyes brightened as he turned the parcel over to see what it said.

"It's from Luke!" he exclaimed. "He told me he would send this, but I did not know if he would remember!"

He sat up straighter and carefully opened the package. Inside was a thick stack of parchments. He pulled it out and turned it over so he could see what was written. As he looked at the first few lines, he smiled, thinking about the last conversation he had with Luke and with Paul.

———————

The morning before they departed for Rome, he and Luke were sitting in this very place, talking. Paul was a short distance away praying. They had become close friends and Luke and Paul had been teaching him much about Jesus. He had asked many questions, and Luke was patient with him, answering all of them. Luke had shared with him much that he had learned about Jesus' life. He had interviewed many who had known Him personally, even Jesus' own mother. He had compiled much of the information during their stay on Malta but was not finished yet.

"Remember, I want to read it!" Temeros had said. "Don't forget to send it to me!"

Luke had agreed to do so. "I'm proud of you deciding to stay here and work with these people. I think you will be a great part of their lives."

"I am ready to stay on solid ground, and Malta is a nice island. I talked to Publius earlier this morning, and he told me he may need my help with some of his governing duties. I believe God is leading me to stay here and serve. Maybe someday I will come to Rome and see the sites, but I'm enjoying it here."

Luke grinned at him, a knowing look on his face. "I'm sure Publius' daughter will be happy with your decision!" He chuckled at Temeros' discomfort around this subject.

Paul had finished praying and had come over to where they were sitting.

"Brother Paul!" Luke had said. "Temeros has decided to stay behind. He plans to work with Publius, and I imagine he will be running this place before long! We'll have to start addressing him as 'Your excellency' or some other fancy title!"

Paul had laughed at that. "Well, with a title like that, you might need to change your name! Temeros doesn't seem like an official name for royalty! I don't think I ever asked you what your formal name actually is."

His smile had faded at this and he had looked out over the bay. After a pause, he had answered. "I've never liked my name. When father was younger, his devotion to Artemis was deep, almost fanatical. Of course that had faded as his devotion to money had increased and his own reputation became more important to him. But when I was born, he was still enthralled with Artemis. He named me ArtemEros, lover of Artemis, to reflect that. You can imagine how much I was teased over that as a child. As I got older, my friends took to calling me Temeros and I never used my full name after that. Now, I'm ashamed to have the name of a false idol."

They sat quietly for a moment and then Paul spoke up. "You know, God gave father Abraham his new name when He made His covenant with him and then did the same thing with Jacob when He named him Israel after he had struggled with the Angel of the Lord. Even for me, He led me to stop calling myself Saul, the name by which everyone knew me when I was a murderer and torturer of His people. I became Paul. I think a renaming is in order for you."

Luke nodded in agreement. "Yes! Instead of being a lover of Artemis, you have become devoted to God. I have a suggestion of what you should be named!"

————

They had all had a laugh about that but then they all seemed to like the sound of it. It had never really become what his friends called him, but now, as he read the first paragraph of this book from Luke, he laughed out loud:

Inasmuch as many have taken in hand to set in order a narrative of those things which have been fulfilled among us, just as those who from the beginning were eyewitnesses and ministers of the word delivered them to us, it seemed good to me also, having had perfect understanding of all things from the very first, to write to you an orderly account, *most excellent Theophilus, ....*[11]

Theophilus, Lover of God. That was truly what he hoped to be for the rest of his life.

Alex leaned her head on his shoulder and asked him to read to her. He started again from the beginning as they settled in.

---

[11] Luke 1:1–3 (NKJV), emphasis added

# FINAL WORD

A nd so The Emir perished. The full name, Emir Al Salaam, means the Prince of Peace. Just like the ship, its namesake, the Prince of Peace, was broken and torn to save humanity and eventually gave in to death. That, however, is where the analogy breaks down. The true Prince of Peace, Jesus, returned from the grave and remains alive still. He is with us to carry us through the storms in our lives, bearing us to our home on heaven's shore. The journey is not always calm, and there are guaranteed to be storms, but this Prince- our Prince- will no longer succumb to the storm. With a word He calms the storms when they are too great, and He never leaves us alone to fight the storm on our own. He longs for us to turn to him, He pursues us, and He reaches out for us.

If you find yourself in stormy waters, in need of an anchor, turn to Jesus, the Prince of Peace. The book of Hebrews tells us our hope of salvation through Jesus is "an anchor of the soul, both sure and steadfast."[12] No matter how dark the storm clouds or how uncertain our circumstances, "If we confess our sins, He is faithful and just to forgive us our sins and to cleanse us from all unrighteousness."[13] When we are worn out from battling life day by day, Jesus himself says, "Come to Me, all you who labor and are heavy laden, and I will give you rest."[14]

---

[12] Hebrews 6:19 (NKJV)

[13] 1 John 1:9 (NKJV)

[14] Matthew 11:28 (NKJV)

If you long to know Christ, I encourage you to read God's word, the Bible. Find a good Bible-believing church, and talk to a pastor. I pray that God will rescue you from whatever storms you face as you turn to Him.

CPSIA information can be obtained
at www.ICGtesting.com
Printed in the USA
LVHW032113050120
642554LV00004B/4